**Praise for the delectable Culinary Mysteries
by Nancy Fairbanks . . .**

"Clever, fast-paced. . . . Food columnist Carolyn Blue is a confident and witty detective with a taste for good food and an eye for murderous detail. . . . A literate, deliciously well-written mystery."
                                                          —Earlene Fowler

"Not your average who-done-it. . . . Extremely funny. . . . A rollicking good time."   —Romance Reviews Today

"*Crime Brûlée* is an entertaining amateur sleuth tale that takes the reader on a mouth-watering tour of New Orleans. . . . Fun."   —*Painted Rock Reviews*

"Fairbanks has a real gift for creating characters based in reality but just the slightest bit wacky in a slyly humorous way. . . . It will tickle your funny bone as well as stimulate your appetite for good food."   —*El Paso Times*

"Nancy Fairbanks has whipped the perfect blend of mystery, vivid setting, and mouthwatering foods . . . *Crime Brûlée* is a luscious start to a delectable series."
                                                  —The Mystery Reader

"Nancy Fairbanks scores again . . . a page-turner."
                                                  —*Las Cruces Sun-News*

Also by Nancy Fairbanks

CRIME BRÛLÉE
TRUFFLED FEATHERS
DEATH À L'ORANGE

Chocolate Quake

Nancy Fairbanks

BERKLEY PRIME CRIME, NEW YORK

CHOCOLATE QUAKE

A Berkley Prime Crime Book / published by arrangement with the author

PRINTING HISTORY
Berkley Prime Crime mass-market edition / April 2003

ISBN: 0-425-18946-5

Berkley Prime Crime Books are published by The Berkley Publishing Group, a division of Penguin Putnam Inc., 375 Hudson Street, New York, New York 10014. The name BERKLEY PRIME CRIME and the BERKLEY PRIME CRIME design are trademarks belonging to Penguin Putnam Inc.

PRINTED IN THE UNITED STATES OF AMERICA

10 9 8 7 6 5 4 3 2 1

Acknowledgments

I would particularly like to thank Eileen Hirst, chief of staff at the San Francisco Sheriff's Department, who provided so much information on the jail; Inspector Sherman Ackerson of the San Francisco Police Department, a wonderful source of information on police procedures in San Francisco; Elizabeth Falkner, executive pastry chef and managing partner of Citizen Cake, who sent me the recipe for the delicious hazelnut and chocolate dessert; Hoss Zaré, owner and chef at Zaré, a restaurant, in San Francisco, who provided recipes for Wild Mushroom Soup and Dungeness Crab Cakes; my son and daughter-in-law, Bill and Anne Herndon, who were my hosts and guides to the city, from the Hall of Justice to the many neighborhoods and wonderful restaurants.

The following books provided information on and pictures of the city and were invaluable research tools: *San Francisco Memoirs, 1835–1851* and *More San Francisco Memoirs, 1852–1899*, compiled and introduced by Malcolm E. Barker; *Reclaiming San Francisco, History, Politics, Culture*, edited by James Brook, Chris Carlsson, and Nancy J. Peters; *A Short History of San Francisco* by Tom Cole; *Fodor's San Francisco*; *San Francisco Victorians*, photographs by Michael Blumensaadt, essay by Randolph Delehanty; and *San Fran-

cisco Points of View, photography by David Wakely, essays by Dan Harder.

Last but never least, thanks to my agent Richard Curtis and my editor Cindy Hwang, both of whom have been so supportive as the series progresses, to my friend Joan Coleman for her friendship and support, to my son Bill for running my website, and to my husband Bill, scientific consultant, travel companion, innovative chef, and walking dictionary. Any words I misspelled are probably his fault. However, he *was* right about the opera in which "Una Furtiva Lagrima" appears and the spelling of the Italian word for *tears*. And I was wrong. It takes a woman to admit that.

N.F.

For Bill and Anne Herndon,
my son and daughter-in-law,
who were my hosts and tour guides in San Francisco

1
San Francisco Shock

Carolyn

We flew into San Francisco, registered at a lovely hotel, and had dinner in the company of several scientific couples at a French restaurant. Of course, it wasn't like the nineteenth-century French restaurants in San Francisco, where male patrons could go upstairs for champagne, poker, and pretty companions from "the finest eastern finishing schools." In fact, after the earthquake of 1906, the mayor was indicted for taking kickbacks from French restaurants. He provided liquor licenses; in return he received money and "finishing school" favors. No one invited us upstairs for champagne, and downstairs we had to pay for our own.

Still it had been a lovely evening, after which I dropped into a comfy chair in our hotel room and did my wifely duty. I called my mother-in-law to say we were in town. This is what I heard on her answering machine: "You have reached the number of Professor Vera Blue. I am not at home because I have been arrested for first-degree murder and am presently housed in San Francisco Jail # 2 at the Hall of Justice, seventh floor, 850 Bryant Street. Visiting hours are 11 A.M. to 2 P.M. on Saturdays, Sundays, and holidays. I am told that a prospective visitor should take the elevator to the sixth floor by 7:30 A.M. and line up for one of the twenty-minute appointments, which fill up rapidly. To avoid this inconvenience, you might prefer to call my lawyer, Margaret Hanrahan, at the Union Street Women's Center, or leave a message after the beep, which I can retrieve and try to return. We are allowed to call out. We are not allowed to receive calls. You may send a letter, but no doubt the San Francisco Police will have realized their error before any exchange of mail can occur."

"*Jason*!" No answer, but I could hear the shower running in the bathroom. I hung up and rushed to inform my husband that his mother was in jail. If it were some feminist protest she'd been involved in, I wouldn't have been so shocked. Not that a woman her age seemed a good candidate for participation in a protest involving police presence and arrests. Mother Blue, as I humorously call her, but not to her face, must be near seventy, when women should be protecting their bones as well as their convictions.

That thought caused me great uneasiness. What if floor number seven was a prison hospital? "*Jason*!" I knocked sharply on the glass shower door. Murder? There had to be a mistake. Aging, if sharp-tongued, professors of women's studies at prestigious universities do not murder people. They just hack their opponents down to size with the daunting power of pen and tongue. Goodness knows, she's done it to me often enough.

For years her disdain was predicated on the fact that I stayed home raising children and giving gourmet dinners for peripatetic scientists visiting my husband instead of contributing my talents to assure the place of women in the power structure. Not that my mother-in-law ever admitted that I have any talents. Lately, with the children off at college and me pursuing a career as a food columnist, she has turned her attention to my size. Just because I'm five-six doesn't make me a giant. Jason's taller than I am—by an inch—and my mother-in-law is simply short. Furthermore, I am not fat. I've taken off the weight I acquired eating at wonderful restaurants in New Orleans, New York, and France. But she sent me a size sixteen dress for my birthday. I wear a ten, and I did not appreciate the gift. "Jason Blue, have you lost your hearing? You're probably letting the shower run into your ears," I shouted.

Jason opened the door an inch and replied, "I don't want to hear about the dangers of wet ears. You nagged Chris and me about wash cloths and wet ears all the way through our tour of Northern France." He grinned at me through the opening. "Has it occurred to you, love, that you're becoming obsessive about a number of things now that you're in your middle years?"

I ignored the reference to middle age and said, "Your mother's in jail."

"Right." Jason laughed and started to shut the shower door.

"No, really. She's charged with murder."

"Terrific. Then we won't have to take her out to dinner. Who did she kill?"

"Jason, I'm not joking. She's in San Francisco Jail #2, seventh floor."

Jason did some noisy splashing, turned off the water, and reappeared wrapped in a towel. "And I suppose she told you this?"

"It was on her answering machine."

"Then you got the wrong number."

"The message began, 'You have reached the apartment of Professor Vera Blue'."

"Someone's playing a joke on you." Towel-wrapped, my husband inspected his beard in the mirror. "Do I need a trim?"

"If you don't believe me, I'll dial the number, and you can listen to the message."

A puzzled frown creased his forehead, and, dripping, he padded bare-footed into the lush bedroom we'd been assigned at the Stanford Court, where a conference on environmental chemistry and toxicology was being held. Jason called the number of his mother's San Francisco sublet. She was spending the summer as a consultant to some much-touted, multipurpose, multiethnic, cutting-edge women's center.

As he listened to the answering machine message, his face expressed absolute astonishment. When it finished, he said, "Mother, it's Jason." He gave her the number of the hotel and our room but explained that he'd be in committee meetings and other first-day activities of the conference until evening the next day, Sunday. "Carolyn will come down to the jail to see you and find out what happened. If you get this message tonight call or leave us a message." Then he paused. "Murder? You're kidding, right? Well, get in touch, or we will."

"*I'm* going to visit her in jail?" I exclaimed. "She doesn't even like me. She sent me a size sixteen dress for my birthday!"

"I know, sweetheart," said my husband soothingly, "and I did mention it to her. I hope you sent it back."

"I certainly did, and I have yet to receive a size ten in that frumpy number or some equally unwelcome replacement gift."

Jason sighed. "The thing is, the editorial committee is meeting tomorrow morning at eight, and there's a meeting of the board at 10:30, after which I'm to meet my graduate students from El Paso for lunch and review the research they've done since I've been in New York. I did tell you that this would be a very busy meeting for me," he added defensively. "After the students, there's registration for the conference."

"I remember your attempt to dissuade me from coming

to San Francisco with you. What you didn't tell me is that I'd have to visit your mother in jail."

"Caro, that's hardly something I could have foreseen, and we can't very well ignore her. I'm sure it's some ridiculous mistake. Maybe you could visit her lawyer." Then a bolt of inspiration struck him. "You could take the lawyer out for lunch after you see Mother at the jail, talk about the case, and eat something wonderful that you can review."

"I can see the column now," I replied. "While investigating a charge of murder against my mother-in-law, famous feminist Gwenivere Blue, I enjoyed a truly excellent example of San Francisco's delicious seafood."

"I don't see that you need to mention my mother," Jason interrupted. "We'll meet back here at six for the welcome mixer. In fact, I'll try to be in the room by 5:30 so you can tell me what you've found out about Mother."

While carrying on this discussion, Jason had finished drying himself off—for a man of forty-seven he does have an admirable physique—and pulled on his pajamas. If Jason hadn't been so inviting to look at, I'd probably have been a lot angrier at the thought of spending my first full day in San Francisco rising early enough to get to the jail and afterward pursuing whatever distressing duties might fall my lot.

I had insisted on accompanying Jason to San Francisco because the day he mentioned the meeting, the temperature was 103 degrees in New York City, where we were summering with our daughter in a small apartment. It wasn't even 103 degrees in El Paso, where we live most of the year and Jason teaches. I had thought: *San Francisco, new restaurants to explore, cool days, light breezes off the bay, fog drifting along the hills, delightful Victorian row houses painted in soft colors with intricate gingerbread wood carving and charming bay windows, and eating at the Cliff House dining room with its view of the seals, sunning themselves on Seal Rocks and barking.*

(My mother took me to a seal show at the St. Louis zoo when I was a little girl visiting my Aunt Virginia. I still remember those seals, balancing balls on their noses and doing cute tricks.) Such were my expectations for San Francisco.

I did not think: *Jail #2, my mother-in-law in a particularly foul mood, talking to policemen and lawyers and opinionated women at the center, women who won't like me unless I volunteer for radical social projects.*

I sighed and looked up the telephone number of Jail #2 to be sure that Gwenivere Blue was really there and that I could visit her tomorrow if I arrived early enough to join other relatives of alleged criminals in the competition for visitation appointments. She was; I could; and murder one was the charge. Good grief.

When I glanced at the bed, my husband, far from lying awake worrying about his mother, was asleep. No doubt dreaming of toxic molecules and committee squabbles over the refereeing of scholarly papers. I considered plugging in my laptop to transcribe the notes I'd made on our dinner. The food had been excellent, but I was too tired for newspaper-column writing. Instead I dropped into bed, secure in the knowledge that Jason would awaken at some ungodly early hour to take a healthful and invigorating run up and down the hills around the hotel, after which he'd awaken me in time to get to the jail by 7:30.

How long will that take? I wondered. I'd use a cab to be sure of arriving in a timely fashion. No doubt the bell captain could accommodate me, and I didn't have to tell him that I was going to the jail. The Stanford Court is a very nice hotel, known for its stellar service, built on the site of the Leland Stanford mansion, whose owner had led the movement to build a cable car line from the financial district up to his Nob Hill house in 1878.

Of course our hotel probably wasn't as posh as the old Palace Hotel, which opened in 1875. The Stanford Court didn't have 7,000 bay windows, a gold dinner service for one hundred, or a chef stolen from Delmonico's. Still, it was expensive. Thank God, Hodge, Brune & Byerson, the company for whom my husband was consulting during the summer, was footing the bill. The only fault I'd found with our lodgings was the terrifying experience of near death by limousine when I alighted from our cab. Their entrance is a chaos of vehicles zooming around under one roof and endangering anyone on foot. It does have a famous restaurant, which might provide me with solace tomorrow after chatting with my jailed mother-in-law. *Look on the bright side, Carolyn,* I told myself and fell asleep.

2
Storming the Hall of Justice

Carolyn

What does one wear to visit a relative in jail? A suit? Jason's mother wore suits. Hoping that the weather would stay cool, I paired a tailored, smoke-blue pants outfit with a white shell and set out for the San Francisco Hall of Justice. The cabby let me out at the corner, the best vantage point from which to examine the building. A hedge and grass ran down one side with a large modern pipe sculpture near the corner. Behind the hall, one could see the handsome, round, glass jail buildings. The front of the Hall of Justice, however, was long and featureless, its only decoration blank windows and a stair to the large entry doors.

The interior was equally utilitarian, although it incorporated pinkish marble floors, walls, and columns. The most interesting features were the weapons-check desk on the left side, an espresso bar with an awning plopped down in the center of the lobby, a snack bar whose selection ran from exotic juice drinks to ordinary junk food, and a number of misleading directories and signs, all of which gave conflicting hours for jail visitation.

Trusting that my mother-in-law's message was accurate, I took an elevator to the sixth floor, where I joined a mob of casually-to-scruffily dressed men, women, and children of various races and ethnicities, largely black and Hispanic. They milled around a desk in front of a red double door manned by deputy sheriffs. The noise was horrendous.

I knew immediately that by the time I made my way to the desk, all the visitation slots would be full. If she had retrieved Jason's message, my mother-in-law would be very irritated when I didn't show up. While I was pondering this new low in our relationship, a strange thing began to happen. People in the crowd noticed me and pushed me forward. Of course, I murmured, "Oh no, I couldn't. . . . Thank you so much, but I couldn't. . . ." and so forth, but I soon found myself standing in front of the deputies' table.

Then I discovered why I had been eased forward. The female officer, Deputy Kinesha Jones, a powerful young black woman whose biceps stretched her sleeves to bursting, said, "You must be new. This ain't the lawyers' entrance."

"I'm just here to visit my mother-in-law," I replied. "Gwenivere Blue."

"Oh Jesus. The professor. Hear that, Nacho? Her mother-in-law's the tight-ass, hundred-year-old slasher I was tellin' you about."

Her Latino partner, Deputy Ignacio Molinar, looked up from his list and said to me, "OK, you're the last of the 11:00 to 11:20 group. Name?"

People behind me were grumbling to each other that I wasn't a lawyer, after all. I suppose the suit had misled them. I was the only person in the crowd wearing one. "Carolyn Blue," I said. "Spelled with an L-Y-N."

"I.D."

I produced my driver's license.

"Texas?" He squinted at me. "The old lady ain't from Texas. I'm from Texas. She ain't."

"No, she's from Chicago, and my husband, her son, and I are here for a scientific conference. Well, I'm actually a food writer, so I'll be visiting local restaurants and, of course, trying to help my mother-in-law."

"Best thing you can do for her," said the female deputy, "is keep her away from them big knives an' tell her to stop tryin' to cause trouble in the women's section."

My heart sank. What had she been up to? Trying to raise the feminist consciousness of her fellow prisoners? Organizing a hunger strike? That would be just like her. She has no interest in food so wouldn't miss it, while her converts, getting hungrier by the day, would also be getting more dangerous.

"Here's your appointment card," said Deputy Molinar. "Be here at eleven. You show up late, you miss your group an' can't see her 'til next Saturday."

I nodded cooperatively. "Could you recommend a restaurant in the area?"

Deputy Jones laughed. Nacho shouted, "Next."

The woman behind the man who stepped up said to me, "Nothin' open around here on Sunday 'cept McDonald's, honey."

McDonald's? I couldn't write a column about the McDonald's near the San Francisco Jail. Or could I? I began to edge my way toward the elevator.

"You're not a lawyer?" asked a young woman with pink hair.

"No," I replied apologetically.

"Maybe you are, but you won't admit it."

"Really, I'm not."

"You know a good one? My sister's in for possession again, an' if she don't get a real lawyer insteada one a them public defenders, she's in deep shit."

"I'm sorry," I replied. "I don't know any lawyers."

"If you're visitin'," said a burly man, whose jeans were riding at a perilously low ebb, "you know a criminal, an' if you know a criminal, you know a lawyer."

"Right," said the woman beside him. Her hair was braided down her back, and she was wearing a cerise flowered muumuu.

Are these people going to prevent me from leaving because I'm not a lawyer and don't know one? I wondered desperately. It wasn't my fault they'd pushed me forward. I'd tried to decline the kindness politely. A chocolate-colored child took her thumb out of her mouth and said, "My granny's upstairs. She's behind the red doors."

At that moment the elevators released another flood of visitors, and I wiggled through that crowd and boarded an elevator. It wasn't going down, but I didn't care. Eventually, I'd reach the first floor, which I did and got directions to McDonald's from the woman at the espresso bar. Had it been the twenties or thirties, I'd have been only a block away from Manilatown, about which I'd read. There I could have eaten something interesting like chicken *adobo*. On the other hand, I wouldn't have been welcome. Manilatown had been a bachelor enclave of Filipino migrant workers, small business owners, and gamblers.

Well, there's nothing like an Egg McMuffin in frightening company while you're waiting to visit the women's floor of the jail. My poor mother-in-law. She wasn't even in one of the fancy, blue glass jails, which probably had much nicer facilities and views.

3
San Francisco Jail #2

Carolyn

The Latino deputy led the first group up the stairs at precisely eleven. Breathless, I reached the top and got my initial view of the visiting facilities, a long glass window with partitions and telephones on either side. No chairs. I sighed and moved down the line to the middle compartment behind whose portion of glass stood my mother-in-law. She wore a v-necked orange shirt, which displayed some of her thin, wrinkled chest and arms, and baggy pants at least a size too big. Nonetheless, she looked as formidable as ever when she picked up the phone and asked where Jason and Gwen were.

"As Jason said, he has meetings all day," I replied, trying to sound pleasant. "Gwen's back in New York."

"You left the girl on her own in New York City?"

"She's staying, under protest, with Charlotte Heydemann, the widow of a friend of Jason's. Gwen's managed to become part of an off-Broadway company for the summer and—"

"I'd hoped the girl would have found some more sensible path in life during her first year at university," interrupted my mother-in-law. "Now, Carolyn, about your accommodations. With me in jail, perhaps you'll see the sense of staying at my sublet. Paying for that fancy hotel when you can stay free at the apartment is—"

"Actually, Hodge, Brune & Byerson is paying."

"Please take down the address. You can get a key from Mr. Valetti, who lives on the second floor. You'll have to call ahead because the outside door requires a key as well. Tell Jason—"

"But Professor Blue, I don't know if Jason will agree. The conference is in the hotel where we're staying."

"Nonsense. And why are you calling me Professor Blue? You've been married to my son for God knows how many years. Isn't it about time—"

"You've never suggested that I call you anything else." I was so embarrassed and irritated that I continued, "What did you have in mind? Mother Blue?"

She gave me a withering look and replied, "I'll have to think about it. Although thinking is hard to do with competing televisions in the day rooms and dormitories, not to mention the hubbub of my fellow prisoners, most of whom are miserably uneducated. The situation of the guards, however, is pathetic. I'm hoping to organize them while I'm here, and of course, I'm telling the prisoners to take their problems to the center *before* they end up in jail. Many are drug addicts, and we do refer addicted women to clinics. More than you'd imagine are mothers, and we have services for mothers in all sorts of situations. This experience has motivated me to insist that a service for women coming out of jail be organized."

"Don't you think we should talk about why you're here?" I interrupted.

"You got a cigarette?" asked the man in the next area.

"Sorry, but I don't smoke," I replied.

"Tell him that smoking isn't allowed, and that it's bad for his health," my mother-in-law said into her phone.

"He should quit immediately and get a chest X ray. The city has free medical services for those who can't afford them."

By then I'd got a second look at him and didn't want to tell him anything. He had tattoos from shoulder to wrist on both arms, which were fully displayed because he was wearing a shirt whose sleeves had been torn off. However, Professor Blue insisted, so I told him. He responded by calling me a nasty name, after which Deputy Jones hauled him away, and the woman he had been visiting screamed at Professor Blue. "About the events that resulted in your arrest—" I began.

"I suppose you could call me Vera," she said, not sounding happy about it.

I nodded reluctantly. "Well . . . ah . . . Vera, just what—"

"Typical police inefficiency," she snapped. "I didn't kill Denise Faulk. I just found her. When I saw her lights on, I stopped at her office—with the idea of renewing our discussion on funding a library of feminist books for our clients. There she was on the floor, covered with blood and moaning, so I called down the hall for help and did what I could for her—trying to stop the bleeding, administering artificial respiration when she stopped breathing. Then other people came in and called 911, a detective arrived from the second floor, and the uniformed police and paramedics finally showed up, much too late, and then the detective who decided that I was the attacker since I was covered with blood. Now, does that make sense? If I'd wanted to kill the woman, I'd have done it and left instead of getting myself covered with blood trying to save her."

"And she died?" I asked, horrified.

"Try to think logically, Carolyn. I wouldn't be charged with murder, if she hadn't."

All right. If my mother-in-law wanted logical thinking, I could provide that. "But she was alive when you got there? Did she say anything?"

"She said *books*. With blood in her mouth, even that

word was hard to understand. I certainly hope she didn't have AIDS. I'm told San Francisco has a high infection rate."

"They're mostly male," I said. "There's evidently a whole district inhabited by male homosexuals, and they call unprotected sex with each other 'the gift of love.' Jason read me an article about that. I must say that I was shocked and disheartened."

"I don't know why you'd be shocked. Men, straight or gay, haven't an ounce of sense when it comes to their penises," said my mother-in-law sharply.

Over the phone I could hear women on the other side of the glass commenting on Vera's opinion of men. One said, "You got that right, Mama," to which my mother-law-law replied, "I am not your mother, young woman."

"More like my gran'ma," retorted the voice.

"You see what I have to put up with," Vera muttered. "Inane wit and abominable pronunciation and grammar."

"Up yours," someone on the other side of the glass shouted.

Oh dear, I thought. Bad enough to be in jail, but my mother-in-law seemed bent on making enemies of everyone in sight.

4
A Much-Interrupted Tale of Arrest

Carolyn

"**I was telling you** about Denise," my mother-in-law continued. "She repeated the word *books* while I tried to stanch the bleeding with Kleenex. Not a successful endeavor, but that's all I had at the time."

"What do you think she meant?" I asked.

"I assume she was referring to the reason for my visit."

"But how could she know why you were visiting?"

"Because that's what we'd discussed the last time I saw her. Books."

"Did you hear anything before you went in or see anyone in the hall?"

"Carolyn, I hope you're not planning to investigate this yourself. I know you and Jason have had some strange experiences with criminals in your recent travels, but that does not make you a detective. I'd be quite embarrassed to think my daughter-in-law was bumbling around, asking questions about Denise's death. The police will find out what really happened."

"But they've already arrested you. Obviously, they

think you did it and they needn't investigate further. Have
you been arraigned?"

"Of course not. It just happened Thursday—or perhaps
Friday morning. I'm not sure what the time was when
they finally took me to the booking facility. My lawyer
tells me that the District Attorney's office has forty-eight
hours, not counting the weekend, to decide whether they
want to change the charge or drop it."

"They ain't gonna drop no murder charge, ole lady,"
shouted a woman from down the row.

"Nonsense," Vera replied, and to me, "No doubt by
Tuesday—"

"You've been in here since Thursday, and could still be
here on Tuesday?"

"Please don't repeat everything I say, Carolyn. These
visits are limited to twenty minutes."

"Are the accommodations . . . are they—"

"Dreadful. A woman my age should not be expected to
wear such revealing clothes—"

"What you care, Chiquita?" called a Hispanic prisoner.
"You ain't got tits no more."

"Or share a barred dormitory cell with three other
women, none of whom have any respect for age or education," my mother-in-law continued, quite unfazed by the
rude comments. "Nor should I be expected to jog around
a rooftop three times a week. I have already lodged a
number of protests and shall certainly lodge more. For
one thing, I want to teach a class in the women's section,
Feminist Awareness in the Twenty-First Century. I've
never encountered a group more in need of such training,—"

"Fuck that," a different voice echoed in the telephone.

"But the jail authorities say that a prisoner can't teach,
no matter how woefully uninformed these poor inmates
are about women's rights and other matters that should be
of concern to them. The jail offers them classes in creative
writing—poetry, no less—and safe sex. Of course, the

latter is useful, although you'd think people would know about safe sex. But *poetry*?"

"Perhaps there's a therapeutic value in learning self-expression," I suggested. Actually, I found the creative writing class an interesting and promising idea.

"Poppycock. And then there is the food, which is quite unacceptable, and you know that I am not fussy about food. To give you an idea of how bad it is, some Irishman held a press conference after being jailed here and said that it was worse than what the English served to imprisoned terrorists."

"What's it like?" I asked. A recipe from the San Francisco jail. Now that would be an unusual addition to my column, "Have Fork, Will Travel."

"The food meets state regulations, I'm told, which, if true, must be very minimal. I'm not the only person in the women's section who considers the meals tantamount to cruel and unusual punishment. Of course, many are complaining about not being served their racial or ethnic cuisines—soul food, tacos, that sort of thing—although it seems to me that we get too much of it. When I said so, my fellow inmates responded very intemperately. The female population is approximately 50 percent black and 30 percent Hispanic. The rest of us are white and Asian."

Heaven help us, I thought. *She's fomenting labor unrest among the guards and insulting members of the minority jail population. We have to get her out of here.*

"Don't look so alarmed, Carolyn. I'm perfectly capable of adjusting to unusual situations, especially when I'm in a position to do underprivileged women some good. Few in the academic world have the opportunity to spend time in jail. But then I was telling you about my arrest: the homicide detectives took me to their enclave on the fourth floor and asked me the same questions repeatedly. As if they thought I'd tell them something different if they asked often enough. Then they walked me underground to the booking facility where deputy sheriffs searched me for weapons, took my fingerprints and photo, and left me for several more hours in a cell by myself. Evidently I got private facilities because I was considered dangerous.

"I must say that I was happy to be alone. Too bad my quarters weren't soundproofed. The holding cells were full of drunken, foul-mouthed persons, many of whom were throwing up and screaming at one another."

"But didn't they let you have a lawyer?" Her description of the situation was horrifying.

"Of course, I called Margaret Bryce Hanrahan, the center's lawyer, but she wasn't available until the next morning, and I really didn't see the sense in asking for a public defender. If I weren't donating my time to the clinic, I wouldn't be in jail, would I? My feeling is that they owe me legal representation."

"But does this lady know anything about criminal law?"

"If she doesn't, someone in her husband's firm will. She quit there because they weren't making women partners. Now they have to do all sorts of pro bono work for the clinic to appease her." My mother-in-law smiled tightly.

"Later, the people in booking spent an inordinate amount of time asking me questions about my gang affiliations and my criminal record. On both counts I had little to offer, so I was turned over to someone who was trying to decide whether I might be psychotic or suicidal. I pointed out that, although not psychotic or suicidal, a woman my age might well drop dead from police harassment and lack of sleep.

"They must have taken that suggestion seriously because they walked me up here for a disgusting breakfast, after which I insisted on taking a nap rather than attending a seminar on breaking a drug habit."

The guard had just announced that we had one minute left, so I asked for the telephone number of the lawyer.

"I don't see why you need that, Carolyn. What you should do is move into my apartment, where I can call you collect. You'll be there awaiting word from me. Presumably, I can leave messages on my own answering machine, which you can retrieve, if you really have to go out."

"But how, if we're not home and there's no one to accept a collect call—"

"I'll purchase a phone card at the commissary if necessary. The telephone charges are outrageous. Over three dollars just for a connection and three minutes."

"At least tell me the name of the lawyer," I begged, afraid it might have been erased from the answering machine.

"There's no need."

"Very well, Vera, I'll tell Jason that you refused to let us help you," I said sternly. "I won't even tell him about the apartment and the phones."

My mother-in-law looked astonished. "Goodness, Carolyn, you just threatened me. I believe you're developing a bit of spunk in your middle years. But don't let that persuade you that you should wander around San Francisco trying to investigate this foolish mistake by the police. They can figure it out on their own. One of the homicide detectives on my case is a woman, so I'm quite optimistic—"

"You gotta leave, ma'am," said Deputy Kinesha Jones. On the other side of the glass, deputies were bearing down on Vera.

"Her name," I demanded in the voice I had used when the children were going through rebellious stages.

"Just tell her, you old bat, so we can get her out of here," snapped the deputy, but it was too late. The telephone had been yanked from Vera's hand, and she was dragged roughly to her feet.

"Well, never mind, honey," said Deputy Jones. "I can get you her lawyer's name. She ain't much nicer with family than anyone else, is she?"

"Thank you so much for your help," I replied, and allowed myself to be escorted away.

5

Citizen Cake

Carolyn

Deputy Jones found both home and office numbers for the lawyer, Margaret Bryce Hanrahan. *Quite an impressive name,* I thought, hoping that her credentials would prove as impressive. First, I called her home number from a public phone booth on the first floor of the Hall of Justice and was told that Mrs. Hanrahan was at the center catching up on work she'd missed Wednesday and Thursday because she'd been passing a kidney stone. Well, that explained why she hadn't come to Vera's rescue Thursday night. Kidney-stone passage, as I understand it, is a very painful experience. *Poor woman,* I thought as I dialed her office number; and after such a debilitating experience, she'd gone right out the next morning to help Vera.

When a booming, low-pitched female voice answered the telephone, I introduced myself and mentioned my visit to my mother-in-law in jail. "I thought I should talk to you as soon as possible since you are her lawyer."

"Well, phooey. When I heard your name, I hoped you were calling to say Vera wanted another lawyer."

"I'm afraid not."

"Ah well. Then we do need to talk. Since I'm in the mood for something sweet, let's meet at Citizen Cake."

What a wonderful name. Perfect for a column. San Francisco had an Italian confectionery in 1849. Was Citizen Cake Italian? Or perhaps it would be like the confectionery shops in 1868 where wealthy women, elaborately dressed, stopped for a lunch of ice cream, cake, and gossip after a hard morning of shopping on Montgomery Street, San Francisco's high-fashion boulevard.

"Just catch a cab to 399 Grove Street. I'll see you there in fifteen minutes."

"Thank you." Would I be able to get there in time? When I finally found a cab three blocks away from the Hall of Justice, I promised the driver a good tip if he'd drive me to Citizen Cake as fast as possible.

"Get in, lady," he said. "I can see you're having a snack attack." And off we went. It turned out to be a short trip, but he did drive fast, so I gave him what I thought was a generous tip (he evidently didn't think so) and carefully wrote the cab fare into my tax deduction notebook. I fully intended to write about whatever I had to eat, unless it was awful. In that case, I'd have to erase the cab expense. Would I have to pay for the lawyer's meal, too? Well, if so, Jason could ask his mother for a refund. Of course, she'd refuse.

The neighborhood was more industrial than high fashion, but the interior was tempting. I stood in the entrance to the right of the bar, looking for Mrs. Hanrahan and taking in the décor. Very modern. A pastry counter behind me full of luscious offerings. A long bar with high stools, bare wooden floors, large black pipes, raftered ceiling, rust-red walls, large windows looking out on greenery with occasional sheer white drapes combating sunlight, peculiar white plastic triangles hanging from the ceiling, and casually dressed employees. A tall girl in worn jeans was coming toward me when I heard, "Blue?" shouted in my direction.

The owner of the voice had risen from a table by the window, waving energetically. Margaret Hanrahan was a very large woman, tall, stout, and bolster-shaped, weighing well over two hundred pounds. I needn't have bothered with my conservative pants suit for her sake; she wore a long, moss-green, fringed dress with beads, and her hair was pinned around her large head in a thick, gray braid. As I headed in her direction, I found myself hoping that she didn't appear in court dressed like that.

Since Mrs. Hanrahan took the chair, I had to squeeze onto the bench seat behind the table and in front of a huge window. "Dessert first, business second," she announced. Then she passed me the dessert menu, and ordered for herself: The "Mixed Berry Shortcake with Rosemary Ice Cream and Vanilla Syrup" and the "Seven Cookies." The first was $8.50 and the second $7.00. I glanced over the menu and chose the "Hazelnut on Chocolate on Hazelnut on Chocolate." It sounded wonderful, pot de crème, hazelnut ice cream, and espresso vinaigrette, $8.50.

"Oh, what the hell," said Mrs. Hanrahan to our waitress. "I'll have the 'Exquisite Tropical Parfait,' too." I glanced back up the menu. Her third choice contained coconut tapioca, mango bavarois, ginger gelee, and caramel, $8.00. There were only two other items on the menu, and I hoped that she wouldn't expect me to order those.

She didn't. Instead, she asked if I wanted a sandwich since I'd only chosen one dessert. The waitress said they weren't serving sandwiches yet. I asked if I could keep the menu. She looked at me askance but agreed. I asked if I could have a recipe for my newspaper column. She shrugged and said she'd consult with management.

While we were waiting to be served, Mrs. Hanrahan told me that Vera's case was a real problem, not the least of which was Vera herself. "She's not taking this seriously. She thinks the police are going to realize she didn't kill Denise and let her go, and in the meantime she's going to do good work among her fellow prisoners and the jail guards. She's already set her sights on two new clients that need my aid, as if I don't have enough grief thinking about her situation.

"Bad enough that someone killed Denise at the center, but to have our big-name consultant charged—well, it looks terrible. Bad publicity for us, bad for poor Denise who got killed, bad for me—maybe I'll stick one of the rainmakers at my husband's firm with Vera's defense. That should make them sorry they never voted another woman after me into the partnership. They're already ruing the day I quit."

Mrs. Hanrahan had a laugh as ear-catching as her voice. When she let out a huge, delighted chortle over the pro bono complaints of her husband's partners, heads turned all over Citizen Cake.

"And of course bad for Vera. If she doesn't get a grip, she's going to find herself in the state prison instead of the San Francisco jail. I'm not sure which would be worse from her point of view."

"Have you ever tried a murder case, Mrs. Hanrahan?" I asked diffidently.

"Call me Margaret. Of course I have, but always women killing men—spousal abuse, battered-wife syndrome. I'm good at those. Never had one with a woman killing a woman. Not that I think Vera killed anyone, but the evidence does look bad."

"What evidence?"

Before she could answer, our desserts arrived. Mine was gorgeous, a tall, narrow tower of delicious-looking nuts and chocolate and whatnot. I was gazing at it with admiration when the plate gave a jump and the luscious tower toppled over. I experienced a moment of queasiness and glanced toward Margaret Hanrahan, who had started to consume, with gusto, the Exquisite Tropical Parfait. I noticed that her Mixed Berry Shortcake with Rosemary Ice Cream seemed to be put together somewhat haphazardly. "What happened?" I asked.

"You mean the murder?" Margaret helped herself to one of the Seven Cookies, the one that was resting on the table.

"The plates—jumped."

"Maybe we had a tremor," she replied nonchalantly, putting the half-eaten cookie back on the plate and scooping up more of the parfait. Noticing that I seemed fascinated by her dessert sampling, she added, "I'm saving the shortcake until last."

"Tremor as in earthquake?" I asked, a tremor in my voice.

"Goodness, dear, it was nothing. We've had five hundred or more since the mid-nineteenth century."

"I'm sitting by a big window. Isn't that dangerous?"

Margaret waved vaguely toward the other customers. "You don't see anyone taking notice, do you? Now eat your hazelnut thing. It looks wonderful." Then she gave into temptation and tried the disheveled shortcake with a sigh of delight.

"What evidence?" I asked, trying not to look and feel terrified. The Hazelnut on Chocolate, etc., helped. Even in disarray, it was delicious. "She didn't kill anyone, so there couldn't be evidence that—"

"Well, she was covered with Denise's blood. Not that I saw her. Pictures, of course. The cops took pictures. But I didn't see the real thing. I was passing a kidney stone at the time, which is, believe me, worse than giving birth, and then you don't have anything to show for it. But that's the last one, believe you-me. They're going to put me in a bathtub and blast my kidneys with a laser. New technique. Turns a kidney stone to powder."

She'd finished off the parfait and two more of the cookies. "Besides the blood all over your mother-in-law, there was the argument. They had a humdinger—Denise and

Vera—just that afternoon. Something about feminist books. Denise said there wasn't enough money for a library of them. Vera got very shirty, as the English say. Lord, I could hear them all the way in my office, one section over and one floor up. And poor Denise. She doesn't like to argue, and she only took over as the center's accountant and fund-raiser because Myra Fox got breast cancer. Myra kept the books before she went under the knife, and Denise headed the Battered Women's Advocacy.

"So there you are. Discovered at the scene of the crime with the victim's blood all over her after a nasty argument just that day, and then Vera admitted to the police that they were back on the subject of books in the office that night."

"No she didn't," I protested. "She told them Denise said the word *books* twice before she died. Vera didn't say anything, except to call out for help when she saw that Denise had been attacked. Did they find the weapon?"

"Not that I know of. If they did, they'll have to say so on discovery."

"Well, how could Vera have used it, got covered with blood, hidden it, and then come back to help her victim? That's both impossible and implausible."

"Very good point, my dear. Something the cops should look into. They won't, of course. They think they've got their murderer."

"A small, elderly woman? That's ridiculous. Couldn't they tell from the angle of the wounds that someone taller did it? In fact, it had to be a man. What woman would kill another with multiple stab wounds?"

"And with a big knife, according to my sources at Homicide."

"There. You see. Where would Vera get a big knife?"

"Beats me. The kitchen?"

"She's not at all domestic."

"Good point. What's your first name, dear?"

"Carolyn."

She had finished off the shortcake and the other cookies as we talked and was draining her coffee cup, which had been refilled twice at her request. "Well, I'll tell you what I'd do, Carolyn. I'd get a good private detective to look into who might have killed Denise if it wasn't Vera. Unfortunately, the center doesn't have a detective. We're lucky to have a rent-a-cop at the front door. So I can't provide one, and Vera would probably refuse if I could. However, I'm sure the city is full of them. The famous detective William Burns, who eventually had his own agency, was hired to help clear out our crooked politicians after the 1906 quake. Sometimes it takes a good shaking up to set things to rights in this town."

I hoped that she wasn't wishing a major earthquake on the city, and I had to agree that my mother-in-law was unlikely to favor hiring a detective. However, I myself could ask questions at the center if the police weren't willing to do so. In fact, I should probably talk to the police. Maybe I could convince them to investigate for me, which would leave me free to explore San Francisco, and its eating establishments.

Margaret and I split the bill. Her suggestion, which wasn't at all fair since she'd had three desserts and three cups of coffee while I'd had only one of each. But I guess it was better than being expected to pay the whole bill because she was offering free legal advice to my mother-in-law.

Hazelnut on Chocolate
on Hazelnut on Chocolate

This recipe is complicated to make, but the end result is delicious. If you visit Citizen Cake in San Francisco, you can just order it and save the trouble. If, however, you have to prepare it yourself, take comfort. You'll have not only the complete dessert, but also hazelnut custard and hazelnut ice cream if you don't use it all.

POT DE CRÈME

- Bring *1 qt. heavy cream* and *4 oz. whole milk* to a simmer in a medium saucepan.

- Whisk *6 egg yolks, 1 whole egg,* and *1/4 cup of brown sugar* together.

- Mix a little hot cream mixture into the egg and sugar mixture; then, pouring slowly, mix the rest in.

- Stir over medium heat until custard begins to thicken.

- Pour over *12 oz. chopped bittersweet chocolate* and *1/4 cup hazelnut paste* (Nutella can be substituted). Stir until chocolate is melted into custard.

- Pour into shallow dish or individual molds and chill until set.

HAZELNUT ICE CREAM

- Combine *24 oz. milk* and *8 oz. cream* in a saucepan with *8 oz. fresh roasted hazelnuts* (roast in oven at 350 degrees for 12 to 15 minutes until browned) and steep for 1/2 hour or more.

- Combine *7 oz. brown sugar* and *6 egg yolks* in a bowl and whisk together.

- Pour hot milk/cream slowly, stirring, into the yolk mix.

- Return to stove and cook over low heat until it begins to thicken.

- Strain and chill.

- Add *1 tsp. salt* and *1 oz. brandy* and churn in ice cream machine.

ESPRESSO VINAIGRETTE

- Whisk together *1 shot fresh espresso, 2 tsp. sugar, pinch of salt, 1 tbs. orange juice,* and *1 tsp. lemon juice.*

- Slowly add *2 tbs. hazelnut oil* and *1/4 cup canola oil* to emulsify.

CHOCOLATE CHOUX

- Preheat oven to 375 degrees.

- Drop to 350 to bake.

- Combine *4 oz. whole milk, 1/4 tsp. salt, 2 tsp. sugar,* and *1.5 oz butter* in a saucepan and bring to boil.

- Add *2 oz. flour* and *2 tsp. cocoa powder* all at once and cook as choux off heat.

- Return to medium heat and stir with a wooden spoon until dough forms a mass.

- Add *2 eggs,* one at a time, and stir until smooth.

- Pipe small discs , 2" diameter, on a baking sheet.

- Bake 20 minutes and cool completely before using.

BUILDING THE DESSERT

- Place the choux on a plate.

- Place a spoonful or quenelle shape of the pot de crème custard on this.

- Place *bittersweet chocolate* shavings on the custard.

- Place another spoon of custard on this and make an impression with the back of a spoon.

- Place a small scoop of the hazelnut ice cream on this and garnish with *fresh roasted hazelnuts* and more chocolate shavings.

- Drizzle vinaigrette around the plate.

This delicious recipe was provided by Elizabeth Falkner, executive pastry chef/managing partner of Citizen Cake in San Francisco.

Carolyn Blue,
"Have Fork, Will Travel,"
San Luis Obispo Weekly Gazette

6
Meeting Harry Yu

Carolyn

Since the drive to Citizen Cake had seemed short, I walked back to the Hall of Justice, a mistake. However, I did arrive eventually and located the Homicide Division on the fourth floor, where my mother-in-law had said it was. Most of the cubicles were empty, but I spotted an Asian person and asked to speak to a detective.

Looking up from his computer, on which he had been playing solitaire, he said, "I'm one. Inspector Harry Yu. There something you'd like to report about a homicide, ma'am? Most people just call us." Although his remarks could have been taken as sarcastic, both his voice and his countenance were expressionless. Asian inscrutability? A stereotype, but perhaps accurate.

"Actually, I was here this morning, visiting my mother-in-law—"

"She a cop?"

"No, a prisoner."

"Complaints about the jail go to the Sheriff's Department. City Hall."

"Well, she didn't make it sound luxurious, but I'm not here to complain about that. Is one of the detectives investigating the murder of Denise Faulk here today? I just got back from lunch at Citizen Cake with my mother-in-law's lawyer and thought perhaps I should talk to—"

"Sit down. Your name would be?" He took out a notebook.

"Carolyn Blue."

"You live here in town?"

"El Paso, Texas."

He looked up. "I got a nephew-in-law teaching at a university out there in West Texas. Millard Fillmore Fong. Ph.D. in psychology. You know him?"

"No, but he certainly has an interesting name."

"Yeah, my wife and her sister are into presidents and first ladies. I got a daughter named Dolly Madison Yu. She's not real happy about that."

"Well, you could point out that it's better than Millard Fillmore. Dolly Madison was a heroine first lady, whereas Millard Fillmore—well, *I* don't know anything about him."

"I'll tell her that. So you got something that would exonerate your mother-in-law? That is one tough lady. Reminds me of my grandmother."

"Well, really what I wanted to say is that she's a professor at the University of Chicago—"

"So she told us."

"And a famous feminist scholar."

"She mentioned that, too."

"And she wouldn't kill anyone. Especially not another woman."

"Mrs. Blue, I was at the scene, and I questioned her, and I've seen the evidence. It's my opinion that she did kill the accountant."

"But have you looked at other suspects?"

"We asked around. She was the only person besides the corpse at the scene, bending over the victim, covered with blood, and the only one who had a loud fight with the woman that same afternoon. Not only did she have the victim's blood all over her, but her bloody fingerprints were here and there in the office."

"Did you search for other fingerprints?"

"Sure. Only the professor's were bloody."

"Well, did you find the murder weapon?"

"Nope, but we will. She must have put it somewhere around the center. It's one of those old Victorians that rambles all over the place. Unless someone else got rid of it for her. But we've turned up no evidence of an accomplice. When they're not taking flack from the ladies about obstructing business, we've got a team turning the place upside down looking for the knife."

"But, detective, you owe it to your own sense of justice to look further than my mother-in-law. She's just not the killer type. Women seldom—"

"Mrs. Blue, in San Francisco, women are as weird as men, although I'll admit they don't commit as many crimes, but your mother-in-law is more aggressive than most. And she's got a record."

"What?"

"Bunch of disturbing the peace charges, one inciting to riot, and an assault with a deadly weapon. She attacked a minister."

"With a phone book," I replied defensively. "He'd been making threats to women's clinics, and then he made some to her. She had caller I.D. and confronted him at the next demonstration."

"She still whacked him on the head with the Chicago phone book. Detective in Chicago says she sprained his neck."

"The charges were dropped."

"Yeah, and she had to drop the telephone harassment charges against him. It was a standoff."

"Detective, she's almost seventy."

"Seventy-two."

"Really? She never has said."

"I'll grant you that the women at that Union Street Center are a wild lot—lesbians, witches, counselors, blacks, whites, Asians, kids, old ladies. They've even got a woman that I'll swear used to be a man. My grandmother thinks San Francisco is an urban nut house."

"From what I read on the Internet, she may be right."

"Grandmother Yu is always right. Look at city government. If I wanted to be a woman, the city health plan would pay for it."

"Do you?" I asked, surprised at the idea. Inspector Yu did not look at all feminine. He had a broad, middle-aged body, a wide nose, and black hair that stood up in bristly clumps. On the other hand, I'd changed my mind about his being inscrutable. He was much too talkative for that.

"No, ma'am. I do not want to change sexes. It upsets friends and relatives, my fellow inspectors wouldn't take it well, even the women, and after all that aggravation, I'd end up being a woman. No offense intended, but who'd want to be a woman?" His phone rang and he answered, "Inspector Yu. . . . You're pulling my leg! . . . Well, tell the guy for me that murderers are supposed to take Sunday off. . . . Yeah, sure. I'm on my way.

"Gotta go." He rose from his blue chair, put on a brown tweed sport coat, and tightened his tie.

"But what about the investigation of Denise Faulk's death?"

"Unless the DA sends the case back in the next two days, I'd say you should get the professor a good lawyer. She's going to trial."

"I really don't think that's fair."

"Confucius say, 'Life not fair.'"

"He did not. That's a Western saying."

"Chinese," he insisted. He patted his gun—to be sure it was there, I suppose—and stuck a cell phone in his pocket.

"Well, if you won't help Vera, I'll have to do it myself," I said, feeling both disappointed and put upon.

"Feel free."

He smiled at me, a very nice, twinkly smile, which gave me the courage to add, "At least you could recommend a good Chinese restaurant. I'm a food writer."

"Eliza," he said as he walked away.

"Eliza?" That didn't sound very Chinese to me.

7
The Aging Tenor of Sacramento Street

Carolyn

As **I waited** for the elevator, I decided that I didn't really *have* to return to the hotel for the welcome mixer until 6:30. That gave me two hours, enough time to check out the apartment my mother-in-law wanted Jason and me to occupy. Although he'd already declined her offer, perhaps I could persuade him.

With that plan in mind, I bought a cup of low-fat latte at the coffee cart and caught a cab. The driver, who was drinking his own cup, didn't mind me bringing mine into the cab. He said, "This is San Francisco, lady. Everyone drinks coffee everywhere." Within ten minutes, moderately invigorated by the coffee, I clambered out onto an intimidating hill. After all the delightful Victorians with ornate bay windows and brightly painted, projecting roofs and woodwork, my Sacramento Street destination was rather plain and had steep stairs leading to the front door. It was locked, as Vera had said it would be.

From above my head a tenor voice was belting out an aria from Puccini's *Turandot*. I rang the bell marked

Bruno Valetti, wondering if it was Mr. Valetti singing "Nessun Dorma" above me. *Must be a record,* I decided, pressing the doorbell more insistently.

"Who'sa dere?" shouted the voice.

I looked up to see, thrust out the window, a brown face topped by curly, white hair.

"Carolyn Blue," I called. "Who was singing Calaf's aria?"

"It'sa me! Bruno Valetti, besta tenor on Sacramento. What you want?"

"My mother-in-law, Professor Blue, wants my husband and me to move into her apartment while she's—"

"Oh sure. *La Professora. Una minuto.* I let you in."

Sunday strollers were staring at me as they passed by with wheeled grocery carts and chic bags from department stores on Union Square. I pretended an overwhelming interest in the names, some illegible, of the other tenants until Mr. Valetti swung open the blue door, grasped my hand, and kissed it. He was a little, wrinkled man with a scratchy chin that left a red mark on my hand, clothes that looked too big for him, and flopping slippers on his feet that did not keep him from bounding up two flights of stairs with me in tow. My lungs were afire and my calves aching by the time he opened the door to an apartment that was not my mother-in-law's. It was his.

"Have a seat, *Bellissima,*" he cried, beaming at me. "I have-a gelato I make-a myself, an' espresso." Before I could protest, he was scurrying out of the room, calling over his shoulder, "I, Bruno Valetti, am-a lose my heart to *la Professora.* Many times I'm-a ask to marry her. You husband, her son?"

"Yes, Jason," I replied, trying to imagine Mr. Valetti proposing to my mother-in-law. He probably didn't even understand feminism.

"*Si, si.* Jason. Maybe him I ask for her hand. Many night, if she come home before it's-a my time for sleep, I serenade her. Puccini, Verde, Donizetti, Bellini. I'm-a sing in the opera chorus here inna San Francisco. You like-a "Va Pensero" from *Nabucco*?"

"Very much," I replied.

"Then I sing for you." He was rattling utensils in his kitchen.

"Mr. Valetti, I just wanted to pick up a key and take a look at the apartment. You really shouldn't go to so much trouble—"

"No trouble, *Bellissima*. I love-a sing for you." And he launched into that beautiful, melancholy chorus sung by the enslaved Hebrews.

Ah, well. Obviously I was going to stay for song, gelato, and espresso, all of which I like. I perched on the edge of a worn, but elegant chair, one of two separated by a small, elaborately carved table. An embroidered scarf picturing the Virgin and Child lay on the tabletop. From that viewpoint, I surveyed the room. Dusty velvet drapes hung at the wide windows on two walls, while darned lace curtains billowed inward in the late afternoon breeze. There was a slightly bald, velvet chaise longue with a box phonograph on a table beside it. Vinyl records in worn covers leaned against the table legs. Opera posters from theaters in Italy and San Francisco decorated the walls. Stretching away at my feet was a bare, but highly waxed wooden floor with a dark wooden inset lining the edges a half-foot from the walls. The only other thing in the room was a large television.

"You like-a my TV?" asked Mr. Valetti, bustling in with a silver tray, which he placed on the table before taking the chair that matched mine. "I sell my pizzeria—is called Bruno's Napoli—an' buy apartment house an' TV. For my old age. Once I make-a best pizza in San Francisco. Gotta place downtown, then sell an' move to Nort Beach, then sell an' retire here. But no stop-a singing."

I nodded. "I read that the first opera was sung at the

Tivoli Gardens, a beer garden. Then the owners opened the Eddy Street Opera House, where you could hear a famous singer for seventy-five cents. Of course, that was in the 1890s."

"Sure," Mr. Valetti responded. "Tetrazzini sing-a *Lucia* there," and he burst into a rendition of *"Tomba Degl' avi Miei."*

I nodded, smiled, and said, "Wonderful gelato."

"I make everyday. Only one flavor. When I have Bruno's Napoli—twenty–thirty flavors. Best gelato in San Francisco. Best pizza. Pizza come from Napoli. Bruno come from Napoli. *La Professora* marry me, I teach her make gelato. Pizza. *Penne all'arrabbiata.* You know it?"

"I'm afraid not," I replied, soaking a biscotti in my espresso.

"I make-a you *penne all' arrabbiata.* You an' you husband an' you husband mother when she come-a back. Ah! What a woman! Smart. Healthy. Hair is-a good as mine. Good woman for take care of Bruno in old age."

I had to stifle a giggle at the thought of Professor Vera Blue learning to cook Italian and taking care of the ebullient Mr. Valetti while he serenaded her with opera arias. "Mr. Valetti, she asked me to look at the apartment. She wants us to move in while she's in the—ah—"

"You no know she's in a jail? I go yesterday. Bring flowers an' a pizza Margherita, but they no let me in. Say only *famiglia.* I say, 'Bringa da priest, we marry, an' I be her *famiglia.*' 'Go away, Bruno,' they say to me. So I take my pizza home an' eat it myself. Is good. I no lose my touch. So you wanna go in *la Professora's appartamento.* Now we gotta problem. I need-a know you really her—"

"Of course," I said quickly and opened my purse. "My driver's license." I handed it to him. "Family pictures." I produced photos of the children and of Jason and myself.

While he studied each item carefully, I sipped the last of my espresso. "That's-a Jason. So we go downstairs." He rose, lifted a key from a board of keys, and led me downstairs, leaving his own door open behind him.

"Shouldn't you lock up?" I asked nervously.

"Anyone try to steal my TV or my espresso machine, I got alarms I bring home when I sell Bruno's Napoli. Make-a noise gonna wake alla dead popes in Rome."

I trotted down the stairs behind him and entered Vera's sublet, which was really quite nice—ledged woodwork high on the walls, the same bordered wooden floors, but these had lovely Persian carpets. There was a center room with a fireplace, although a dining room set and china cabinet occupied it, a bedroom and living room to the right, and a bathroom, office, and kitchen to the left. The office had built-in, glass-fronted cabinets. As I peered into the kitchen, which had a ground-level door leading to a backyard with flowers, a birdbath, and a separate garage, Mr. Valetti called, "Telephone winking. *La Professora* call an' leave message. I come down an' call someone else she wants to call."

I scooted back into the office in time to hear a male voice saying, "God damn it, Vera, your dog got knocked up. And don't blame me. She howled two nights in a row, so I thought she needed a walk and took her out. How the hell was I supposed to know she was in heat? This big lout of a rottweiler knocked me over to get to her. I damn near had a heart attack. Thought he was after me until he jumped her. So what should I do? Is there a morning-after pill for dogs? Should I get her an abortion? It's Lawrence. Call me back."

"No *la Professora*." Bruno punched skip and cut off Lawrence. "Carolyn," said Vera's voice sternly, "I hope you've made arrangements to move into the apartment. Margaret came to visit me this afternoon and said you planned to ask questions at the center. Don't. Someone killed Ms. Faulk. If you go poking around, they might decide to kill you. Believe me, Jason would not thank me if you were murdered on my behalf. Leave the matter to the police. And pay no attention to Margaret and her television-inspired idea about hiring a private detective. The police get paid to investigate murders. And please leave me a message on the telephone in case you're not there when I next call. The instruction book is in the drawer to the right of the computer. Mr. Valetti, if it's you checking the messages, please do not leave flowers for me at the jail. The guards complained." There was a pause; then the machine said, "End of messages."

"No flowers?" cried Mr. Valetti. "What kind jail no let flowers stay. The guard, he's-a Latino. Why he no understand romance?"

While the landlord chatted on, I fished out the instruction book, discovered that I could change the answering message, thereby communicating with my mother-in-law, and pushed the necessary buttons before recording my message. "I'm here, Vera, but I haven't seen Jason yet. If he agrees, I don't think we can move in until tomorrow. Someone named Lawrence called to say Clara has been impregnated by a rottweiler. He wants to know if there's a morning-after pill for dogs, and if you want it administered. Let Mr. Valetti know if you call before tomorrow, and tell him Lawrence's number. Hope to talk to you soon. This is Carolyn. Bye."

Then I turned to Mr. Valetti. "Could I call you around nine to see if she's left any messages?"

"Hey, I'm-a retired. Inna bed by nine. Call eight-thirty."

"Eight-thirty," I agreed and summoned a cab. As I sat on the front steps waiting, I mused on the situation. My mother-in-law was in jail, Clara needed a doggie abortion, Vera expected me to talk Jason into moving over here, and tomorrow, no matter what she said, I'd have to start asking questions at the crime scene since she'd never agree to a private detective.

So who could have inflicted multiple stab wounds on a women's center accountant? Perhaps some crazy person off the street. Maybe Denise had had a crazy boyfriend. Yes, that made more sense. Multiple stab wounds sounded like a crime of passion to me.

8
Husband Abandoned

Jason

After twenty-plus years of marriage I wasn't even sure how I ended up by myself in a hotel room with my usually good-humored wife, suitcase in hand, slamming the door in my face. It started when Carolyn arrived at 6:25. I had been waiting since 5:45 to tell her about one of those perfect days in a scientist's life: old friends rediscovered, fascinating research ideas discussed, exciting plans for our organization on environmental toxicology, my nomination to become next year's president of the group. Instead, I spent the forty minutes worrying about what could have happened to her. Carolyn is rarely late and always considerate about calling if she's been held up. Could she have been run down by a car? Or mugged?

"My God, Carolyn," I cried when she finally let herself into the room, "where have you been? The mixer starts in five minutes. I've been worried that—"

"Oh, goodness," my wife murmured, "heaven forbid we should miss a minute of what will undoubtedly be the social event of the year." With that remark, she kicked off her shoes and began to unbutton her jacket.

"You were supposed to be here at 5:30," I pointed out, taken aback by her snippy tone when I was expecting an apology.

"Jason, goodness knows you've been late often enough, and as for my being late, keep in mind that I had to be at the jail at 7:30 this morning, or have you forgotten about your mother?"

The truth is that it had slipped my mind—perhaps because the idea of my mother charged with murder was too nonsensical to be taken seriously.

"Well, she's in jail, and I went there, and then I had to eat an Egg McMuffin because McDonald's is the only place open on Sunday in that area, and then I had to go back to the jail and wait on the sixth floor with a very strange group of people, some with tattoos, until I could go upstairs and stand—not sit, stand—for twenty minutes while your mother demanded to know where you were and why I'd left Gwen unprotected in New York City."

"Didn't you tell her Gwen is with Charlotte?"

"Of course I did. And then she told me that we have to move into her apartment while she's in jail."

"We can't do that. The meeting is—"

"Here. I know. You tell her. And then I had to meet her lawyer because your mother refuses to take the situation seriously. She's too busy preaching feminism to the prisoners and guards to—"

I had to laugh at that point because it was so like my mother to see being jailed as an opportunity rather than a cause for dismay.

"Oh, you think it's funny? Well, her lawyer says they have a good case."

"That's ridiculous."

"And that we should hire a private detective to find out who really killed Denise Faulk because the police, who think your mother did it, aren't going to. And that means, since neither of you is taking this seriously, that I'll have to find the murderer myself."

"You'll do no such thing," I protested, remembering with a shudder various dangerous situations my wife had exposed herself to since she started traveling with me. "Mother's quite right. The police will—"

"I went to see them. That was my fifth stop. It seems that your mother was found kneeling over a body with multiple stab wounds, covered with the victim's blood, her bloody fingerprints all over the office, and that she had a loud quarrel with the victim just that afternoon. Homicide Inspector Harry Yu is convinced that your mother is guilty. By the way, he has a nephew named Fong teaching psychology somewhere in West Texas."

"That would be Millard Fong," I replied, astonished. "I've met him."

"Good for you! When we get back to El Paso, you can tell him that his uncle arrested your mother. After Harry Yu, I had to go to your mother's apartment and have espresso with an elderly tenor named Valetti in order to get a key to her place."

"Look, Carolyn, perhaps we should talk about this later."

"And then someone named Lawrence in Chicago called about the rape of your mother's dog."

"Carolyn, are you making this stuff up? We don't have time for jokes. We have to get downstairs. Are you going to change?"

"Certainly I'm going to change, and bathe. I'm exhausted and dirty and—well, why don't you just go downstairs, Jason, if the mixer is more important than your mother's—"

"I didn't say that, but—"

"Run along. I'll meet you down there."

I sighed and allowed myself to be pushed out the door by my grumpy wife. Two hours later she showed up at the mixer, just as I was considering a return to the room to see what had happened to her. Evidently she'd taken a nap, bathed, changed clothes, and called my mother's landlord before venturing downstairs. The mixer was winding down, and we'd been invited to visit North Beach for Maine lobster at some Italian restaurant that provided discount coupons to conference participants. Hoping to cheer Carolyn up—she does love Maine lobster—I mentioned the plans and the friends with whom we'd be going.

"If I wanted to write about Maine lobster, I'd go to Maine," she muttered, but she did agree to accompany us after making two more calls.

"Were you calling local master chefs for reservations and recipes?" asked Jeannie Lohman, young trophy wife of a Ron Lohman from Penn State. "Jason's been telling us about your column. I'm going to demand that our local paper run it. It sounds like so much fun, Carolyn. Are you going to write about the dinner tonight? You could quote each of us." She turned to Ron. "Wouldn't that be awesome, Ron? We'll clip it and send it to your mother." Ron mumbled a response having to do with his mother's refusal to read his scientific papers much less his opinions on Maine lobster.

My wife sighed, smiled, and off we went. On the way she told us that North Beach had been, from the fifties, the Beatnik enclave, Jack Kerouac and company, but before that the Italian community, a den of anarchism and café socializing. I did feel a bit conscience-stricken because Carolyn looked tired, and the restaurant was crowded and noisy. We had to wait a half hour for seats, but the price of lobster, purchased with our tourist coupons, was amazingly good. Fifteen dollars for a whole meal: minestrone, salad, garlic bread, three-quarter-pound lobster, clarified butter, and coffee.

Given the amount of alcohol consumed at the mixer, cocktails from the bar while we waited for a table, and wine during dinner, we were a merry group by the end of the evening. Carolyn dutifully took down quotations on

the meal from various members of our party: Bob Timo-
thy, University of Illinois, Urbana, said, "There are no
beans in this minestrone. Aren't there supposed to be
beans, Carolyn? Those tasty white ones?" Al Mahmoud,
University of Vermont, said, "What's wrong with these
people? Every restaurant should have a vegetarian plate,
and a dinner salad just doesn't do it." Margie Forman, University of New Orleans, said, "God, I love lobster. Eating it
makes me feel so prehistoric. Look at it. It's scarier-looking
than a crab. Paul, honey, if we were Neanderthals, would
you dismantle my lobster for me with a rock?" Paul Forman, Tulane, replied, "Lobsters are deep water creatures,
Margie. I doubt that Neanderthals ever got any." Collie
Mertz, Oregon State said, "I'd recommend this particular
merlot to any of your picky wine connoisseurs." I added,
"The retail price at Sam's Club is around fifteen dollars."
And so forth. Carolyn surreptitiously ripped her notes
from the notebook and slipped them under her dessert
plate.

When we finally returned to our hotel room, she said
wearily, "I repacked for you, Jason. We need to check out
and move to your mother's apartment."

"Carolyn, I see no reason—"

"It costs her over three dollars for the connection and
three minutes from the jail. We can't call her there, and
she can't call us here collect. I phoned Mr. Valetti at 8:25
and promised we'd do it. I'd still be on the telephone with
him if I hadn't agreed, and you'd have missed the cheap
lobster dinner. He'll put the message on her machine."

"What good would it do for us to move there? I certainly can't stay waiting for my mother to call. This is an
important meeting, and Hodge, Brune is paying for it."

"Fine. I'll get the calls."

"You're planning to give up your food research and sit
home—"

"No, actually, I'm planning to find out who killed
Denise Faulk so your mother can get out of jail. As for her

calls, I can pick them up and leave her messages on the answering machine, but I have to be there to do it."

"Carolyn, I forbid you to endanger yourself by—"

"Jason, I'm much too tired to put up with ultimatums."

"And as for moving, we can talk about that tomorrow."

"Fine. You can leave a message telling me what you decide." With that, my wife grasped the handle of her suitcase and wheeled it out. Before I could get there, she had slammed the door in my face. I was so irritated that I let her go. However, by the time I had taken a shower, I began to worry about her taking cabs at night by herself. What if the landlord wouldn't let her in? There she'd be, out on the street with her suitcase, and no way to call a cab to get back here, maybe too proud to do so if she could.

I called my mother's number. Carolyn answered. When I admitted that I was simply calling to find out if she had arrived safely, she hung up, then put the phone on automatic answering machine and refused to pick up. Obviously, I was going to have to move to Sacramento Street tomorrow.

Heretofore, I hadn't taken my mother's situation seriously. She'd been in jail before. In fact, she has a felony conviction for leading a group of women into a psychiatrist's office and demonstrating how to protect oneself against a rapist by kneeing him in the balls. The psychiatrist had been drugging his patients and having sex with them and was saved from jail himself by promising to take no more female patients. He got probation and lost his license to practice. He also had to have a testicle removed after my mother's visit.

She got probation because hordes of Chicago women hounded judges, police, and city politicians on her behalf. Then a female judge, who hated psychiatrists, arranged a pardon and the expunging of Mother's felony from the public record. Carolyn doesn't even know about that episode. Maybe my mother did need help, no matter how invulnerable she thought herself. But I did not want my wife chasing after a murderer. The very idea terrified me. So how was I to help my mother and derail Carolyn? I mulled over the problem and then called my father in Naperville, waking him up, midnight in San Francisco being 2 A.M. in Chicago. Although my parents have been divorced since I was twelve and my father remarried and had two more children not much older than my kids, he always had sensible advice to offer when it came to dealing with my mother.

"God damn it!" Dad said when I'd explained the situation. "I can't believe she's in jail again. What's the charge?"

"She's accused of killing someone at the women's center with a big knife."

"Why do they think Vera did it?"

"She had an argument with the woman and—"

"The victim was a woman? Christ! Vera wouldn't stab a woman. They must be hard up for a suspect."

"Carolyn talked to them, and they're sure they've got the right person."

"You believe your mother killed someone?"

"Of course not, Dad, but Carolyn has decided she has to save Mother by finding the real murderer. She walked out when I told her to stay out of it."

"Well, that's good. She's gone home?"

"No, she's moved to Mother's sublet and plans to start asking questions at the center tomorrow. Dad, she could get herself killed."

"Right," my father agreed crisply. "As soon as I can get a flight, I'll fly in and hire a private detective."

"Funny, that's evidently what Mother's lawyer suggested. Of course, Mother said no."

"Well, Vera's safely in jail, and she can't tell me what to do, anyway."

"How would we find one?"

"My people do a lot of lab work for a company in San

Francisco. They'll have a security outfit that can recommend someone. Meanwhile, you get on the line and tell your wife we'll take care of it."

I tried the number again and got the answering machine. No doubt my wife was fast asleep in my mother's bed while I stayed up worrying about the two of them, not to mention all the problems I could see developing out of my father's appearance on the scene. Mother would be furious if anyone told her about it, and when she did get out of jail, he'd have gone home, and I'd get jumped for interfering in her business.

Well, hell! Hard to believe how much I'd looked forward to this meeting, how cheerful I'd felt at 5:30, and how tired I was now. If I didn't get to sleep, I'd have to skip my morning run.

9

The Duty to Detect

Carolyn

I woke to find myself in a strange bed without my husband. After a moment of panic, I remembered: Vera's sublet, the violent murder, the quarrel with Jason. In all our years together, I'd never walked out on him. What had gotten into me? Well, I had been very tired when I got back to the hotel—all the stress, the walking and riding in taxis, not to mention three cups of coffee. Jason can do that, but I'm definitely a one-cup woman, and not near bedtime. No wonder I was awake in the middle of the night.

Then I had to admit how much I resented feeling responsible for the exoneration of Jason's mother. Both of them had told me to stay out of it. Yet someone had to do something, and I was the only someone with sense enough to realize it. I had a perfectly good reason to be angry with Jason. She was *his* mother.

And what about Gwen and Chris? They'd be horribly embarrassed to have their grandmother on trial for murder, and even more so if she were convicted. Innocent people got convicted; I'd seen it in the newspapers and on TV. Having a grandmother imprisoned for a violent murder could ruin their lives. People would whisper behind their backs. People they wanted to date would shy away. They would be denied fellowships and jobs for reasons that were never mentioned.

And Jason—didn't he realize his career could be affected? Or mine? I could see the headline: *Food writer related to feminist knife-murderer.* Who would want to follow my recipes? On the other hand, my agent, Loretta Blum, would probably say that any publicity is better than no publicity. She'd say the notoriety would help the sales of my book, *Eating Out in the Big Easy*, when it came out.

I had to have it in by early fall. How was I supposed to concentrate with my mother-in-law accused of murder? And I had to prove her innocence before our family was destroyed.

I'd go straight to that women's center tomorrow morning and ask questions. It was my duty! Flopping over on my side, I gave my pillow a punch, determined to go back to sleep. I'm happy to say that, worries and espresso aside, I did—probably out of sheer perversity.

"Carolyn? Carolyn? For Pete's sake would you pick up?"

I woke with a start, heart racing, and recognized Jason's voice. He must have been shouting into his telephone at the hotel because I could hear him from Vera's office in the far corner of the apartment.

"All right. You're still mad at me. I'm sorry I wasn't more sympathetic. But don't go out investigating. Please! I called my dad. He's flying in this morning. He'll hire a detective. So just—just have some great meals and write about them. OK? I'll check out of the hotel and join you on Sacramento Street by 6:30. I love you, sweetheart. . . . Well, I guess you're not going to pick up. OK. Bye."

He'd already hung up by the time I managed to disentangle myself from the sheets—I must have had a very restless night—and stagger out of the bedroom, around the dining room table, and into the office, where a lighted digital clock told me that it was 6:30. He'd called me before going out to run. Only a mad man would consider running up and down the hills of San Francisco. Only a mad man couldn't wait to call until he got back and I might be up. I punched the replay button and listened to his message. *Have some great meals and write about them* indeed! He was still trying to tell me I shouldn't look into the murder of what's-her-name. And Jason's father was going to hire a detective to help his ex-wife? Like I believed *that*!

I stumbled back across the apartment and fell into bed. I still planned to go straight over to the center, but nine o'clock should be quite early enough.

10
Frittata with the Pizza Man

Carolyn

Showered and dressed, I was peering into the refrigerator to see what Vera had in stock, hardly anything, when someone knocked at my door. A voice called, "*Bellissima,* is-a me. Bruno Valetti. Answer the door. I'm-a hear you toilet an' you shower, so I'm-a fix you a tasty frittata. Is omelet *Italiano. Si?*"

Saved by the neighborhood tenor, I thought and dashed to the front door.

Mr. Valetti stood before me with the lovely aroma of an Italian kitchen wafting from his spatula. Or was it imagination that made me think that I could already smell the frittata? "Come!" he cried. "The mozzarella is-a almost melt."

We scampered downstairs. Feeling mildly vindictive, I thought of my husband who, by staying at the hotel, was going to miss a lovely breakfast. The omelet, fresh from the oven, was creamy and dripping with cheese, flavored with mushroom, onion, and ham chunks that had probably been sliced from a delicious product of Parma. I glanced around, but no such ham hung from his ceiling. However, braids of garlic and onion festooned his kitchen, and his table was tiled like an ancient Roman mosaic and surrounded by four of those miserably uncomfortable, rush-bottomed chairs whose seats are rimmed by hardwood. Such rims have left indentations on the bottoms of generations in Mediterranean Europe.

While I complimented Mr. Valetti on his delectable frittata, I glanced surreptitiously at the design on his table. I had read recently about pornographic mosaics found that year in a unisex Pompeii bathhouse, which information prompted the thought that I might be eating my breakfast on an embarrassing depiction of ancient sexual practices.

"I see you look-a my tile. I'm-a do it myself. A hobby. *Si*? I get furniture that don't look good on top. I'm-a tile it like an old mosaic in a picture book. You wanna see the one inna my bedroom?"

"No, thanks," I said hastily. The kitchen table didn't seem to be pornographic, but it was hard to tell because it was covered with the cast-iron frying pan in which he had made the frittata; plates, cups and saucers, wildly painted in red and yellow; a vase of purple flowers that I'd seen growing on bushes around the city; and a stack of magazines. But goodness knows what mosaics he had in the bedroom and whether he'd showed them to my mother-in-law. I almost choked on a bite of garlic toast when I thought of Vera casting a jaundiced eye on some ancient Roman courtesan and her lover cavorting on a ledge in a bathhouse. I'd seen some of those mosaics myself. They caught you by surprise, especially if you were fourteen years old and accompanied by your father, a rather stern history professor.

Mr. Valetti sighed. "You mother-in-law, the beautiful *professora,* she no want to see either. My wife Anna, God cherish her soul, she's-a like the tiles. Her grandfather on the mama's side make-a tiles in Ravenna, for fix up the basilica there. Very old. Her father, he's a longshoreman, beat up scabs on Bloody Thursday in 1934 with Harry Bridges, the *communista*. He no wanna my Anna marry me. He don't like guys like me jus' over from Napoli. I'm-a say, 'I can cook, I gotta job, I'm-a no *communista*,'" so Anna an' me elope an' finda priest in the Mission to marry us. Her papa hire a witch to put a curse on us. No babies. We never forgive him. But that's many years ago. Anna an' me make many mosaics together."

I was sorry then that I'd refused to see the ones in his bedroom. Probably his late wife made them.

"I'm-a got a new project. Emperors' heads around the sink. When I'm-a chop tomatoes, alla bad emperors, they get splashed behind my sink." He laughed heartily.

"Tell me, Mr. Valetti, did my mother-in-law ever talk to you about the women's center?"

"Oh sure. She's-a say they got too many social-worker types, an' no one who's-a know nothing about theory. That's-a some theory about women an' how they should forget cookin' the pasta, an' go out an' make more money than their husbands. So I say, "*Cara mia,* I'm-a no make money no more. I'm-a retired, an' I'm-a make pasta like you never eat in you whole life. You an' me, we be perfect *famiglia.*" He sighed. "She no say yes, but she's gonna do it. You see."

"Did she ever say anything about people not getting along at the center?" I asked.

"Oh sure. Alla women talkin' bad about alla other women. Jus' like in the old country. My sister, rest in peace, she insult a neighbor, an' they—"

"Did anyone have a grudge against my mother-in-law?" I interrupted. Perhaps Vera had been "set up to take the fall" as they say on TV.

"Naw. Why someone have a grudge against you mama? She's-a smart woman. She's-a famous *professora.*"

And an irritating one, I thought. "Well, what about the woman who got killed? Did my mother-in-law ever mention her?"

"Oh sure. She say Denise, she's-a got such a stone head; she's-a need a hammer behind the ear to tell her anything."

Oh dear, I thought. *I'll have to keep him away from the police.*

"So what you gonna do today, *Bellissima*?" He refilled my espresso cup and passed the plate of sautéed tomato slices, a dish I had always associated with the English— and pleasantly so. I like their fried tomatoes much better than their raw bacon or their gray sausage. Not that England isn't rapidly overcoming its reputation for inedible food.

"You go to Fisherman's Wharf? Everyone wanna go to—"

"No, Mr. Valetti, I intend to visit the center and find out who killed Denise Faulk."

He nodded solemnly. "I go too. We—how you say?— spring *la Professora* from the jail. How you gonna find out who kill the poor dead lady?"

"Well, I thought I'd talk to the security man. He guards the front door and makes everyone sign in. After I find out who was in the building that night, I'll know whom to investigate."

"You're a smart girl, jus' like you mama."

"In-law," I added. "And as kind as it is of you to offer to go with me, you really shouldn't feel that I need either help or protection." As I said this, I was thinking of my husband, who didn't want me to get involved.

"Oh sure, you need-a my help," protested Mr. Valetti as he rose and carried his plate to the sink. "Only in books is-a detectives women. I'm-a go with you because you a woman, an' my daughter when my *professora* marry me. How can-a she no marry me if I get her outa the jail?"

"Mr. Valetti, Vera's been divorced for a long time, speaking of which, doesn't your church forbid you to marry a divorced person?"

"How they gonna know if I don' tell 'em? No, I go

with you. What if the guard he don' wanna tell you who sign his paper? I'm-a tell him I'm a *mafioso*."

"Are you?" I asked, alarmed.

"No, *cara mia*." Bruno laughed. "I'm-a pizza man. But the guard, he don' know. He's gonna tell us anything we wanna know, cause he's-a think I'm a *mafioso*." He took my plate, from which I managed to fork up the last tomato before he could remove it. "An' how you gonna get there? I'm-a got a truck. I drive you. I see no one gives you no trouble. I take care of you like you my own daughter. It's-a my duty, because I'm-a love *la Professora*."

And that's how I ended up beginning my investigation with Mr. Valetti at my side. He refused to be left behind no matter what arguments I used. We went downstairs and out into the backyard, behind which was a garage that housed his vehicle, a brown truck of some ancient vintage, but well maintained and preserved, as he was himself. Within minutes we were chugging off to the Union Street Women's Center, a delightful Victorian building, two stories high and narrow in front, but rising behind to three stories as it descended a hill for almost a full block. It was adorned with bay windows, rounded turret corners, intricate gingerbread trim, stained glass, and a stunning light-blue exterior with maroon and white accents. My mother-in-law must have hated the décor. Fussy Victoriana was not her style!

Italian Omelet

- Preheat oven to 450 degrees F.

- Sauté *1/2 cup sliced mushrooms* and *1/2 chopped medium onion* in *1 tbs. butter,* and set aside.

- Mix *6 beaten eggs, 3 tbs. heavy cream, salt and ground black pepper to taste, 1/4 tsp. basil, 2 sprigs chopped parsley,* and *1 tbs. grated Parmesan cheese.*

- Heat *1 tbs. olive oil* and *1 tbs. butter* in a large cast-iron skillet or other heavy ovenproof frying pan until butter turns white. Pour in egg mixture and cook over a very low heat until mixture is soft on top. Remove from heat.

- Sprinkle the top with the sautéed mushrooms and onion, *1/2 cup diced cooked ham, 1 tbs. grated Parmesan cheese, several drops of lemon juice, 4 oz. cubed mozzarella cheese,* and *1 tbs. butter melted.*

- Place skillet in oven and bake until the cheese has melted (about 4 minutes). Remove to a hot platter and serve with *parsley garnish, toasted garlic bread,* and a side of *sautéed tomato slices* sprinkled with *fine bread crumbs, olive oil,* and *herbs of choice.*

- Serves 4.

11
Sleuths: Day One

Carolyn

Once parked, Mr. Valetti and I had to climb a very steep stair to reach the front door of the center. For no sensible reason, the city fathers, several centuries earlier, had laid the streets straight up and down the hills, perhaps as an exercise in sheer perversity. San Francisco is known as a contrarian society for more reasons than its city planning.

I was panting by the time we arrived but not too incapacitated to admire the double doors with their stained glass insets and fan window above. At the same time it occurred to me the glass would make the center easy to break into. Perhaps the person who killed Denise Faulk had done just that. I'd have to investigate.

We entered a wide hall with an uncarpeted, scuffed, wooden floor. Immediately to our left was a table with a sign that invited us to state our business to "center security" and sign in. The chair behind the table was empty. Another indication that an outsider could have entered, unremarked, and killed Denise.

On the wall behind hung a large directory board giving floor and room numbers for the services offered by the center. I skimmed over such ordinary items as Director and Business Office, which I could see down the hall on the right cordoned off by crime scene tape. Battered Women's Advocacy, Child-Care Referrals, and Nutrition Central didn't cause me much speculation, but what had my mother-in-law made of Lesbian and Transsexual Support? Or the Crone Cohort, which brought bizarre pictures of witches to mind?

To my immediate right was a door that announced in elaborate gold letters: Office of the Director and below that, Marina Chavez-Timberlite. I decided to call on her first, but my knock went unanswered. However, a head popped out from the second door on the left, and the woman called, "Kelani's on maternity leave. She's probably giving birth as we speak."

"We're looking for Ms. Chavez-Timberlite," I called back.

"Knock on the inside door." The woman then ducked back into her office.

With Mr. Valetti in tow, muttering about "that bastard Eric Timberlite," I entered the first door and found a tiny anteroom—presumably the domain of the absent Kelani. The room had been carved out of the corner tower of the building.

"I doubt that Ms. Chavez-Timberlite is related to the man you dislike," I murmured to Mr. Valetti, "but either way, please exercise discretion." Then I knocked on the director's door and was invited in.

A tiny woman in very high heels, an expensive dark-red suit, and a head of shining black hair pulled back into a chignon turned from her many paned, five-sided window alcove and looked at us without pleasure. I judged her to be a good six inches shorter than I, probably five to ten years older. Even in middle age she was a beautiful woman. Or was she the poster patient of some expensive cosmetic surgeon? That light tan skin stretched rather too tightly over good bones.

"Ms. Chavez-Timberlite?"

"Mrs.," she corrected. "My husband is Eric Timberlite. The city's foremost developer." She sounded very pleased with herself and him.

"See," hissed Mr. Valetti.

"Sh-sh," I murmured and introduced myself. Possibly Mr. Timberlite was, as Mr. Valetti had suggested, Satan in an Armani suit, guilty of evicting widows and orphans from their apartments and supporting rent laws that would benefit him and destroy small landlords like Mr. Valetti. Still, I couldn't afford to offend Mrs. Timberlite when my investigation would have to be conducted on the lady's turf.

"Blue?" said Mrs. Chavez-Timberlite. "Are you related to Vera Blue?"

"She's my mother-in-law."

"Well, let me tell you, I wish I'd never let Lila Epersen talk me into inviting that woman to come here as a consultant. She's been nothing but trouble since she arrived. She talked the Women of Color into harassing my husband. They're picketing his office building."

"Good for them," said Mr. Valetti. "Maybe I'm-a go help." He turned to me. "We take some pizza. That picketing, it's-a hungry work."

Mrs. Chavez-Timberlite turned on Mr. Valetti, whom I hadn't had the chance to introduce. "My husband is doing nothing wrong. He just wants to beautify the city by tearing down old tenements."

"Sure. He's-a throw poor people inna the street."

"There's housing in Daly City for such people," snapped the director.

She didn't sound to me like a sympathetic do-gooder type. "Be that as it may," I interrupted, "my mother-in-law—"

"Is a murderer," the director finished for me, "and I'm

not at all surprised. She's been a thorn in everyone's side since the day she arrived. A rude and troublesome woman. "

True, I thought, feeling discouraged. "But she's not a murderer," I said stoutly.

"She's-a *mio amore,*" said Mr. Valetti, not a sentiment likely to endear him to the director.

"Why am I not surprised?" she retorted. "Only a disgusting little immigrant would find Vera Blue attractive."

"Sure. I'm-a come over from Italy, an' I'm-a make a lotta money. Honest money. Not like you husband. So where *you* come from? Mexico? Puerto Rico?"

She looked down her nose at Mr. Valetti and claimed that she was descended from the Californios, the ranchers who preceded the Yankees who stole the land from Spain.

"Actually," I said, unable to resist an historical tidbit, "California was owned by Mexico before it became part of the United States." She did not look pleased. "At any rate, I can assure you that my mother-in-law did not kill your business manager. Since I hope to find out who did commit the murder, I thought the best place to start would be here at the center where people knew the victim. I wonder if you would be so kind as to help me with information."

"I certainly would not, and you do not have permission to disturb our staff. We provide an important community service, and I do not want the relative of a criminal with no expertise in investigating—" She stopped and smirked at me. "What are you, Mrs. Blue? A housewife?"

"I'm a writer and expert on gourmet food."

"Really. Can you cook?"

"Certainly," I replied, not mentioning that I did it as seldom as possible.

"Desserts?"

"I'm famous for my chocolate-walnut cake."

"Excellent. We're celebrating our tenth anniversary on Saturday, and Nutrition Central is providing refreshments, which will be made by our three cooking classes, Easy

Ethnic, Working Mom Cookery, and Food Stamp Gourmet. Perhaps you could teach the Thursday group to make that chocolate-walnut cake. We'll need about ten. Talk to Alicia Rovere. Nutrition Central. The kitchen is in the third building, first floor."

Although amazed at her presumption, I said, "I could do that, but in return you'll have to agree to my investigation."

"Done," said the director with a sly look. "Of course, you'll need permission from the chairman of our board."

Mean Marina was looking shifty, and it occurred to me that she didn't expect the chairman to agree.

"Let me give you her name and number."

She wrote busily on a pad, one of those from-the-desk-of models. You'd think a charitable institution could save some money by dispensing with such perks.

"Go right down to Alicia's office and sign up for that cake class. She'll be so pleased. Oh, and when you get through, maybe you can use her phone to contact our chairwoman. I'd let you use mine, but I have important calls to make. And if you don't get Nora the first time, don't give up." She then waved us out of the office.

"Is a scam," Mr. Valetti said to me. "She get you to teach-a the cake, an' the lady she say you call probably never home or say no when you ask. Rovere now, that's a good Italian name. Maybe she help."

I glanced at the note: Nora Farraday Hollis. There were two numbers. "Oh, there's the security man. He's the first person we need to talk to." I suppose I should have tried to get permission from Ms. Hollis before commencing my investigation, but I didn't want to miss this opportunity now that the guard was finally at his station.

12

The Happy Russian

Carolyn

The man at the security desk was thin and middle-aged with pale, ropy arms that projected from the short sleeves of a badly ironed shirt. Pouched dark circles under his eyes, sunken cheeks, and graying blond hair, very badly cut, completed the picture. His nametag read Alexi Timatovich. I was reminded of Richard Henry Dana's description of a Christmas celebration on a Russian brig in the bay. They drank a barrel of gin, ate a sack of tallow, and made soup from the skin. The guard looked as if he might have been subsisting on that diet. His face bore lines of pessimism and disaffection. *He must be very badly paid,* I thought, *not to mention unreliable about manning his post.*

"Good morning," I said cheerily. "I'm Carolyn Blue, and I'm here to investigate the death of Denise Faulk. Were you here the night of her murder?"

"*Da,*" he replied, squinting at me suspiciously. "Vassily an' me. My son." He showed his first sign of animation.

"Vassily is math genius. Is being computer millionaire while still young like Microsoft," he predicted.

"That's wonderful," I replied. "I didn't catch your name."

"Alexi Timatovich."

"So, Mr. Timatovich, while you were on duty that night did you see any suspicious people in the center, someone who might have killed Denise Faulk?"

"Lady professor after she is killing Mrs. Faulk. Got blood all over when police taking her away to prison."

"Professor Blue didn't kill Mrs. Faulk."

"No?" He looked puzzled. "Maybe police killing her and blaming old lady. In Russia such things happening, but not so much in Siberia where my family living. Everyone busy keeping warm, even police. Got no time for killing ladies and blaming other ladies."

"Siberia? You a criminal?" asked Mr. Valetti, who had been listening closely.

"No criminal. Engineer," said Mr. Timatovich. "Build things. Is hard in cold."

"Sure, engineer," said Mr. Valetti sarcastically. "An' now a guard."

"Guard is good job," said Mr. Timatovich. "Guard in United States making more money and living better than engineer in Russia. And here no cold, no snow. Is good job. Only bad that having to pay for son's university."

"Maybe he'll get a scholarship," I suggested. "Did you see anyone entering Mrs. Faulk's office before Professor Blue went in?"

"Seeing no one."

"You see *la Professora* go in?" asked Mr. Valetti suspiciously.

"No see professor until coming out all over blood with police. I watching door into building, not more doors. I signing in peoples coming in and peoples going out, not looking at peoples inside."

I was discouraged to hear that he'd paid no attention to

events down the hall, but if he checked visitors both in
and out—well, that information would be helpful.

"Were any of the people you signed in given to violence? Or particular enemies of Mrs. Faulk?"

"Not letting in bad peoples. Bad husband coming to
look for wife, I sending away."

"One came that evening?" I asked eagerly. That would
be an important clue. Denise Faulk had headed the Battered Women's Advocacy before she took over as business
manager, and abusive husbands have been known to attack whose who help their wives.

"*Da*. Man always beating up wife coming to find her.
Very mad. Very drunk. Thinking we got her here. I am
saying, 'She not here. Go away, or I call police.'"

"And what happened?" I asked.

Mr. Timatovich shrugged. "He going away."

"Could he have gotten in some other way, or perhaps at
some time when you were away from your desk?"

"No one coming in or going out from Alexi Timatovich
without signing name. Always I am being here."

"You wasn't here when we came in, an' we ain't sign-a
your book," said Mr. Valetti.

"So I am taking a piss. I sitting here or in toilet. You
saying Alexi Timatovich not good security?"

"Not at all," I interjected hastily. No need to alienate
the man; I could check on his reliability through other
avenues. "What was the name of the angry husband?"

"Freddie Piñon. Everyone here knowing him. Bad
man. Alla bosses say not letting him in."

I wrote the name down. A definite lead. "Could I see
the list of people who were in the building that night?"

Mr. Timatovich patted the book in front of him. "Here
is book."

He was certainly helpful. Wondering what Mrs.
Chavez-Timberlite would think of his accommodating be-
havior, I flipped back to Thursday and found, to my dismay, several pages of names. Obviously I couldn't copy

all those down. "Perhaps I could make a photocopy of these pages, Mr. Timatovich."

"Why not? Just so you not taking book off desk. I am having pencil." The security man produced it. "And pen." He pointed to the pen, lodged by the page for the present day. Either I'd have to copy all those names or find someone with a copy machine and the authority to order Mr. Timatovich to let me take his sign-in log away. And do it without the director's knowledge. It seemed to me that, even if she didn't like Vera, she should have been interested in seeing the actual murderer arrested for the crime. Or maybe not.

13
Help at Nutrition Central

Carolyn

Following Mr. Timatovich's directions, we walked along the hall of the A-building. On the right side were the offices of the director and the crime-scene-taped Business Office; on the left beyond the security guard's table were an office for the Chairman of the Board, a boardroom, and stairs to the second floor, under which was an area, obviously walled off as an afterthought, marked *Toilet*. Were men allowed to use the facilities? Or did they have to go elsewhere? If so, it was no wonder Mr. Timatovich had been away from his desk. Of course, the bathrooms might be unisex.

At the end of the hall side-by-side steps and a ramp led down to the next building, which contained, on the left, the Crone Cohort, the toilet, and a storage room, and, on the right, Female and Fit, which had two doors. Conversations could be heard behind office doors, and music accompanied by thumps from the second door on the right, perhaps people getting fit.

We descended to the third section and found a huge

room crowded with cooking and dishwashing equipment, sinks and food preparation areas, refrigerators, a long table with chairs to our immediate right and to the left a small, partitioned-off office. It's door bore the legend, *Alicia Rovere, Food Lady.* In various parts of the room, each decorated with appropriate, if somewhat garish murals, women were preparing food. I longed to scoot over to the Food Stamp Gourmet section, where something involving cheese and bananas seemed to be underway, but Mr. Valetti had exclaimed, "Alicia? Is-a you? *Mia bellissima*!" He was hugging a barrel-shaped lady in the office doorway.

"Is-a Alicia Rovere," he cried with delight. "*Moglie de mio amico* Alberto Rovere, who's-a make-a the gelato even better than mine, better than God's."

"Bite your tongue, you heretic," said Mrs. Rovere. "You want God to send a bolt of lightning through my door?"

"God an' me, we got an agreement. I make-a the pizza, Alberto make-a the gelato, and God, he make-a the beautiful women like you to keep us happy."

"Always the flatterer," she said, and then to me, "Are you Bruno's *professora*? You're too young and pretty for an old goat like Bruno."

"That's very kind of you," I mumbled. We forty-something ladies are always happy to be called young and pretty, "But Mr. Valetti—"

"Is-a her mother-in-law I'm-a lose my heart to," Bruno explained. "This pretty girl is-a *Carolyn. Mio amore,* she's-a name Gwenivere. Soon as we get her outa the jail, you an' Alberto come-a my house for pizza an' meet her."

"What's she doing in jail?" Mrs. Rovere looked astounded.

"She was arrested for murdering your business manager," I replied for Mr. Valetti.

"Mother of God," gasped Mrs. Rovere. "Bruno's in love with the consultant from Chicago? She'll break your heart, Bruno. I never met a woman with less romance in her soul. Why, she doesn't believe in God. She doesn't even like opera." Mrs. Rovere shoved her hands into the capacious pockets of her apron, which she wore over a severe navy blue dress that came almost to her ankles, and frowned.

"My mother-in-law doesn't seem like Mr. Valetti's type," I agreed. "Nonetheless, he's been so kind as to offer his help in my efforts to exonerate her."

"Hasn't she got a husband to help her? Or a son? Is she a widow?"

"Divorced," I replied.

"Bruno, you can't marry a divorced woman!" Mrs. Rovere warned.

"What the church don't know, don't hurt," said Mr. Valetti. "So, you think my sweet *professora* killed the woman here?"

"Sweet *professora,* my sainted aunt Agata. But no, I don't think she killed Denise. She's not big enough."

"My thought exactly," I agreed. "My mother-in-law, if she wanted to stab someone to death, would have to pick on a dwarf. And since you're on our side, Mrs. Rovere, could I use your telephone? In return—" I sighed at what I'd agreed to do. "In return, I've promised the director to teach a class to make chocolate-walnut cakes for the anniversary celebration."

"You know how to bake?" she asked suspiciously.

"She's-a the famous food writer in the newspaper," said Mr. Valetti proudly. "She gonna put one-a my pizza recipes in her column. Maybe you nice to her, she put one of Alberto's gelato recipes in, too."

"Alberto keeps his secret," said Mrs. Rovere, "but she could print one of our Food Stamp Gourmet dishes. Those poor girls are hard to motivate. Who wouldn't be, trying to make decent meals out of government surplus and no money." She beamed at me. "My telephone is yours. You teach the dessert class, put one of our recipes in the paper, and get copies for our girls, and I'll even help you find out who killed Denise."

Although I thought that I might be giving more than I was getting in this bargain, I allowed myself to be waved into her office. It was very small with shelves of recipe books in various languages and loose-leaf notebooks that evidently held class rolls of cooking students. After removing a stack of calendars penciled with the names of teachers and class hours, I sat down and dialed the first number for Nora Farraday Hollis.

Would you believe it? The director had given me two wrong numbers. One wasn't a working number, and the other connected me to an astrologist. A phone book lay on the window seat of Nutrition Central, so I tried that. Without success. Maybe she had an unlisted number or was listed under her husband's name. Or maybe the director made her up as an excuse for evading my request while tricking me into teaching welfare mothers.

When I left the office, Mr. Valetti was gone, and Mrs. Rovere was having a heated discussion with the banana-and-cheese instructor. When she noted my forlorn presence outside her office, she bustled past me to make a call. "Alexi, this is Alicia Rovere. Give that little Italian fellow your sign-in book. We need to photocopy a couple of pages. . . . Don't argue with me, or I'll tell the director you've been sending your son to sit in for you evenings so you can get overtime without working it yourself. . . . Just tear out a sheet, and have people sign in on that. You can tape it back when Bruno returns the book."

She hung up and waved me in. "Russians are such sneaks. He couldn't get away with that scam if the director ever showed her face here after five in the afternoon. Still, his boy wants to go to Cal Tech. If the overtime gets him there, I guess it's in a good cause, but I'll tell you, if Denise hadn't been killed, she'd have turned him in and put a stop to it. She was really worried about the money. Told me there should have been more in our accounts."

"You're the second person who's said that," I murmured. "I wonder if someone killed her over center money."

"I doubt it," said Mrs. Rovere. "She was just too new to the job to realize how much this old building eats up in maintenance."

Having had one theory shot down, I kept to myself the thought that Mr. Timatovich might have killed Denise Faulk to keep her from revealing his overtime scam. "The director seems to have given me the wrong numbers for the chairwoman of the center's board."

"Oh, I have Nora's number. No reason to believe she'll be home. The woman volunteers and donates to every charitable and cultural cause in town. Or just plain runs them." She pushed the phone across the desk to me. "Hit memory and 07." With that, she bustled out again to greet Bruno, who had returned with the sign-in book. I called the chairwoman while they came into the office and began to photocopy pages from last Thursday.

Someone with a Spanish accent answered "Hollis residence" and informed me that Señora Hollis was out. When I mentioned that I was calling from the center, I was given another number to call, which initially seemed to be yet a third misdirection.

"Legion of Honor. May I help you?" I was dumbstruck, believing the Legion of Honor to be a French award. I stammered out the chairwoman's name and was asked to hold. During the ensuing wait, Alicia, Bruno, and I argued about whether the whole day's sign-ins should be copied or just those from the night of the murder. Finally the Legion of Honor lady came back, apologized for the delay, and told me that Mrs. Hollis was accompanying a group of art lovers through the Henry Moore exhibit and would return my call as soon as she was free. *Henry Moore? The sculptor?* I left Alicia's number.

"What's the Legion of Honor?" I asked after hanging up.

"A museum up in Lincoln Park. Beautiful view," said Alicia. "Now let's look at these names, although you wouldn't think a killer would sign in when he arrived to murder someone."

14
The List

Carolyn

I decided to start two lists, one for suspects, one for people who had been in the building when Denise Faulk was killed. First, I wrote in Freddie Piñon, an abuser whose wife had been sent to a shelter by Denise. No matter what Timatovich said, Piñon might have returned. Then I added Timatovich because Denise had threatened to have him fired for claiming unearned overtime pay. These notations I made while trailing Bruno and Alicia to the long table across from her office.

He and I sat down on either side of "the food lady" with the photocopies of the sign-in list in front of us. First, Alicia read the names of people who had checked in during the day while Bruno and I searched other pages to determine whether they had left before the murder. Finally, we narrowed our list to those who had been in the building during the event. Alicia knew nothing about many of the clients on the list, but she did have helpful observations on staff members and volunteers.

Kebra Zenawi, for instance, was a volunteer in the Bat-

tered Women's Advocacy. "She'd never have killed
Denise. Margaret Hanrahan and Denise managed to save
her from an abusive husband and get her the ownership of
the family restaurant, an Ethiopian place." Alicia had been
tapping a pencil on the name. "Isn't everyone in Ethiopia
starving? What do they serve at an Ethiopian restaurant?"
she mused.

We certainly had no Ethiopian restaurants in El Paso. I
wrote *Kebra Zenawi* on my list of people to interview,
then flipped to the back of the notebook and wrote, "Try
Ethiopian food."

"Kara Meyerhof is the head of Lesbian and Transsexual Support," Alicia continued. "She had no quarrel with
Denise."

I wrote *Kara Meyerhof* on the to-interview list.

"Patrick Baker O'Finn's a lawyer in Margaret's husband's firm. Margaret recruited him to defend the center
against a woman in the Crone Cohort who's suing us.
Something about toilets. You'd have to ask Maria Fortuni
for the details, but I don't see why O'Finn would have
any quarrel with Denise. He's working pro bono."

I wrote his name and Maria Fortuni's on the interview
list.

"Maria had a big fight with Denise. Poor Denise didn't
much like being the center accountant. She said she met
more angry people there than in Battered Women, and believe you-me, some of those batterers can be terrifying
when they're deprived of a beloved punching bag."

I transferred Maria Fortuni to the suspect list.

"Maria and Denise got into it about costs for the old
ladies' ramp, but I don't think Maria could have killed
anyone. She's frail and must be eighty at least."

I put a question mark beside the Crone Cohort lady.

"Marcus Croker. Now there's an unforgiving man, a
policeman who teaches the self-defense class for Female
and Fit. Turns out he was running the name of every
woman who signed up through the police computer. We

found out when he refused to let one poor soul into his class because she'd called the police on a spousal abuse case and then refused to file charges. He and Denise had a real row about it."

Marcus Croker went onto my suspect list.

"Then we've got Denise and Vera. They had words, but your mother-in-law had words with just about everyone here. She's not exactly Lady Tactful, but I don't know that she ever inflicted physical injury on anyone. Last, there's Yasmin Atta. She's a volunteer who teaches clothing and makeup to women looking for work. Doubt she even knew Denise."

I wrote Yasmin Atta in as an interviewee. She might have seen something. Because Alicia didn't know most of the clients, I took charge of the photocopy with the idea that I might follow up on them if I hadn't found the real murderer on the list I'd already concocted.

The Food Stamp Gourmet class had finished their project, so Bruno and I were invited for lunch. Naturally, I accepted, seeing the possibility of a column. Not that cheese and bananas sounded promising. While the table was set and food put in place, I went back to Alicia's office to take a call from Nora Farraday Hollis, a very gracious woman. She said, in response to my request, "Investigate to your heart's content, my dear. I'm so glad that someone is coming to Vera's defense. Obviously a woman of her renown can't be a murderer, but no one seems to be able to convince the police of that. And I do hope you'll keep me informed on your progress. Why don't you join me for lunch at the museum on, say, Thursday? Have you seen our Henry Moore exhibit?"

Of course, I hadn't. I'd never been to her museum. When Mrs. Hollis heard that I was unfamiliar with his drawings, she offered to show me through the exhibit herself. I accepted with pleasure. Even if I didn't have time or news by then, I would be entitled to a respite from investigation.

The cheese and banana casserole was not a delectable dish, although if your family was on welfare and going hungry, it might seem tasty. As we ate, Alicia remarked that Denise had had a touchy family situation. "She was a widow and inherited a lot from her husband, enough so she could quit her job and volunteer here. I heard a rumor that her stepson was an abuser, and his wife came to the center for help. That probably caused some problems."

As I wrote *stepson* on my suspect list, apple pie was being served. Evidently the federal government was giving away apples. The crust left something to be desired.

"You could check with Penny Widdister for files on the stepson and his wife," Alicia added. She pushed her pie plate away after one bite, but Bruno took it as a second helping. He had been eating steadily and without complaint. Maybe he had the same attitude that I do: if you don't have to cook it yourself, eat up and don't complain.

"Also I heard that Denise and Dr. Tagalong at Female and Fit had words. Rosamunda's heart was set on a mammogram machine. She even had volunteers set to run it, so she could do everyone's breasts. Of course, Denise had to say there wasn't enough money."

"Who's-a have the job before the dead lady?" asked Bruno, having finished his second piece of pie. He interrupted advice to a black, unwed mother on the intricacies of pasta making to ask his question. The young woman had just told him that she thought making your own pasta when you could get it in a box was "a dumb idea."

"Good thought," I agreed. "We need to find out why there were so many financial problems."

"I already told you that a building like this gobbles up money," Alicia replied.

"Yes, but the problems seem to have led to many of Denise's—"

"Myra Fox. Denise took over from Myra because Myra had to have a mastectomy. If you want to talk to her, do it on the phone. The poor woman looks dreadful—almost bald from the follow-up radiation, dreadfully thin even before she was diagnosed—and she's very sensitive about the whole thing."

I felt terrible at the thought of bothering a woman who had been through such an ordeal. Obviously, she hadn't killed Denise. I wouldn't call her unless I had to. Instead I made other calls.

First I tried Kebra Zenawi at her restaurant, but she couldn't come to the telephone because she was busy. I left my name and number. Then I called Yasmin Atta and discovered, to my astonishment, that she was the CEO of a company called Nightshades. Surely they didn't make poison? And there was that terrorist named Atta. I had to admonish myself not to be silly. If she were the CEO of a terrorist poison-making establishment, she wouldn't announce it in the firm name. And probably nightshade isn't a weapon of mass destruction. More like something in a Shakespearean play.

After I had stated my business, the executive secretary said Miss Atta was booked solid all week, but if I wanted to meet her at Zaré for lunch at one on Wednesday, she'd work me in. I agreed and got the address of Zaré, hoping it would be a place I could use for a column. Last I called Marcus Croker at his police station. They said he wasn't on duty today and that they did not give out home phone numbers. Even if my telephone calls hadn't produced much, Alicia Rovere had been a trove of information, for which I thanked her profusely.

"I will find out who killed Denise," I promised. I had to drag Bruno away from a second young welfare recipient, who was getting a lecture on the proper way to make tomato sauce.

"Go help your girlfriend's daughter-in-law ask questions," Alicia told him. "Anyone wants to make tomato sauce, I can tell them."

"That comes in a can," said the boxed-pasta enthusiast, "but you don't have to put nothin' on the pasta. The kids like it plain."

15
Canvassing 1-B

Carolyn

We climbed the steps between C and B buildings, knocked, and entered the office of the Crone Cohort. What a dreadful name! I had gathered from Alicia that it was the service arm for older women, but what aging woman wanted to be called a crone? We found a tiny lady with white hair and a thin face that displayed the vestiges of former beauty. Maria Fortuni. She told me that I wasn't old enough for her group, then said to Bruno, "Don't you know the meaning of the word *crone*, old man? It means old *woman*."

"I'm-a think it mean ugly, old woman, but you are a beautiful lady." He clasped his hands over his heart. "An' from Italia, too."

"My father was from Italy," she said crossly. "I see you know of the Fortunis. Maybe you think you can get your hands on my money."

Bruno looked stricken. "You break-a my heart, pretty lady." Then he burst into a sobbing rendition of "Una Furtiva Lagrima" from *Elisir D'Amore*. That means "one furtive tear," and Mr. Valetti produced several as he sang to her.

Before he could launch into a second verse, I cleared my throat, and Mrs. Fortuni said, "I don't like tenors. My late husband was a tenor, not to mention a lecher, who cared for nothing but sex and money." Mr. Valetti looked shocked. "As soon as he died, I took my family name back, and I intend to keep it to the end of my days."

"Excuse me, ma'am," I interrupted politely, "but I'm investigating the murder of Denise Faulk."

"Why? She was a horrible person. Determined to call off building the ramp for women my age. How can they expect us to climb those dreadful steps in front? But then they obviously don't care about our problems. If they did, they wouldn't have given us such an offensive name. *Crone Cohort.* My mission in life is to get it changed. Someone should murder Pansy Bouquet, or whatever the witch is called. The name was her idea."

"Witch?" I echoed weakly.

"Oh yes, we have witches and lesbians and men who've had their privates cut off. The only sensible thing the center has done is put them up there in the attic where no one sees much of them. It's a scandal. Almost as bad as Denise saying we couldn't have a ramp because it would run insurance rates up. Security concerns or some such."

"There's an unguarded entrance that anyone can use?" I asked.

"Of course not. Only we *crones* are supposed to use it."

So much for security and knowing who was in the building that night, I thought, greatly discouraged.

"Well, I beat her on that. And if she hadn't been stabbed to death—probably by someone whose project she cancelled—I'd have won on getting female-only legal assistance and financial counseling. Have you any idea how many old ladies are cheated by men, particularly their own male children or their lawyers? Declared incompetent so the families or lawyers can grab all the money and put them away in nursing homes? My clients aren't all as sharp as I am. I've got women who can't remember which office I'm in, much less what's going on with their money. What are you staring at, old man? Did you just realize that your children are stealing you blind?"

"Bruno of Bruno's Napoli got lots of money an' no children," Bruno retorted. "Now I got a nice apartment house, bring in rents for my old age."

"In that case you can ask me for a date, but I'm not saying I'll go."

"Were you in the building the night Denise was killed, Ms. Fortuni?" I asked, unable to think of any more subtle way to put it. She could have been here. All she had to do was climb the middle ramp.

Maria Fortuni snorted. "You think I killed her? I don't go out after dark."

I'd have to check on that.

"You hear, old man? You want to take me out, you have to ask for an afternoon. On the weekend. The only one of us old folks who was here was Yolanda Minarez. She's suing the center, so she came to see some lawyer. You can bet he'll take her for a pretty penny. The silly twit forgot to lock the bathroom door when she was in there, and the Russian walked in on her. Now she's suing to keep men out of the toilets, and Denise said we couldn't afford both men's and women's toilets. She'll probably say we can't afford water if the place catches fire."

"She's dead," I murmured. Yolanda Minarez hadn't been on the list. She'd obviously come in the side door too. I wrote the names of both women down on my list. Before I could ask any further questions of Maria Fortuni, we were interrupted by a high-pitched tirade in a foreign language. It seemed to be coming from across the hall, Female and Fit, if I remembered correctly.

"It's the Chinese," snapped Mrs. Fortuni. She pushed herself up from her desk and hobbled, using a cane, to the door, where she shouted, "Be quiet in there!"

Obviously Maria Fortuni had not killed Denise Faulk. Ms. Fortuni was no taller than my mother-in-law and considerably less mobile. Bruno whispered in my ear, "As if I'm-a date her. Does she look-a like she go dancing? Anyway, I'm inna love with you mother."

"*In-law,*" I corrected. I thanked Ms. Fortuni for her time and crossed to the enclave of Female and Fit, where an elderly Chinese lady was shouting at a Chinese girl while a woman in a white doctor's jacket, big black-framed glasses, and long, black hair looked on with interest. I imagined the Chinese grandmother as a young bride in an embroidered satin dress and slippers, wearing an elaborate hairdo, one of the "first chop ladies," being led from a steamer by her husband, a Chinese merchant in the city. Their pictures on rice paper had been for sale in Chinese stores, but they themselves were never seen again outside their husband's houses. A romantic idea, but this lady would have to be about 150 years old to fit that scenario.

When she saw us, Dr. Rosamunda Tagalong skirted the warring Chinese, and offered her hand for a brisk shake.

"Isn't Tagalong a Philippine language?" I asked with interest.

"It is," said the doctor crisply, "and I am from the Philippines. When I came to this country for my medical training, your immigration service was so kind as to mistake one of the languages I speak for my family name, which was, in a past life, de Corona. My student visa, my work visa, and finally my citizenship papers are forever in the name of Rosamunda Tagalong."

"Many Americans," I replied pleasantly, "carry names that are the result of mistakes by immigration officers.

I'm Carolyn Blue, and I'm investigating the murder of Denise Faulk."

"Ah, the estimable Mrs. Faulk, may she rest in peace. Are you related to the murderer?"

"*La professora* is-a no murderer," said Mr. Valetti.

"Well, she certainly wasn't the only person to exchange words with Mrs. Faulk, just the one at the scene of the crime with blood all over her. I myself had a much better reason for resenting Denise. Our late business manager was unbelievably shortsighted. In fact, had the mammogram machine I requested been financed earlier, Denise wouldn't have died."

Is she confessing? I wondered.

"Two years ago when I first suggested it, a mammography facility here would have caught Myra Fox's cancer early so that she wouldn't have had to undergo radiation after surgery. In that case, she'd have been back at work before someone could kill Denise."

While I was trying out that line of reasoning, Dr. Tagalong said, "Every woman over forty should have a yearly mammogram, not to mention learning self-examination techniques, and—" She noticed at that point that the old Chinese woman was glaring at her and said, "That includes you, Mrs. Yu. At your age mammography is a necessity."

A stream of Chinese issued from the old lady, and the young one translated, "Grandmother says she will not have people taking pictures of her private parts, and she will not do exercises in a swimming pool wearing an immodest garment that even a concubine would shun." The young woman sighed. "I'd hoped you could convince her, Dr. Tagalong, but Grandmother is very stubborn and old-fashioned."

"Are you and your grandmother, by any chance, related to Homicide Inspector Harry Yu?" I asked. "He mentioned his grandmother when I talked to him about my mother-in-law's arrest."

"You know my father?" The young woman looked astonished. "I'm Ginger Yu. Well, Dolly Madison Yu."

"Ah yes, the presidential and first-lady naming tradition. I'm Carolyn Blue. My husband knows your cousin, Millard Fillmore Fong."

"My cousin! Wait. Blue? And you said my father arrested your mother-in-law? I can't believe it." Tears filled her eyes. "He did it on purpose. To keep me from living in the dorms."

"I beg your pardon?"

"You said he arrested your mother-in-law. That has to be Professor Vera Blue. She was going to get me another scholarship so I won't have to live at home when I start at Berkeley this fall. Daddy doesn't want me to live in the dorms, and he claims he can't afford to pay for a dormitory room. Now he's—" She couldn't continue because her grandmother began to lecture her in Chinese.

"What did she say?" I asked, hoping more light might be shed on Inspector Yu's ignoble reasons for arresting my mother-in-law.

"She says only if I live at home can my family protect my virginity so that I will be marriageable when they find a suitable husband for me. Have you ever heard anything so hopelessly retro?"

I smiled at Grandmother Yu and replied, "I know just what you mean, Mrs. Yu. I worry about my daughter every day she's away at school, but there does come a time when we have to let them find their way, trusting that we have raised our daughters to act according to what we taught them."

Both Yu's nodded, each evidently thinking I supported her position. Dr. Tagalong said, "What young women need to be taught is safe sex. And, of course, breast self-examination. It's never too early to start, you know." This last was addressed to Ginger. "If you practice safe sex, your grandmother won't have to worry about you, and self-examination will keep you from dying of cancer."

Evidently Mrs. Yu not only understood English but again disagreed with the doctor.

Ginger disagreed as well. "The experts are saying that self-examination is a waste of time."

"They're wrong," snapped the doctor.

"Dr. Tagalong, were you in the building the night Denise Faulk was killed?" I asked.

"No, I was attending a meeting on STDs. That's sexually transmitted diseases. Many of our clients either have them or are at risk. And, as I believe I said, I did not kill Mrs. Faulk. I respect my oath as a doctor—do no harm."

More sharp words from Mrs. Yu.

"Grandmother wants to see the garden," said Ginger. "She likes gardens."

"Fine. Fresh air is good for the elderly," said the doctor, "but you must convince her to get a mammogram and start water exercise at the Y. Small-boned, elderly Asian women are at risk for osteoporosis. Tell your grandmother that a few hours every week in the pool are much better than a broken hip."

Mrs. Yu glared and left; her granddaughter trailed along after telling me how proud I must be to have such a wonderful woman as my mother-in-law.

"I believe that Marcus Croker teaches a class in your division," I said to the doctor.

"Indeed. The Centers for Disease Control have declared violence an epidemic in this country. Consequently, I feel that our clients should be able to protect themselves."

"Would you have his home phone number?"

"You think Marcus killed Denise?"

"Since he was here that night, maybe he saw something."

"Being a policeman, he'd have reported it if he saw something."

"Still, I'd like to talk to him."

"I don't give out the home numbers of our volunteers."

"She's-a no gonna help," said Bruno. "We try the second floor. Maybe murderer there."

Old houses certainly have their drawbacks, foremost among them the high ceilings, which make for steep stairs. If Dr. Tagalong could have seen me puffing up those stairs, she'd have wanted to put me in an exercise class.

16
Canvassing on Two

Carolyn

The Working Women and Child-Care Referral offices were closed for a meeting upstairs. In the B section, Legal Services was closed, but Penny Widdister, a slender, jittery, cocoa-colored woman, was manning the Battered Women's Advocacy. A lush philodendron decorated her bay window and an array of delicate glass figures, some broken and glued back together, adorned her desk. When we knocked, she jumped nervously and eyed Bruno as if he meant her harm.

After introductions, I explained our mission. She said, "Thank God, I wasn't here that night. I hate violence." The poor woman blinked back tears. "In fact, I'd never have let the director talk me into this job, even on an interim basis, if I hadn't thought Myra would be well sooner so Denise could come back. Now Denise is dead, Myra is still sick, and I'm terrified. I'll just have to find some other volunteer activity to satisfy N.A.P.C.P. requirements."

P.C.P.? Wasn't that a dangerous chemical? I'd have to ask Jason.

". . . Association for the Protection of Colored People, all ladies of good family and strong church affiliation. Unfortunately, many women of color, not our members of course, are abused by men. It's very sad. But I don't care. I'm not doing this anymore."

"I can understand that the plight of the clients must break your heart," I said sympathetically.

"Well, yes, but it's the men. They come in here and threaten me because I'm not allowed to tell them where we've housed their wives for safekeeping and their poor little children."

"And you weren't here last Thursday?"

"No, Kebra was. And I wish I hadn't been here Wednesday, either. That's the night a man named Piñon came in and screamed at me. I told him to go away or I'd call the police. I had my hand on the telephone. He said he'd kill me if I called the police. I—I panicked and threw the telephone at him."

"Good for you," said Bruno. "Is a smart move."

"No, it wasn't. Denise was irritated because I broke the phone, and I was terrified because I had to run by him while he was cursing and staggering around with his head bleeding, and Margaret said we might get sued because I injured him, and I locked myself in the bathroom until he went away, but by the time the police arrived, he was gone, and the director was peeved because she said the police and sirens made the center look like a dangerous place." Penny then burst into tears. "And he broke four of my glass figurines before he left."

I asked gently, "Would you have a name or address for Freddie Piñon?" Why hadn't Timatovich told me Piñon had been here Wednesday night? Maybe Piñon had slipped in twice.

"Do you think he killed Denise?" Penny asked. "I hope he goes to jail forever. It's so silly to think the professor killed her. Old ladies don't kill people." She rummaged through a drawer and pulled out the file on Frederico and Graciella Piñon. "Denise got Gracie into a shelter the first time, but he found her and went to jail because he hit the director of the shelter. Then Gracie went to another shelter; I don't even know which one. That information is in the safe. When he got paroled, he came right back here. I consider him very dangerous."

I agreed and wrote down the telephone number and address of the evil Freddie's mother, the name of his halfway house, at which he would no longer be residing, and the name and number of his parole officer. Obviously he had to be investigated, but I didn't want to do it. "Do you have a home number for Kebra Zenawi? Since she was here Thursday, I'd like to talk to her."

"Oh, Kebra wouldn't have killed Denise. She adored her. Denise is the reason Kebra volunteers here."

"Yes, but she might have seen someone suspicious."

"Of course. What a good idea! It's so frightening to think a murderer may still be lurking around. Waiting to kill someone else." She started to tremble.

I patted her hand and told her she was a very brave woman, a little white lie, but it seemed to make her feel better. When she'd calmed down, I went next door to the Women of Color office, and Bruno stayed to talk philodendron care with Penny. Bertha Harley, a sturdy black woman, possibly fifty or so, greeted me. She was going gray, but her skin was completely unwrinkled. Twin children sat on her floor playing jacks and giggling.

To me she said, "Wrong color, honey." To the children, she said, "Stop with the gigglin', babies. We got us some company." The children stopped giggling, looked at me, round-eyed, and then went back to their game. *Very well behaved,* I thought, *especially for preschoolers.*

I repeated my standard introduction and statement of purpose, then smiled down at the little ones. "Your twins?" I asked.

"Lord no, honey. My grandbabies. My no-good daughter got herself hooked on crack cocaine. I beat up her dealer, but she jus' went out an' got herself another one, so I took the babies to raise. No baby should hafta live with a crackhead mother. Sounds like you're related to Vera, so I'll jus' tell you up front, no way Vera Blue killed poor ole Denise. Vera is good folks. 'Fore she went off to jail, she was helpin' with our protest against the Timberlite people. Knows a lot about protestin', she does. Also knows a lot about gettin' the goods on no-good exploiters of poor women in need of cheap housin'. That Mr. Eric Timberlite, he gonna end up in jail himself if Vera still on his case."

"I see." My lord, what if Denise was killed and Vera framed to get them off the land developer's back. No wonder his wife had tried to keep me from investigating. "Was Denise involved in the protest movement as well?"

"Lord no, honey. Wouldn't even cough up money for picket signs, but I got 'em made in the neighborhood, so we're in good shape for the demonstration. Hope you can get Vera out in time to march with us."

"Yes, I hope so too. Were you here the night of the murder, Mrs. Harley?"

"God bless you, no, chile. Got choir practice at the church on Thursday nights. My clients know not to come then. Doubt there was a woman a color in the house."

She was wrong about that. "Do you know of anyone who disliked Denise?"

"Sure do. Denise was a real penny pincher, jus' sayin' no to everybody need money, but none of 'em be killin' her. I give it some thought, and I figgered maybe Bad Girl. Denise tole Doctor Rosie that puttin' a psycho in the art class like to raise the insurance rates an' scare off clients. That Bad Girl is some mean chile, an' she hear what Denise say 'bout her an' come out screamin' words no Christian woman would use, but then likely the closest that one git to God be one fallen angel name Satan."

"What's her real name?"

"Don' know that. She live in a shelter over in the Haight, or sometime on the street. Gets her pills from a free clinic. Doctor Rosie say she fine if she take them meds, but I swear she don' take 'em much. Bad Girl prob'ly be over there paintin' murals in C buildin' right this minute. Part of therapy, tha's Doctor Rosie's dumb idea. Bad Girl, she like to scare poor ole Fiona half to death, but maybe they know her real name over there. You could try."

I thanked Mrs. Harley, who called after me, "Jus' look for the T-shirt. It say *Bad Girl* front an' back, an' she wear it everyday." Then I collected Bruno and made my way, reluctantly, down the stairs to 2-C, another large room like the kitchen. What a sight it was! On the far side by the bay window stood a huge grand piano, badly scarred and so heavy it caused the floor to sag. The rest of the room had large plasterboard wall sections used for mural painting, tables, easels, music stands, boxes of supplies, and a lady wearing a pink shirtwaist dress trying to encourage a group of black and Hispanic women in the art of flower painting on dishes.

I introduced myself and Bruno in a furtive whisper while I glanced around. Several of the painters looked scary. "Do you have a student called Bad Girl?" I asked. "Mrs. Harley in Women of Color mentioned her."

Fiona Morell sighed. "She's the one painting knives on a teacup."

"Knives?"

"Yes, she simply has no interest in flowers or any other *nice* subject. Even the mural painters, who aren't usually that fussy, become irritated when she paints knives into the hands of their figures. Those who don't think they're twenty-first-century Diego Riveras want to emulate gang graffiti artists. It's very distressing to me, I must say."

"Perhaps you could tell me her real name."

"Well, she *says* it's Martina L. King, but that's just a

lie. Dr. King believed in the peaceful principles of Mahatma Ghandi. If you want to speak to her, I can call her over, but that's not a guarantee she'll come. I don't think she likes other white people. Even when she's taking her medication."

"We gotta go upstairs," said Bruno, who had been listening to the conversation and looking from Mrs. Morell to a white girl three easels to the rear wearing a black T-shirt and a head of dusty dreadlocks. Since Martina L. King looked terrifying and seemed to make those around her nervous, I cravenly allowed myself to be urged away. Had she been here Thursday? I'd ask around, and if she had, I'd suggest that Dr. Tagalong talk to her, or her psychiatrist, if she had one.

17
Canvassing the Attic

Carolyn

The child-care and working women were stampeding down from the meeting as we took the stairs to the third floor. One asked Bruno if he was planning to change his sex, which he took amiss. For just one horrified moment, I thought they did the operations upstairs, but of course that was nonsense. They probably provided counseling. A wave of exhaustion washed over me. It had been a long day, and instead of more interviews, I'd rather have gone home for a nice, end-of-the-afternoon nap.

Our first encounter was with Kara Meyerhof, a blonde in the Lesbian and Transsexual office. She was alone and typing industriously at a computer. When she noticed us, she saved her work and rose for a hearty introduction and handshake. My, she was tall. At least six feet. Bruno's mouth dropped open.

When I told her who we were, her whole face brightened. "Vera's daughter-in-law. A fellow *writer*!"

"Well, yes, but her writing is much more academic

than mine. Not that I don't try to add some history to my columns, but—"

"No dear, *I'm* a fellow writer. Historical romances."

"Really," I said weakly. Was she writing lesbian romances?

"Yes indeed. I have at least *twenty* in print. I was just finishing a scene for my newest, *Frontier Passion*."

Had there been lesbians on the frontier?

"I've been winning awards for romance for *years*," she added proudly. "I just couldn't attend the conferences to pick them up. It's so much *easier* now that I'm a woman. Although the formal banquets *can* be a problem. I can't seem to find an evening gown that looks good on me because of my wide shoulders."

Evidently she wasn't a lesbian. "Maybe you could get some advice from Yasmin Atta," I suggested. "She teaches classes here on makeup and clothing selection."

"I had no *idea*. Yasmin, the famous model and founder of Nightshades, Inc.? We never hear *anything* up here on three. And I can't *thank* you enough for the suggestion. Yasmin would be *perfect*. She's *very* tall, you know."

"Actually, I don't, but I'm having lunch with her Wednesday."

"Isn't that *exciting*!" Kara sat down and said, "Would you like to hear an excerpt from my chapter. It's really *hot,* if I do say so myself. I'm sure the reviewers will put this book in the *very sensual* category. Isn't that ironic? Women all over the country love my romances, and I can't even get a *date*. Men just don't want us to be *really* tall. Unless we look like Yasmin, of course." She peered at her screen and began to read, "Parker rolled his muscular body over onto her slender—"

Bruno sputtered and turned red. I quickly intervened, saying, "I'm afraid I wouldn't be any help at all as a critic. I don't read romances."

Kara giggled. "I should have known. *Vera* probably won't let you. She gives me *such* a hard time about writing things that objectify women as sexual objects, instead of providing role models that will inspire them to overcome the prejudices of the patriarchy. I just tell her that I need a *date* more than I need a *lecture*."

"Actually, I'm trying to find out who killed Denise Faulk," I said.

"Well, *I* certainly didn't. Denise was always *very* nice to me. Not everybody here is. And *Vera* certainly didn't kill Denise. The police should be ashamed of themselves, and I told them so. I said it was probably some *dope addict* trying to rob the business office. Of course, they didn't pay any attention to *me,* except for the black policewoman, who said, 'Jesus, you're tall. How tall are you?' I *hate* that."

"Did the center keep money in the business office?" I asked hopefully.

"I have *no* idea, but it's a good theory, don't you think? It makes more sense than blaming Vera. I *tried* to visit her over the weekend, but you have to have an appointment, and I didn't get there in time. They *did* let me leave the cookies I baked for her. Does she like cookies?"

"Who doesn't?" I replied diplomatically, and Bruno and I left to check out the other office on the third floor, Interfaith Women. He was very upset that the jail deputies had taken Kara's cookies but refused his pizza.

I must have misunderstood the remark about witches. Interfaith Women sounded like an ecumenical organization. A lady in sandals and flowing clothes let us in. She wasn't wearing a flower crown, but she looked like a participant in an outdoor sixties wedding, and she introduced herself as Marigold Garland (Maria Fortuni's Pansy Bouquet?). Still, she didn't look like a witch. Not that I'd ever met one.

Once we'd stated our business, Marigold sighed and said, "Vera wouldn't want my help. She called me an idiot the last time I saw her. Goodness, she acts as if we're a bunch of fruitcakes. Even the army—or is it the air force?—recognizes Wicca as an established religion. They authorized services at a base in Texas. It came out in our newsletter several years ago."

Marigold offered us chairs and provided cups of tea, each of which had a flower petal floating in it. "I bring the flowers from home," said Marigold, "and I buy the tea at Crystals and Teas in the Haight."

I just hoped that the tea wasn't a hallucinogen and the flowers poisonous. I have bushes in El Paso, oleanders, whose leaves and petals can kill a cat or even a baby, but Jason wouldn't let me have them cut down. He said our children are too old and sensible to eat the leaves off our bushes when they come home from college.

"I don't know how I can help in finding Denise's killer. No one from our group was here that night. Of course, we held a ceremony over the weekend to cleanse the building—spiritual cleansing. We didn't actually scrub it down. I'm not sure they've been allowed to clean up the blood in the office. The police wouldn't even let us in that room to chant."

"Maybe you've heard of someone who had a grudge against Denise," I suggested.

"Denise was well liked. She's saved many women from. . . . Wait!" She held her hand up dramatically. "I've just had an idea. Why don't you attend our ceremony tomorrow night? Maybe the Goddess will send us a sign to help with your investigation."

What goddess? I wondered. *What kind of ceremony?* "Actually, I just wanted to talk to people who might be able to help." I emphasized the word *people*.

"Then you must come. After the ceremony we have a social hour, herb tea and cookies. We have a channeler. Perhaps Jeanine could put you in contact with Denise herself. Denise probably knows who killed her."

"Well, I . . ."

"Be here just before moonrise. The ceremony is in the backyard and the social hour in the kitchen. I just had *an-*

other thought! Perhaps you mother's arrest is punishment from the Goddess for her unkind words about our faith."

"My mother died when I was a child. Vera is my mother-in-*law*."

"You poor dear. Have you heard from her since she died? If you haven't, our channeler will certainly have to try to put you in touch. That's much more likely to be successful than trying to contact Denise, unless you were close to her."

"I never met her."

"There, you see." Marigold beamed at me. "I'm sure you'll find it very helpful to talk to your mother. Children who lose their parents at an early age so often have unresolved issues with the departed. It does help to talk it out with the late parent."

I fled. Bruno was right behind me, muttering that the church used to burn women like that. He wondered if the pope had heard that witchcraft was making a comeback.

I was thinking that I shouldn't let these strange encounters upset me. This was, after all, San Francisco.

18
The Perversity of Husbands and Mothers-in-Law

Carolyn

Back in the apartment at 4:30, I had to forego a nap to call Jason about dinner plans. The conference desk was reluctant to summon him from a session, but I assured them that it was an emergency concerning his mother. I didn't mention that she was in jail, not in a hospital, as they undoubtedly surmised. Jason must have thought the same thing because he came on the line, saying, "What's happened? Did the guards beat her up? Or the inmates?"

Good! I thought. If he hadn't yet realized how dangerous the murder accusation was, at least it had dawned on him that his mother, in jail among hardened criminals at her advanced age, was in danger. Not that I envied the hardened criminals, who were undoubtedly being subjected to feminist lectures. "I haven't heard from Vera," I replied. "Did your father hire the detective?"

"You called me from a meeting to ask about a detective?" he exclaimed. "Well, the answer is yes. Dad's friend recommended one, and he hired the fellow, so you don't have to feel responsible for the investigation. I hope you haven't been doing anything dangerous today."

"I had a lunch concocted by the Food Stamp Gourmet group, which was dangerous to the sensibilities of anyone who doesn't relish banana and cheese casseroles."

Jason laughed. "That should make a good column, but don't say you're planning to subject me to the dish."

"Never," I promised.

"Look, I've got to get back. I'll be home between 6:30 and 7:00."

"Just meet me at a restaurant called Eliza on Eighteenth Street. They're reputed to have wonderful Chinese food, an interesting décor, and a collection of art glass. Invite your father and the detective."

"Well, Dad, sure I'll invite him, but you don't need to meet the detective."

"Of course I do. I have information to pass on."

"Carolyn, what have you been doing? I specifically asked you not to—"

"If you don't care what happens to your mother, you might at least consider the effect on our children of having a grandmother convicted of a particularly gruesome murder."

"*Gruesome?* All the more reason for you to—"

"I'm sure a few more days in jail will lure your mother to my point of view. I'm told that the food is so bad an Irish terrorist, accustomed to English dungeon food, filed a complaint."

"Mother doesn't care about—"

"I'll make the reservation for four people. See you at 7:00." I then hung up to avoid further argument, and settled down for a nap. I should have known better. I had no more than fallen into a comfy doze when the phone rang. In case it was Jason, I let the answering machine pick up, the result of which was that I had to scramble to the office before Vera hung up.

"Did you just get in?" she asked, sounding peeved.

"No, I just hit my arm on a dining room chair," I replied, rubbing a painful bruise. "But I have spent the day at the center, Vera, and I have some good leads on Denise's murder."

"Didn't I tell you to leave it to the police?" she snapped. "If the murderer hears that you're nosing around, you'll be the next person dead. Denise was a veritable sieve when I got to her. And blood. You wouldn't believe—"

"Don't tell me what to do," I retorted peevishly. "We're going to get you freed, no matter how much fun you're having in jail."

"My goodness, you're in a bad mood. Still, I don't want you getting yourself murdered. Gwen and Chris will blame me, and I'd never hear the end of it from Jason. On the other hand, since you've been to the center, I have an errand for you. Did you meet Maude Kosinski? She's the head of Working Women."

"No, they were having a meeting on three when I stopped by her office."

"Meetings are the ultimate waste of time. If organizations would stop having meetings, they'd get twice as much done. Tell Maude I'm sending her a client. Have you got a pencil?"

I found one in a side drawer and took down the information. *Hispanic female. Jesusita Gomez. Nineteen. Single mother. Two children. To be released from jail Wednesday. Find her a job, housing, child care. Vera suggests starting a Jail-to-Work program in addition to the other three.*

"Will the head of the program want to deal with a criminal?" I asked.

"I should hope so," Vera snapped. "There are all sorts of organizations to help male parolees. We need to help the women, too. And assure Maude that this girl isn't some dangerous psychopath." She snorted with laughter, and I thought how few times I'd heard Vera laugh. Jail seemed to have improved her sense of humor. "Jesusita stupidly fell in love with a drug dealer and got scooped up when they arrested him. Poor girl's frantic because her children have gone into foster care."

"Doesn't she have any relatives who could take them?" I asked, imagining the horror of being unjustly arrested and then having one's babies put in foster care. If she was only nineteen, the children had to be very young. One might even be nursing. "I'll talk to Ms. Kowolski tomorrow."

"*Kosinski*," Vera corrected. "Maybe you can help Maude while you're here. That should keep you out of trouble if you can't find enough restaurants to review."

"You are so irritating, Vera. If you want me to help your friend Jesusita, you'll just have to let me schedule my time as I please. And since I've asked everyone else, I'll ask you. Who had a reason to kill Denise?"

"Nobody that I know had any better reason than I did," said Vera sharply. "If you actually have some suspects, give their names to the police. It's perfectly ridiculous for a housewife to be out looking for a murderer."

"I'm not a housewife anymore. I'm a professional writer. Just like you. Except more people read what I write."

Vera was chuckling when I hung up. Too bad I hadn't fought back from the beginning. We might have been friends.

19
Pot Stickers with Clients

Sam

Having lucked into a parking place for the bike, I arrived extra early. Tourists can usually be counted on to choose a restaurant with high prices and mediocre food, but the clients had chosen a good place. That's why I planned to get there early enough to order and eat some pot stickers before the Blues could decide on three plates for four people, no appetizers, and, if I was lucky, something alcoholic—not, pray God, plum wine. I ordered beer.

This didn't look like my kind of case. An old lady arrested for knifing some woman at a middle-class-women-getting-their-jollies-helping-out-welfare-mothers kind of do-gooder center? I took it as a favor to a bunch of scientists paranoid about industrial espionage and coughing up big bucks for my services. Not too sexy, but it pays my share on a great Victorian in the Castro. Since I got hired by Bay Tech, Inc., even my portfolio going down the toilet with the bear market hasn't affected my standard of living.

So here I am, dunking the world's greatest spicy pork pot stickers into a great hot sauce that looks like berries but isn't and waiting for my new clients, an old scientist from Chicago, the ex of the alleged knifer; a middle-aged science prof from Texas, who'll probably want his Mongolian beef cooked to shoe leather; and the Texas guy's wife. The scientists' wives at B.T., Inc., cocktail parties aren't my idea of a jolly bunch. Most of them would faint if I took it into my head to discuss the gay lifestyle.

I looked up from pot sticker number three and saw a woman who could be the Texas guy's wife—blonde hair tied back with a scarf that matched her jacket and slacks—chatting politely with the Chinese waitress, who spoke little or no English because she was actually a busgirl. A real waitress hustled over to point the lady in my direction.

Bad luck. I'd have to share the last of the pot stickers with her. Maybe she'd be too polite to take one. She looked sort of shocked when she saw me, and I hadn't even stood up yet, but hell, I'd put on a tie and sport jacket, so what was her problem? Still, she headed gamely in my direction, introduced herself—Carolyn Blue—and held out her hand. By then I'd stood up, prepared to shake it. "Sam Flamboise."

Her eyes widened. Well, I'm 6'6" and weigh 280, and since my hair started to recede, I shaved my head. I suppose she thought she'd introduced herself to some pro wrestler by mistake.

"I'm the P.I.," I said to ease her mind. I didn't want her to run off screaming before the paying customers showed up, so I held her chair for her, and she sat down. Then she spotted my pot stickers. Hell! She was going to want a taste, maybe a whole pot sticker.

"Have you eaten here before, Mr. Framboise?" she asked, whipping out a notebook.

"That's *Flam*boise," I corrected. "Like a French combination of flamboyant and raspberry, and yeah, I've eaten here before. I'm eating my favorite dish right now."

"I'm a food writer. Can I have one?"

I pushed the plate toward her. "Dip it in the sauce if you don't mind hot."

"Not at all," she replied, dipped, and tasted. "Oh, yummy." She flipped the notebook open to the middle pages and began to make notes. "What a wonderful sauce! Let's order another plate."

That was fine with me. You can't ever get enough Eliza pot stickers. I waved the waitress over and reordered. Mrs. Blue devoured her first and reached for another.

"You don't mind, do you?" she asked, but not before she'd taken a bite, so what could I say? I grabbed the last one before she could scarf that down too. "I'm really starving. I spent too much time at the center, but a man your size probably requires a lot of food. Maybe I should have waited for the second plate. Are you starving?"

"Sweetie, I'm always starving." I grabbed two pot stickers off the new plate, just in case the food writer thought she was supposed to get the whole bunch. She looked pretty surprised to be called *sweetie*. "So what were you doing at the center? That's the site of the murder, right?"

"I was detecting. I didn't really believe they—my husband and father-in-law—were going to hire anyone. I wonder what's in this sauce. If I knew, I might try to make it. Do you cook?"

"Every other day, except when we're going out to dinner."

"Really? Your wife is a lucky woman."

"Guy."

"I beg your pardon."

"I live with a guy."

"And he cooks, too? I wish Jason would get interested. Thirty years of cooking was enough for me. I cooked for my father and then for Jason and the children. Now that

I'm writing about food, I'm even less interested in cooking."

A food writer who doesn't cook. Well, why not? "So why were you over there detecting?"

"Because the police aren't going to do it. Inspector Yu is quite sure he has the murderer. Of course, his daughter Ginger—whom I met today and whose name is really Dolly Madison Yu—oh, miss, could I have some plum wine?" She'd waved energetically at the waitress. "When his daughter Ginger gets hold of him, the inspector may be very sorry that he arrested the wrong person. Ginger is a great admirer of my mother-in-law. Anyway, I can't just let Vera rot in jail for a crime she didn't commit. For one thing, it would be hard on my children. Even my husband might wake up and get serious about this when he realizes Vera could actually be convicted." She sipped the plum wine, and her face lit up. "Why, this is actually good!" she exclaimed. "I'm not usually a fan of plum wine, at least not what I've had in the Southwest, but this has a sharp, fruity flavor. A touch of cherry, but not the cough-syrup kind." She made a few more notes. "Would you like a sip?"

"Can't stand the stuff." I quickly ordered another beer before she could insist that I try her plum wine. "And did you find the murderer?" I asked, probably sounding sarcastic.

"In one day? With Mr. Valetti trailing along? He's Vera's neighbor. I'm not a professional, after all." She sounded a little huffy. "But I do have some suspects. Let me just flip over to my investigation notes, and I'll bring you up to date."

She didn't get a chance because the two men arrived before she could start telling me my business. Her husband looked surprised to see us eating. "We're not that late," he said defensively. A short guy who looked to be in good shape for someone in his forties. I just hit the big 4-

0 so I don't consider myself *in the forties*. More like thirty-nine plus.

They sat down and did just what I'd expected. Ordered three dishes. The older guy insisted on Scotch, and the younger one asked for hot *sake,* which didn't go over well with the Chinese waitress.

Mrs. Blue, God bless her, refused to share the pot stickers and told them to get their own. I was starting to like the lady. She was funnier and less picky than your average faculty wife—not that I know that many, but I sure as hell remember the wife of a professor I had in college. She used to serve us tea and cookies after seminars at their house. That woman was a real ball-buster. Mrs. Blue, who invited me to call her Carolyn halfway through dinner, seemed a lot less uptight than my old prof's wife.

Evidently the two male Blues weren't really interested in discussing the case. They just wanted Carolyn to approve of me so they could get her off their backs about rescuing the woman in jail. Well, that was OK. One of the things I insisted they order, since they were being so stingy about the number of dishes, was the Mango Beef, which thank God, they didn't like. She did, and told me I had good taste in food. By that time she seemed to have gotten over her shock at my size. I'm still all muscle and no fat, so I guess I do look intimidating.

Carolyn and I shared the Mango Beef, and she did more note taking than eating, so I figured I wouldn't have to cook when I got home. She also tried to introduce the investigation a couple of times, but she didn't get anywhere. The Blues, father and son, talked science, football, and how the city had changed since they were last here. I made a few suggestions for tourist activities, like the Henry Moore exhibition up at the museum in Lincoln Park, funky places to eat, stuff like that.

She seemed a lot more interested in those topics than football and science and remarked that San Francisco tourism obviously wasn't what it once had been since I hadn't mentioned bullfights, bear and bull fights, or tours of opium dens and Barbary Coast dives, or the half-year performance at the Joss House in Chinatown. Her husband thought she'd enjoy the Henry Moore exhibit more than an opium den and tried to move the conversation back to football. She was shooting him reproachful looks by mid-meal.

Toward the end, when we'd mopped up every scrap of food in sight and were down to scraping our rice bowls, he told her that he and his dad had to go back to the Stanford Court for some frontier-busting research scheduled to be revealed at nine. "We'll drop you off on Sacramento Street, and I'll be back by 10:30 if you don't mind staying up to let me in." The husband looked a little nervous about that. "I'm packed. Left my bags with the concierge."

Ah, trouble on straight street. They hadn't shared a bed last night.

"Don't bother," she said, a cube or two of ice in the voice. "Since you haven't wanted to talk to Sam about your mother's situation, I certainly must. I have all kinds of information to pass on. I'll just call a cab."

"Well, Carolyn, I don't think—"

"I can give her a ride home," I offered, being careful not to laugh or give any indication of how I was going to do that. "You're in an apartment house, Carolyn? You can buzz my cell phone to let me know you got in all right. Or I'll go up with you and take a look around. If women at this center are being targeted, we shouldn't take chances."

"I can wave to you out the front window," she suggested, grinning.

Her husband wasn't at all amused, but what the hell. This case was turning out to be more fun than I'd expected. "Quarter to nine," I said, looking at my watch. "You two will be wanting to get to that meeting. Who do I report to when I learn something?"

"Me," both men said.

"I'm paying," said the old man. "I'm at the Stanford Court."

When they'd left, Carolyn said, "You can report to me. I'm the only one who's really interested." Then she made a few more food notes while the plates were being cleared. The old man had provided his credit card number before he left so we wouldn't get stuck with the bill. She said, "Let's have dessert."

"What do you want?"

"Anything without rice. I hate sweet rice." She was flipping through to the back of her notebook where she'd evidently recorded all the clues she'd turned up that day. I wish I'd been there to see her at work. It was probably a hoot.

20
Networking over Ginger Ice Cream

Carolyn

After Sam ordered ginger ice cream, he went off to the men's room, having drunk four bottles of beer with dinner. I took the opportunity to make notes on the décor of the restaurant. Very modern, glass-topped tables held up by aluminum stands, big pastel blocks on the ceiling and walls, cubist, and an amazing glass triptych featuring huge teal waves with aqua foam. It hid the kitchen from the dining areas. Was that the art glass? I asked the waitress and was directed past the triptych to the back dining room, where I discovered blown glass asparagus sculptures in cases and on high ledges. Or did they represent bamboo? They came in various colors, but I liked the lime-green ones best and was sorry I hadn't brought a camera. The owner evidently collected them.

I didn't see him but couldn't help picturing the first proprietor of a Chinese restaurant in the United States. He's reported to have worn a queue and a stovepipe hat and claimed baptism in South Carolina. The gold rush days saw a lot of Chinese restaurants opening after his. They were said to be the best deal in town—clean premises, tasty food, and all you could eat cheap. I wonder what their proprietors and customers would make of Eliza. The food, no doubt, is more various and delicious, but there are no all-you-can-eat dollar dinners.

Back in the front dining room, Sam stood by our table scowling. "Thought you'd taken off," he said.

"Why would I do that? I didn't spend the day talking to peculiar people at the center for the fun of it."

"You must be pretty fond of your mother-in-law."

"No more than most people," I mumbled evasively. "So." I put my finger on the first name. "Marina Chavez-Timberlite. She's the director of the center and the wife of the developer Eric Timberlite." Sam whistled through his teeth. "Mrs. Timberlite tried to keep me from conducting an investigation by insisting that I get permission from the board chairwoman. I did, no thanks to Mrs. Timberlite, who gave me two wrong numbers to call."

"Probably doesn't like people nosing around her operation, particularly amateurs and especially after an embarrassing murder."

"I'm sure that's true, Mr. Flamboise," I said rather stiffly.

"Sam."

"Yes. Later I discovered that center staffers, my mother-in-law among them, are organizing a protest against Mr. Timberlite's development company because he's planning to tear down low-rent housing to put up condominiums. If Denise, the victim, was involved, which Bertha Harley denies, or he thought she was involved, he might have hired a hit person to kill Denise and to frame my mother-in-law."

"A hit person?" Sam grinned. "OK, Timberlite. I can nose around. Money and power are motives for murder. Maybe this business manager was trying to blackmail him. She'd call off the protesters if he'd give a bundle to the center."

"What an interesting idea! Everyone says Denise was having trouble making ends meet and having to deny various department heads project money. She made enemies, but I doubt they'd kill her over budget problems." I scooped up some ginger ice cream, which was actually quite good and certainly deserved a note in my food section.

"Next is the security guard, Mr. Alexi Timatovich. He claims to have been an engineer in Siberia before immigrating. He also claims to always be at his post, but he wasn't when Mr. Valetti and I arrived, and I discovered that several people were in the building who hadn't signed in. Of course, that could be because the Crone Cohort insisted on a ramp entrance to the middle section to save seniors from the front stairs."

"The Crone Cohort? OK, I believe you. The place is full of nut cases. But just because Timatovich is a lousy security guard doesn't make him a murderer."

"No, it doesn't, but he is claiming overtime for night shifts that his son actually works, and someone or other said Denise was going to tell the director about his fraudulent overtime claims and get him fired."

Sam nodded and made another note. "I'll find out about Timatovich. Was he there the night of the murder?"

"Yes. Also he needs money to send his math genius son to Cal Tech, and he wouldn't let me take the sign-in book away to photocopy the pages for the day of the crime. Mrs. Rovere at Nutrition Central made him give it to us. Maybe his son was in on the murder too."

"I doubt that overtime at the center would pay the kid's way through Cal Tech, but it's still a lead. They could have other scams going."

"And there's Freddie Piñon. He's a wife abuser on parole who came to the center that night, drunk, angry, and wanting to know where his wife was. Denise, who was head of the Battered Women's Advocacy before she took over the business office, had gotten the man's wife into shelters. Twice. The guard said he sent Piñon away, but Piñon could have slipped in the side door and killed Denise when she wouldn't tell him where to find his wife. He just got out on parole for attacking the director of his wife's first shelter. Oh, and he sneaked into the center the night before and threatened to kill Penny Widdister, present head of the Battered Women's Advocacy. She hit him with a telephone, locked herself in the bathroom, and someone called the police, but he was gone by the time they arrived."

"Now, there's a good prospect." Sam wrote down Piñon's name and the other material I had on him, particularly pleased to know who the parole officer was.

"Now, this woman," I said, flipping a page, "was in the center that night but not the day I was there, so I need to interview her. Kebra Zenawi."

"Sure, I know Kebra. I'll talk to her. Good chance to eat Ethiopian."

"I'll go with you. Ethiopian food would make an interesting column."

"Listen, Carolyn, I don't know about your hanging with me. Whoever did the job on Mrs. Faulk is obviously dangerous. This Piñon. You don't want to go interview him, do you?"

"Of course I wouldn't go on *all* your investigations. I have some of my own people to question. I'm meeting one lady at Zaré in the financial district, and another at the Legion of Honor. I wouldn't expect you to go on those interviews with me, anymore than I'd expect to go with you to—"

"Gotcha. So I'll take you to the Ethiopian place. We can both eat on your father-in-law's dime, but fair warning. Lots of people get the trots because the food is really hot. I mean really—"

"I live in El Paso where the best restaurants are Mexican." Back to my list. "Patrick Baker O'Finn, pro bono lawyer. He was there but had no reason to kill Denise. I can call him and let you know what he says."

Sam nodded.

"Maria Fortuni. She had a quarrel with Denise about money, but she's about eighty years old, very frail, and walks with a cane. I don't think she could have done it."

"I'll get the crime scene photos from Harry Yu. I take it you talked to her?"

"Yes. I got O'Finn's number from her. Next. Marcus Croker."

Sam glanced up, surprised.

"You know him? He's a policeman who teaches self-defense. He and Denise had words because he wasn't allowing women in his classes who'd reported spousal abuse and then refused to testify against their husbands."

"I'll do Croker."

"Do you think—" Sam gave me such a quelling look that I didn't pursue it. After we became better acquainted, and he realized that I wasn't a wimp, I'd ask again.

"Yasmin Atta. I'm seeing her Wednesday."

"Lucky you. Suspect or witness?"

"Witness, if she saw anything. Next, Denise's family. She was a widow, but Mrs. Rovere said that she inherited a lot of money from her husband and that there was bad blood between her and her stepson because he abused his wife. That might be worth looking into. We could talk to the wife about the abuse. Another possibility: the son might be angry because Denise got a lot of his father's money. Maybe he wanted to get it back by killing her."

"OK. I'll follow up." He wrote *Faulk* in his notebook.

"I could talk to the wife. Or both of us could if you're worried that he might come in while I'm questioning her." I hoped that I was being cooperative enough to ingratiate myself into his investigation.

He didn't reply, so I didn't push it. "Then there's Dr.

Tagalong, who was angry when Denise wouldn't fund a mammogram machine for the center. She actually said she had a better reason for killing Denise than my mother-in-law did. Still, I don't consider her a good suspect. She was at a meeting on sexually transmitted diseases while Denise was being killed." I paused for comment. He said nothing, so I went on. "There's an elderly woman named Yolanda Minarez who is suing the center over the unisex toilets. She was there that night to talk to O'Finn, and she wasn't on the sign-in list. I could call her."

"You trying to save your father-in-law money by doing all the work yourself for free because I bill by the hour?"

"Not at all, Mr. Flamboise. I'd be happy to have your company for any call or visit I make, and I'll certainly turn the information I get over to you, so you can bill lots of hours studying it." I wanted to ask him how much he charged per hour, but decided that wouldn't endear me to him as a prospective fellow investigator. "In fact, this conversation will go on your bill, I presume."

Sam chuckled. "Sweetie, you are one prissy, smart-ass woman. But cute."

Since I couldn't afford to take offense, I opted for a playful approach. "Mr. Flamboise, are you flirting with me?"

"Well, I sure would be, honeybunch, but the fact is I'm gay."

He didn't look like my idea of a gay man. He looked like—a street fighter? I guess I showed my surprise because he felt the need to enlarge on the subject.

"They call me the Sam Spade of the Castro," he added and gave me his card, which actually did say that. Even I know that the Castro is the gay enclave.

"You really give out this card?" I stammered, not, I'm afraid, a very tactful question.

"Only to special friends, chickie. So. Now that we've

eliminated sexual tension as a barrier to good detective work, you got any more suspects?"

"One," I replied, wishing I could fall through the floor. That is absolutely the last time I try my hand at flirting. "There's a mental patient named Bad Girl or Martina L. King, which no one believes is her real name. She paints pictures of knives no matter what the assignment is. Dr. Tagalong put her in an art class for therapy. Then Denise said she'd have to be dropped because of the insurance, and Bad Girl took it amiss. Because of the knives and the psychosis and the bad blood between them, I thought she might be a good prospect."

"Got an address?"

"She sometimes lives in a homeless shelter in Haight-Asbury and gets her medication from a free clinic, although I'm told she doesn't always take the medication. She's my last suspect."

"OK." He closed his book.

Curiosity overcame me. "Since you're gay, did you take part in the riots in 1979? When the Twinkie man got a light sentence for killing Harvey Milk?"

"I know what riots you mean, and no, I was just a kid playing high school football then. My parents didn't let me take part in riots."

"Oh." I wondered how old he was.

"So now I'll give you that ride home."

He looked so amused about the offer that I felt a bit uneasy. We left and walked along Eighteenth Street for about a block. "Here we are." He stopped by a black motorcycle, buckled a helmet on his head, and handed one to me.

"I—I can't ride on a motorcycle," I stammered.

"Well, I can get you a cab, but if you're too chicken to ride on the bike with me, I don't see how we can team up on the investigation."

I'm sure his wide smile was smug rather than good-humored. I took a deep breath, wondered whether he'd really pursue the exoneration of my mother-in-law if I weren't there to see that he did, thought about my children, and then ruined my hair by pulling on his rotten helmet. "What next?" I asked, trying to sound courageous and cheerful when I was really furious and scared to death.

21
Sleuths: Day Two

Carolyn

All the way from Eliza to the apartment, I clung to the substantial bulk of "the Sam Spade of the Castro." As the motorcycle vibrated and roared, I pictured my husband, sitting on the steps, his luggage beside him, waiting for me to return and let him in, little knowing that I would arrive on a Harley, wearing a black helmet.

Lucky me. Jason had lingered to discuss the exciting research presented at the meeting. I'd been home a half hour, typing culinary notes into my computer, when he rang the bell downstairs and I buzzed him in. He was so eager to tell me about the amazing discoveries made at Ohio State that he completely forgot to ask about my conversation with Sam. Which was fine with me. We went to bed, happy with one another once again. He kissed me before he left this morning and asked if I had exciting plans for the day.

"Ethiopian food," I mumbled.

"Good for you. I should be back by 6:30." With that he was gone, and I didn't feel obliged to tell him that I would be eating Ethiopian food with Sam while we interviewed Kebra Zenawi, proprietor of the restaurant and possible witness to murder.

Now wide-awake and ready to begin a day of investigation, I jumped out of bed, showered and dressed, and left to buy breakfast supplies for Vera's empty fridge. Over fresh croissants, coffee, and a cup of mixed fruit that came peeled, chopped, and enclosed in plastic, I looked over my list of people. Whatever Sam was doing this morning—riding in motorcycle races, spying on adulterers, marching in gay pride parades—I intended to get on with the exoneration of Vera.

First, I called Patrick Baker O'Finn and introduced myself as an acquaintance of Margaret Hanrahan. Because Margaret's husband was the senior partner, O'Finn took my call. Yes, he had been at the center the night of the murder, using Margaret's office to negotiate a settlement with one Yolanda Minarez, a very successful negotiation, he added in a self-congratulatory tone.

"Did she agree to share the toilets with men?" I asked.

"No, the center will put up a Women Only sign on the first-floor toilet, directing men upstairs, and Mrs. Minarez will stay away from facilities on the top floors."

"She probably can't get upstairs anyway," I remarked.

"Not easily," said Mr. O'Finn, "but the point is that no money changed hands. Was that what you wanted to know?"

"No, I'm interested in anything you might have seen relative to the murder, someone lurking around, someone who shouldn't have been there, someone escaping."

"With bloody knife in hand?" Mr. O'Finn asked sarcastically. "I was on the second floor, Mrs. Blue. I saw no one in the front section of the building, except your mother-in-law, who was coming down from an upper floor about 7:15 when I arrived."

"Didn't you see the guard?"

"You mean the teenager at the desk? I signed in there.

Then I nodded to Professor Blue and went upstairs, where I stayed to meet Minarez. She arrived perhaps five minutes later. When we heard the screams and ruckus downstairs, Mrs. Minarez became hysterical and wanted to back away from the agreement. I suggested that she sign and then I would drive her home. She did, we went down the stairs in the middle section and exited by the outside ramp, where we climbed into my car and left."

"You left the scene of a crime? As an officer of the court, shouldn't you have waited for the police?"

"I didn't know there had been a crime. I assume, since my name is on the sign-in list, the police will contact me if they want my input. In the meantime, I had an elderly, hysterical woman on my hands. She could have had a heart attack. I felt that it was my duty as a gentleman and a pro bono lawyer for the center to see to her welfare."

I thanked him for his time. One interesting fact stood out: the presence of a high school boy at the sign-in desk. Timatovich had claimed *he* was on duty that night. Had both of them been there, or just the son? Or was the high school boy someone else posing as a security guard until he could murder Denise? He might have been Denise Faulk's stepgrandson.

I wrote down my thoughts and called Yolanda Minarez, who said, "Eef the lawyer din' get me outa there, I could be dead like Denise, who was very mean to me about my lawsuit. She should have known I deedn't want no money, just a safe bathroom to pee in. That lawyer, he talk an' talk about money, when all I want is a toilet *por las damas,* no *por los hombres.* Eef he let me talk, maybe I could be home in my house before anyone get keelled. My husband, he no like strange Anglo man breeng me home at night. He no like I go out at night. An' he really don' like I want *damas* toilet instead of money."

Mrs. Minarez hadn't seen anyone on the first floor or the first-floor ramp to the street or on her way up the stairs to the second floor, a hard climb for an old lady.

And she hadn't seen anyone when she and Mr. O'Finn escaped out the side exit.

O'Finn and Minarez alibied each other. What else could I find out while waiting for Sam Flamboise to pick me up? Dr. Tagalong. Had she really been at a meeting? I booted up Vera's computer and looked through August meeting calendars on a San Francisco Internet site, marveling that I had become computer literate enough to do an Internet investigation.

Three meetings on sexually transmitted diseases had been held last Thursday, only one for health professionals. I called that number and identified myself as a writer doing a story on the meeting and looking for comments from attendees. The person who answered the phone couldn't have been more helpful. I will never again naively trust any stranger who telephones me. After she had suggested several people I could interview, I thanked her and said I also had a Dr. Rosamunda Tagalong on my list.

My informant responded enthusiastically that Dr. Rosa had been one of the panelists, a wonderful source. She was very active in organizations seeking to stem the tide of sexually transmitted diseases in the Bay area. How long a meeting had it been? I asked. The panel had talked from 7:00 to 9:00, then thrown the discussion open to questions from the audience.

Well, that takes care of Dr. Tagalong, I thought. Denise had died while the doctor was talking about STDs in front of, according to my source, fifty people.

My next thought was to research the Timberlite organization. If Denise had been blackmailing Mr. Timberlite for a big contribution, who would know about that? His wife wasn't likely to tell me that they had, in fact, arranged for Denise's murder. I looked up his company and asked to be connected with their Public Relations Department, where I inquired about rumors of a "large contribution by Timberlite to the Union Street Women's

Center." The director believed me to be a volunteer looking for a contribution to Bay Area Women at Risk, my own invention.

"Just between us," she said, chuckling, "I don't think Mr. Timberlite will be making more contributions of that sort this year. One of his charities has organized a protest against one of his projects." I thanked her and said we at Bay Area Women would try again when Mr. Timberlite was feeling more tolerant of women's groups.

Having investigated O'Finn, Minarez, Tagalong, and Timberlite, I was left with Bad Girl. That was a tough one. She might not be back at the center until next Monday, and I had no idea where to find her. Without much hope, I called some free clinics. Two weren't even in Haight-Asbury, and the two that were weren't impressed with my story that Bad Girl, otherwise known as Martina L. King, had won the hundred-dollar food lottery at the center. I was told that they didn't give out information of any kind on their patients, even a yes or no as to whether the person in question was one of theirs.

Here I'd told all those lies, and I hadn't learned anything from the people I'd lied to. Just what I deserved. I gave up and went to dress for my Ethiopian lunch. How formal would an Ethiopian restaurant be? *When in doubt, err on the side of conservative but attractive clothes* the mother of a high school friend used to tell me. Of course, I had to wear slacks since Sam might show up on his motorcycle.

22

Morning of a Professional Sleuth

Sam

Tuesday, and I had some big-profit clients to see to, but what I couldn't stop poking at in my mind was the murder of Denise Faulk and the oddball list of suspects and witnesses turned up by the amusing Mrs. Blue, the last person you'd expect to find seriously hunting a murderer. At breakfast, after I described the events of the evening and my plan to pick her up for lunch at Kebra's, Paul accused me of having a crush on Carolyn. I assured him that I wasn't changing my sexual orientation, just having fun luring a sedate lady onto the back of a Harley. She was game. I'll have to give her that.

At the office I delegated the security jobs, signed some papers, and turned a couple of my computer geeks loose on Eric Timberlite and the Faulk son. I wanted probate information on the Faulk family and rumors of criminal association or activity on Timberlite. I called Freddie Piñon's parole officer myself. Like you might expect, Freddie was in the wind. He hadn't reported in yesterday like he was supposed to, and he hadn't been seen at his halfway house since Thursday. It looked bad for Freddie.

"You think he'd kill anyone?" I asked Burl Kalton.

"Hasn't yet, but he's gone after his old lady a couple of times. He even took a crack at this woman who runs a shelter." Burl laughed. "She shot him in the ass. Missed the first shot an' got him when he tried to run. That's how he ended up in jail this last time. Got his sentence plea-bargained down for ratting out some mutt who was running meth labs in the basements of day care facilities."

"Lucky none of the labs blew up a bunch of kids," I remarked. "So if I wanted to get hold of Freddie, where would I look?"

"If I knew, I'd pick him up myself," Burl retorted.

"Yeah, right. How many parolees you got on your list right now?"

"Point taken. You could ask Araña Morales at the Tres Hermanos pool hall. He used to hang with Freddie."

"Thanks, Kalton. I owe you one." Should I take the neatly turned out Mrs. Blue to Tres Hermanos with me? I'd give it some thought.

Next I called the cell phone of a contact in the Russian community, hanger-on to better-connected criminal types. "Boris, my friend, it's Sam Flamboise. How're they hangin'? You sellin' lots of rock to kids on street corners?" Boris wasn't amused, although I could tell by the background noise that he was on a street corner. "Listen, *tovarish*, you wanna do a little job for me?" Boris was interested. "Ask around about a guy named Alexi Timatovich, immigrant from Siberia, works security for a women's center on Union, might have something going there. I wanna know if he's killed anyone lately, or ever. If he knows anyone who would. If he's been drinking too much and telling stories about illegal activities. . . . Yeah, call me back. There's a couple a hundred in it if you find me anything good."

Then I dialed our architecturally challenged Hall of

•Justice. What can you say about a city that builds a jail that's better looking than its courthouse? "Harry Yu in?" I was transferred. "Harry, it's Sam Flamboise. I've been hired to prove you made a mistake in hanging that old lady out to dry for the Faulk killing. . . . Yeah, well, I would too if I saw that much blood on someone kneeling over the body, but a job is a job, and this one was wished on me by a client with deep pockets. . . . No, he never met your alleged murderer. He's old buddies with the lady's ex, who doesn't want his grandkids embarrassed by a killer grandma. You know how it goes.

"How about I come down and take a look at the evidence? Or have you really got a hard-on over sending the old girl up for the rest of her golden years? . . . Hell, you know me, Harry. I find it's someone else did the crime, you'll get the credit. I'm only in this for the money. . . . So I'll see you in fifteen, OK?"

Five minutes, and I was heading out, enjoying the nice weather and the rumble of my Harley. I parked in back where the cops do and went through the open grassed area to the hall and an elevator up to Homicide. While I was there, I'd see what Harry knew about Marcus Croker. What I knew wasn't that great, like some brutality complaints in the past, but not against women as far as I knew.

I'll swear Harry was chunkier than ever. "Hey, man, how're they hanging?"

"No use asking a guy my age that question, Sam. Here, take a quick look." He handed me a folder of photos. "My partner wouldn't approve, but she's out on a case with Kliner, arm in a Dumpster. No body attached."

"Better her than you." I flipped through the photos. "Jesus, Harry, this poor woman was cut to pieces. You really think an old lady could have done this?"

"Take a look at the pictures of the old lady," Harry advised.

He had a point. She was not only bloody, but she had a

mean look to her. Carolyn Blue would be disappointed if I proved her mother-in-law really was the murderer.

"Coroner thinks Faulk was down for some of the wounds," Harry added.

"I guess the old lady could have inflicted that much damage if she managed to knock the victim down first, but how'd she do that?" I asked.

"Threw a glass paperweight at her? We found one on the floor."

"Bruises?"

"One."

"Could have happened when she went down."

"Could have."

"Prints on the paperweight?"

"The victim's were the only usable ones. It was broken, and she bled on it."

"No knife?"

"Not yet."

"How about other people? You find anyone else who could have done it?"

"No one else was seen in or near Faulk's office."

"Listen, you know a cop named Marcus Croker?"

"Sam, are you saying you think one of ours did it? The only cop in the building was my partner. She was upstairs taking a makeup class from some big-time black model, heard the commotion, and went down. And she didn't see any suspects except the one we arrested."

"Croker was signed in, Harry. And he wasn't signed out."

Harry gave me a disgusted look and began to tap computer keys. "Marcus Croker was on duty. Four to twelve. That pretty much eliminates him as a suspect, unless you think Arbus Penn, his partner, was in on the murder, too."

"Yeah. Well, thanks, Harry. I'll be in touch if I get anything."

"You won't," said Harry.

As I was leaving, I ran into Harry's partner, Camron Cheever. "Hey, Cam," I called. "Lookin' good."

She liked that. Cammie is a real pretty black woman, and she knows it. Late twenties, early thirties, and a smart detective. Not many women that young make inspector. "What were you doing over at that center Thursday night? You don't need any lessons on looking first-rate."

"How come you know about my case?" she demanded. "Harry an' me don't need any hotshot, football-player private eyes screwing with our busts."

"Oh, now you're hurting my feelings, baby. I thought we were in love."

"Yeah?" She gave me a saucy grin. "If you weren't white an' gay, we would be, Sammie."

23

An Exotic Kind of Hot

Carolyn

Did Sam have a car, I wondered, but choose the motor-cycle to, as my son Chris says, "yank my chain?" Off we went, riding the hills to the Lower Haight and Gondar, the Ethiopian restaurant. Fortunately, I couldn't see over Sam's shoulder, so I was spared the sensation one experiences when almost at the crest of a hill in San Francisco, a queasy conviction that there is nothing beyond the skyline but sky and that one's vehicle will simply fly off into nothingness. Rudyard Kipling described San Francisco as a city one-fourth reclaimed from the sea and the rest, sand hills held down by houses with no attempt to grade the hills and build streets at sensible angles.

"You OK, chickie?" Sam shouted.

My imaginings had caused me to tighten my grip. "Fine," I shouted back.

"Then retract your nails. You just hit flesh."

"Sorry." I tried to relax one hand, then the other, without, of course, letting go.

I needn't have worried about proper attire. The staff at

Gondar wore tunic-like garments, under which the women had long skirts and the men tight trousers. The customers were numerous and dressed, to say the least, casually. Very reasonable menu prices explained Gondar's popularity.

"Combination plates for three and diet Cokes," said Sam to a young waitress. Obviously I was not to be allowed my own selections. "Tell Kebra we'd like to talk to her when she's free," he continued. When the silent girl nodded, he turned back to me. "Since we'll be eating with our hands, it's considered impolite not to wash first."

I followed him to the restrooms and washed my hands, keeping an interested eye on the "décor" both coming and going. The tables were topped with aging linoleum. The mismatched chairs had plastic-covered seats and backs, with aluminum legs and frames. Exotic, pseudo-Tibetan lanterns hung from the ceiling. On walls painted as yellow as a desert sun were paintings and enlarged photos: two men in rags and chains, dark-skinned and bearded, being led away from an ancient, oar-powered ship; another man in monk's robes, wearing a high, white, brimless hat; photos of castle ruins; a round church; and ancient, humble dwellings among large rocks on the curve of a river. Last was a framed flag: green, yellow, and red horizontal bands with a yellow pentagram sending out rays on a light-blue disk.

Our waitress followed us to our table with cans of diet Coke and a large, round platter lined with *injerra,* the flat, unleavened bread of the country. It was topped with varieties of *wat,* hot curries made in different colors and from different vegetables. All burned the throat, but many were enchantingly tasty. We tore pieces off the bread to dip in the pastes. I disliked the spinach but liked the chewy and flavorful cabbage, also the beany hot lentils, chickpeas that tasted slightly of vinegar, and best of all, the mushrooms. Never had mushrooms burned so rich or so hot on the tongue. "Amazing," I said when I had tried each selection and washed them down with Coke. Between us we had almost finished the platter.

No sooner had we wiped up the last smudges with bread than a different woman arrived with another platter. "Kebra, love. Join us. This is Carolyn Blue. It's her mother-in-law who was arrested for Denise's murder. Carolyn, Kebra Zenawi."

She was a beautiful woman with a thin, fine-featured face, creamy brown skin, full lips, and the most amazing dark eyes, large and thickly lashed. Kebra slid the platter onto the table and sat down with us. "My heart aches at the terrible death of my friend Denise, and I pray for her soul each day." She spoke very precise English, but with an interesting lilt. "Nor do I believe, Mrs. Blue, that the mother of your husband would have killed Denise. A scholar does not wield a knife, nor does a woman who speaks for all women kill a sister."

"Thank you. Since you were in the building that night, we—"

Sam cut me off by saying, "We'll eat first." Evidently I had committed a faux pas, so I scooped up some mushrooms and complimented Mrs. Zenawi on the dish. "I'm a food writer," I explained. "I'd love to write a column about Ethiopian food and include a recipe if you'd be willing to provide me with one."

"I am desolated to say that the recipes are shared only among women of my family. If I were ever to have a daughter, I could tell her, or if I returned to my country, I could tell the daughter of my sister, but—"

"Of course," I interrupted hurriedly. "I shouldn't have asked."

"How could you know?" she replied politely.

"So what do you hear from Menelik?" Sam asked. "Did they send him off to the border to fight the evil Eritreans?"

Before she answered Sam, she explained to me, "Menelik Zenawi was my husband. Together we fled to the United States because our lives were endangered during the coups that racked our country. However, Menelik was not happy here, although San Francisco is, in some ways, like Ethiopia—because of the earthquakes and droughts."

"Earthquakes here are caused by the tectonic plates grinding together," said Sam. "In Ethiopia the Great Rift, where the land pulls apart, causes quakes."

"To the man who is killed by the heaving and splitting of the earth, it little matters what happens far below to cause his death," she replied serenely.

"What she's telling you, in a roundabout way, is that Menelik, who thought he was hot stuff because he was named after some king who was the son of Solomon and Sheba—"

"I too am proud of my name," said Kebra, "for I was named for a queen in that dynasty. Mesqel Kebra is a saint in our church, as well." She turned to me. "Ethiopia is a Christian country, and the Ethiopian Orthodox Church is one of the oldest Christian denominations, although we are Monophysites and have some differences of belief from the Western sects."

Wondering what a Monophysite was, I smiled and looked interested.

To Sam she said, "Will you come for the feast of Mesqel?"

"Wouldn't miss it," he replied. "And if I forget, Paul will remind me." Then he explained to me, "It's the celebration of somebody going to the Holy Land and finding the True Cross."

"St. Helena," said Kebra. "But we were speaking of Menelik, whose unhappiness in the United States was not so much that no one recognized the importance of his name and family, but that no one had any interest in his academic credentials. Menelik is a noted scholar of Ge'ez, the ancient religious and literary language of our country. Alas, there was no job in San Francisco for a scholar of

Ge'ez, so we opened a restaurant, a calling which he felt beneath him."

"Then he took it out on Kebra by beating her up," said Sam.

"True. Menelik did not feel that I was a properly humble woman. He felt that I was picking up unseemly attitudes here in the United States, which he thought to beat out of me. It was then that Denise came to my rescue. She secreted me in a house for women in danger of being killed by their husbands and sent the police to remonstrate with mine. Unhappily, Menelik would not be appeased or turned from what he considered his right and duty as a husband. Then Margaret Hanrahan was recruited by my friend and defender, Denise. Margaret had my husband deported and our restaurant put legally into my hands. I am a very lucky woman to have such friends."

"And Menelik?" asked Sam.

"Menelik too is safe and happy, for his political enemies are no longer in power, and the church has granted him an annulment from his undutiful, barren wife. He has become a monk and will no doubt find a life of chastity and scholarship to his taste."

"All's well that ends well," said Sam, grinning. "If he's taken vows, he's not likely to show up and give you grief."

"Indeed," said Kebra and turned to me. "I observed when you came in that you took note of my pictures. Would you like to know what they represent?"

"Yes, please." Anything to keep on a subject that wasn't impolite.

She nodded. "The two men led from their boat in captivity are St. Frumentius and his brother, who became favorites of the king and converted my country to Christianity in the fourth century A.D. The bearded man in the white hat and robe is a monk, such as my former husband is now. The castle is in Gondar, once the capital of our country. The picture of the round dwellings with conical roofs is of Aksum, a holy city. These photos I took from the Internet and had made large. The paintings I commissioned from a fellow Ethiopian."

"Fascinating," I murmured and embarrassed myself by impolitely scooping up the last of the mushroom curry. I was distracted by trying to reconcile the idea of this exotic woman, with her unusual clothing and adventurous history, decorating her walls with photos from the Internet.

"And now that we have broken bread together, of what help can I be to you in your search for the true murderer of my friend?"

"Did you see anyone that night who might have killed her?" Sam asked. "Who had something against her? Who shouldn't have been there?"

Kebra folded long fingers on the plastic table—ours was a bilious green—and bowed her head in thought. Then she said, "I was in the office of the Battered Women's Advocacy that night. It is on the second floor. A very bad man named Piñon came in and screamed at me many rude things in demand that I tell him in which shelter we had hidden his wife. Do you know him?"

"By reputation," said Sam. "What did you do?"

"I told him to leave or I would call upon the police to remove him."

"What did he do?"

"He left, of course. I pointed my weapon at him. No doubt, he was afraid of injury and humiliation, having been previously shot by another woman whom he attempted to frighten."

To my astonishment, when she mentioned her weapon, she pulled a black metal, rather squared-off gun from the folds of her robe. Several customers at surrounding tables noticed and became agitated.

"Do not be alarmed," she said to them. "I am authorized to carry this weapon by the city of San Francisco, because I am the proprietor of a business and because my former husband was a man of violence." She smiled at the customers, then resumed her description of last Thursday night.

"Once Mr. Piñon had departed, I closed the office and went downstairs to the kitchen to speak to Bebe Takashima, who had just finished teaching an ethnic cuisine class. I wished her to take a class for me tomorrow night because we are having a family party here to celebrate the birth of a child. In the kitchen I saw a person I did not expect to see, Mr. Charles Desmond, who was flirting most outrageously with my friend Bebe."

"He wasn't on the sign-in list," I remarked to Sam.

"Neither was this Bebe," Sam replied. "So who's Charles Desmond, Kebra?"

"He is the love of Myra Fox, who was once our accountant before she was afflicted with cancer of a female sort. How unkind of him to flirt with another woman when his love is in danger of dying and subjected to dreadful medical treatments. I felt very sorry for Myra, whom I know from before Denise replaced her in financial matters.

"I believe this Desmond could see my disapproval of his unfaithful conduct, even though he has not married Myra Fox, as would be proper. He hurried to tell me that he had come to the center to secure financial papers for Myra to work on at home because inactivity has caused her depression. He seemed angry that the center had replaced her, even temporarily, while she was sick and said it would be good if she were to come back to work and take over her old duties.

"I wondered, if he was on an errand for Myra, why he was in the Nutrition Central smiling with lascivious intent at Bebe Takashima. His conduct embarrassed me, and I left. And now I must return to my duties. Please give my regards to the mother of your husband, Mrs. Blue. Perhaps you would care to join us here in September for the celebration of Mesqel."

"Thank you, but we'll be back in Texas by then," I

replied and complimented her on a lovely lunch. Sam got the name of the company Ms. Takashima worked for.

"Two more people to see," I remarked as we walked to his motorcycle. "I wonder if Mr. Desmond saw Denise that night before she was killed? Or saw the murderer?"

"Or was the murderer," Sam suggested.

"It wasn't as if Denise had taken Myra's job for good," I pointed out, "only until she was well enough to come back. Several people said Denise was anxious to return to the battered women, and the interim head is certainly anxious to have her back."

"What if someone didn't want Myra to get her old job back?"

"Ah, maybe the director, Mrs. Timberlite. Maybe they had to keep Denise in place so she'd head off the Women of Color protest against his project."

"In that case Denise would still be alive, chickie. We're getting our suspects mixed up here."

"Well, *Sammie*," I replied sarcastically. "What do you think we should do next?"

"Find Bebe and see what she says about Desmond."

"Could we stop somewhere and get a glass of milk? My mouth is on fire."

Sam grinned as he handed me a helmet. "Then you shouldn't have eaten so much."

24
Chat with a Window Dresser

Carolyn

Bebe Takashima, a designer of store windows, was setting one up for a shop on Union Street. The window contained interesting furniture, ornamental objects, and a young Japanese woman directing two men while a super-thin older woman looked on. Saying he had an interview to conduct himself, Sam promised to pick me up at the center, which was nearby, in an hour to an hour and a half. I agreed to that vague plan because if he wasn't back promptly, I could pass on Vera's message to one of the Working Women about Jesusita Gomez's imminent arrival from jail.

Sam roared off, and I tried to pat my hair into shape using a small hand mirror. The super-thin woman spotted me and beckoned me inside. "I saw you looking at the teak and rosewood cabinet. It's stunning, isn't it?"

I peered at the window from inside and agreed. The cabinet *was* stunning, the price tag even more so. "Actually, I'm here to see Bebe."

"We mustn't disturb her in midcreation. Why don't you look around until she's done?"

How long will that be? I wondered. While looking, I spotted a wonderful black and white dress in an abstract print with the fitted body and flaring skirt of a flamenco costume. Now the *dress* was stunning! And probably very expensive. I needn't have worried because the proprietor snatched it off the hanger. "Not for you, darling. Eight is the biggest size we carry in this one, and Bebe wants it for the window."

My dress disappeared toward the front of the store, while I checked the size tags on the other two. Six and four. Were all the woman's customers as skinny as she? And did she, like my mother-in-law, think that I wore a size sixteen? I took a peek into the window, but Bebe was now draping the dress over a very modern black chaise longue while the two men moved the $7,500 cabinet into another position, the skinny proprietor fussing at them as they grunted and heaved.

I moved off again and found a collection of bizarre stuffed animals from which I chose, as a present for my daughter Gwen, a lime-green and purple fish with puffed lips and crossed eyes. By the time I'd paid for the fish, Bebe had finished the window, hopped down onto the showroom floor, and flitted in my direction.

She was a tiny thing—the dresses here would fit her— wearing green sandals, tight green pants, and a huge green and white polka-dot shirt that reached almost to her knees. Long bangs and straight, black, shoulder-length hair completed the look. "So what's up?" she asked. "Hedwig said you wanted to talk to me." Then she looked at the clear plastic bag the clerk handed me and said, "*Cool* fish!"

"Thank you." If she liked it, maybe Gwen would. "I just had lunch at Gondar—"

"And you're looking for a bathroom," Bebe interposed with a giggle. "If you ask nicely, Hedwig will let you use hers."

"I'm fine," I said, embarrassed. "I'm investigating the murder of Denise—"

"You're a P.I.? That's *so* cool."

"No." I sighed. "I'm Vera Blue's daughter-in-law, and Kebra Zenawi mentioned that you were there that night and talking to a man named Charles Desmond, who is evidently Myra Fox's . . . ah—"

"Right. They're shacked up. So which one of us do you think murdered Denise? It wasn't me. I headed on home as soon as Charlie took off."

"In what direction did Mr. Desmond—"

"I don't know, but he didn't kill her. He's a high-end techie type. They don't kill people. They play with their computers and found companies that go bust. Not that he has a job just now. Wow, the dot.com blowout left half the people I know unemployed. There's lofts here in town fixed up for dot.coms that never even got rented."

"You think well of Mr. Desmond, then?"

"He's not so bad. Except he comes on to anyone in a skirt, and after all, he's got Myra. She's supporting him. He ought to keep his big, smarmy smile where it belongs. Still, he was there for Myra's sake, so I guess he's OK."

"Perhaps he went to Denise's office after he left you?"

She thought a minute. "I don't think so. He came in from the stairs. I think he was headed for the backdoor."

"*That's* open at night?" Good heavens, I'd never find everyone who'd been in the center last Thursday if anyone could get in anywhere.

"Hey you," Miss Takashima yelled at one of the departing workmen. "You changed the line of that dress." She sprinted toward the window with me behind, hoping for an answer to my question. While she rearranged the flamenco gown on the black chaise, I noticed the area rug on the floor. It was delightful, and I needed one, although of a bigger size, for my dining room.

"Does—ah—Hedwig sell these rugs?" I asked the window decorator.

"No, I brought it along. Why, you like it?"

"Very much, and I'm in the market for a rug that would go with a dark blue and silver color scheme."

"California Carpet. You want me to go with you? I love to pick out rugs."

"Do they ship?"

"Sure. Come on. We'll hop in my truck and head down there."

I glanced at my watch. Forty-five minutes before Sam returned. I accepted Bebe's offer and soon found myself zipping through the streets in a blush-pink pickup truck. Bebe confided, as we ran yellow lights and even reds, that security at the center was a joke. There were open doors and windows everywhere, including the upper floors where you could climb a fire escape and wiggle in through a window. "Alexi's always in the john, and his son, Vassily, who fills in for him and is a cute kid and very smart—he's more interested in talking to the unwed mothers, as long as they're pretty, than manning the security desk."

Bebe hadn't seen anyone suspicious that night, including Charlie Desmond, and she picked out a wonderful rug for me. After flipping through about three hundred, she said, "How about this one?" in reference to a cream-colored design with purple-blue outlined leaves and blocks of color. It was very subdued, and I loved it. She even waited while I arranged to have it shipped home, chatting about how much she loved shopping and various great shops in which to do it.

Her favorite was evidently a place called Recycled Chic that sold "adorable clothes" and was very near the center. "I got a pair of leather pants there for a song, and they are *so* cute. Everything's secondhand but in very good condition. That's what the name means. Recycled Chic. They don't take anything frumpy."

I put my rug receipts in my purse, and Bebe generously drove me back to Union Street, where I went straight to

Working Women and told them about Jesusita and Vera's idea for a Jail-to-Work department. Then I climbed from floor to floor checking for unlocked windows by fire escapes. Bebe had been right. Any would-be murderer who wanted to get in and stab someone would have had an easy job of it. Should I mention the security problem to the director? Would she get snippy and demand that I leave if I told her?

25
Police Station Gossip

Sam

The last I saw of Carolyn was a glimpse of a lady trying to refurbish a hairdo flattened by a motorcycle helmet. Men have it easier than women, which is probably why we're easier to get along with. Although I wouldn't give Marcus Croker any prizes for geniality, which is why I wanted to ditch Carolyn before I went to see him. She ought to be safe enough interviewing a Japanese girl who decorated shop windows. Come to think of it, I'd have to tell Paul about that chest. He'd like it.

Croker and his partner work out of the North Station. If they weren't in, I'd still find out something because cops love to gossip. The partner was there doing paperwork, probably because Croker stuck him with it. Arbus is a big black guy. Played ball in high school, but he wasn't fast enough to get an athletic scholarship. Did a couple of years in junior college and went into the cops. He seems happy enough, and we get on OK. Share a beer now and then and talk sports.

He's always asking me when the "next fuckin' quake is

comin','" like I know any more than anyone else about it. I majored in geology at Stanford because it sounded pretty interesting, but it's not like I figured on anything but going into the pros after college. You're dumb at that age. Don't think about not getting picked in the draft, or if you do, getting hurt, getting old. Happens to all of us. "Hey, Arbus, man, how ya doin'?"

"Sammie." Arbus emerged from the squad room and shook my hand. "Say, the police athletic league's lookin' for a coach—football—for a middle school team. You interested? Them little suckers, they'd shit bricks they thought they was gettin' a big-time pro for a coach."

"Arbus, I remember what junior high school kids are like, an' I'm not gettin' near a whole team of 'em. Hey, is Marcus around?" Arbus said Croker wasn't. "Well, maybe you can help me. Marcus say anything to you about the murder at the Union Street Center? He was there that night."

"Nah, man, I heard about that, but Marcus an' me was on patrol, an' we didn't take that call. Homicide got there before the uniforms."

"So Marcus was with you the whole time? Four to midnight?"

Arbus Penn scratched his head, which was shaven as close as you could get and still have hair. Then he scratched his nose. Arbus is a slow thinker, but he gets there. "Well, he took an hour of personal time. Otherwise, he was with me. We took down a couple of dealers that night an' hauled in some street girls who was tryin' to hustle tourists. I 'member cause one a them girls was *sweet choc'late*. I wasn't a married man, I wouldn't mind bein' hustled by that one. Know what I mean?"

"Who me? I'm gay."

"Always hard for me to believe that, Sammie. I seen you crackin' skulls for the 49ers in your day. You sure don't look like none a them gay fellas down in the Castro all dressed up in girls' clothes or wearin' them chains an' boots on parade day."

"You gonna march with us this year, Arbus?"

"They tell me to march, I march. Always a good show down there. You want me to have Croker call you?"

"Not if you can tell me what his personal time was for."

Arbus looked uneasy and shrugged. "Personal time is personal, man. Ask him, you wanna know, but he didn't kill no one at that center. He teaches a class there. He gets real pissed off 'bout them domestic calls. Me, I jus' get nervous. Croker gets mad. Mad at the guys hittin' their women. Mad at the women not bringin' charges. Callin' us out an' then sayin', 'Oh he didn't mean nothin'. Don' take him away, Officer. How we gonna eat, he be in jail?'"

Arbus did a good imitation of the women. I'd have laughed if it weren't so pathetic. "Come on, man. Whatever he's doin', it can't be that bad. If I ask him myself, he's gonna get all mean, maybe call me names. An' then I'll have to beat the crap out of him, an' then he'll be twice as mad 'cause he won't want to admit he got beat up by a gay, and our whole relationship will just go all to hell."

Arbus sighed. "OK, but you ever tell him I told you 'bout this, you an' me will git into it, an' don't be sure you can take *me*." I agreed that it might be a close call between the two of us.

Then Arbus told me the tale Croker had been telling him every Thursday night for a year or more, which was that he liked to sneak off duty and get it on with his wife for an hour because it added spice to their love life. "Don't that beat all?" said Arbus. "He wanna risk him an' me gittin' in trouble, so he can go home an' ball his own wife. Every Thursday night I gotta let him off at the corner at eight an' pick him up an hour later. I go call in a dinner break an' git me some ribs, an' Croker, he has sex with his ole lady."

Like I believed that. I had to wonder whether Arbus did. We promised to get together for a beer when there was a good game on TV, and I headed back to Union to pick up Carolyn at the shop. She wasn't there. I went on to the center and asked the Russian whether he'd seen her. He hadn't, and she wasn't on the sign-in list.

Deciding to give her a few more minutes, I sat down by the Russian guy and made conversation. Did he like his job? Did he know this guy and that guy in the Russian mob? He looked pretty nervous and insisted he didn't. Well, I'd have to wait for my contact to call back.

What had he seen the night of the murder? Same old people coming and going, then a lot of shrieking down the hall and people running around and cops and paramedics coming in and carrying out the dead, bloody woman and taking the live, bloody woman away in handcuffs. Obviously, they'd got the right person. Ya-ta-ya-ta-ya-ta.

"Where the hell have you been?" I asked Carolyn, who was coming down the stairs as if she wasn't fifteen minutes late and unaccounted for.

"Please don't swear at me," she retorted in that prissy voice.

"Please tell me where you've been, chickie. I was worried about you."

"And don't call me chickie. I talked to Bebe, as you well know, and then we went to California Carpet, and I bought a gorgeous area rug. Bebe has excellent taste. I'd never have picked that one, but once she recommended it, I could see that she was right."

"You went shopping when you were supposed to meet me?"

"You said an hour and a half."

"You'd have been here on time if you hadn't gone shopping."

"And then I came here, as we agreed, and delivered a message from my mother-in-law to a woman upstairs."

"You went to see your mother-in-law, too?"

"Visitors are only allowed on weekends. She *called* me yesterday."

"Jesus Christ!" I grabbed her arm and hustled her toward the front door.

"Where are we going?" she asked.

"To a pool hall to talk to a man about Freddie Piñon."

"I've never been to a pool hall." Carolyn looked intrigued.

"Well, you'll love this one. The ambiance is memorable." I had been so irritated that I decided on the spur of the moment to take her to Tres Hermanos to meet Araña Morales, A-number-one pool hustler and fence, occasional hijacker of trucks carrying worthwhile merchandise. He'd love Carolyn. She was blonde. Araña would probably go for a bearded lady if the beard was blonde.

26

Pool Halls and Dragon Rolls

Carolyn

It **was hard** to feel remorse for keeping Sam waiting when I had found such a perfect rug and after he had sworn at me. Back on the motorcycle, I wanted to ask why we were going to a pool hall but didn't push my luck. I had been invited along, and it did sound exciting. Once there, however, I wasn't so sure. Tres Hermanos was in a very rundown neighborhood with dangerous-looking tattooed youths lounging on street corners and boarded storefronts covered with graffiti.

The pool hall itself was an even greater shock. It reeked of beer and smoke and wasn't at all the dark wood and stained glass milieu I had pictured. Happily, there weren't many people in it, but those who were did not look particularly respectable. One fellow at a pool table looked absolutely sinister, with a cigarette hanging from the corner of his mouth and a ragged undershirt that exposed a mass of tattooed spiders on his arms and shoulders. Sam headed in his direction.

I panicked and murmured that I needed to use a telephone, dismissing my first idea, escape to a bathroom, for fear of what I'd find there. Sam handed me his cell phone and said, "Order two Coronas and bring them over, will you?"

I sat down rather timidly at the bar and gave the order to a dark-skinned man with a belly that overlapped his trousers. He drew two beers into glasses of dubious cleanliness. And he didn't provide napkins. Sighing, I made a call to Vera's sublet. It was the only number I could think of, and she might have left a message on the answering machine.

Much to my dismay, the message was from my husband. Apologizing for ruining any plans I might have had for the evening, he said that he and his father had managed to set up a meeting for a collaborative research project that promised to open a fascinating new avenue for him and be profitable to Calvin's company. Did I mind eating at home? He'd be back by 10:00 or so, and there was surely something in the refrigerator. Or failing that, I could order pizza. In fact, wouldn't a column on San Francisco takeout pizza be a good idea? He actually chuckled. I clicked off without checking for further messages. Here I'd been busy all day trying to save his mother, and he couldn't even be bothered to take me out to dinner.

I stuck the phone into my purse and picked up the beer. When I arrived at the pool table, Sam was in conversation with the dreadful spider man, who took one of the glasses from me and said, "Thanks, *Chica*. Nice hair. *Muy bonita*." Then he leered.

Sam said, "You take the second beer, Carolyn, while I go back to the bar. This is Araña Morales. Spider, meet Mrs. Carolyn Blue. Treat her nice. She's a lady." Then he left me with that man.

"You wanna a game, Señora?" he asked.

"Knock it off, Spider. You try to hustle the lady, I'll

knock you on your skinny ass," Sam called over his shoulder.

Mr. Morales called back, "That ain't no way to talk in front of a lady." Then he clicked his beer glass against mine and took a long swallow, after which he smacked his lips. "That Sam, he knows his beer. Lotsa guys doin' the buyin', they order some cheap shit. Corona now, it's good beer."

Then he stared at me. For lack of anything better to say, I asked if he'd read about Lola Montez, who arrived from Panama in 1853 and was famous for her "Spider Dance."

He said he didn't do much reading and added, "I hear you wanna know about Freddie Piñon? When Sam say that, I think why should I tell him anythin' about *mi amigo* Freddie, but for a pretty lady with blonde hair, maybe I got some information."

I backed up. Sam returned, beer in hand. "So Spider, my man, you know where Freddie is?"

Araña grinned at me with what I took to be lustful intent. He had a very strange drooping mustache, thin and straggling. It was hard not to shudder, and I did edge closer to Sam, who draped his arm over my shoulder companionably. "Quit looking at my lady like a goat in rut, Freddie. I don't like it."

"Hey, you don't dig women. You think Araña not know you're a—"

Some Spanish word followed that I certainly didn't recognize but took, because of Sam's expression, to be a rude term. "Watch your mouth, Morales," Sam said in a threatening rumble. Mr. Morales looked alarmed and launched into apologies, which were met with Sam's harsh "Shut up."

What would I do if they came to blows? Run for my life? Or was I obligated to hit Mr. Morales with a beer bottle or some such thing? Actually, all I had was my purse, Sam's cell phone, and my glass.

"When did you last see Freddie?"

Morales rolled his shoulders, which made the spiders on his upper arms appear to creep around. Keeping a wary eye on Sam, he said, "I ain't seen him myself since, like, Wednesday, but I hear he want his sister to take him in Friday night an' she tell him to fuck off 'cause if he was out of the halfway house, he was breakin' parole, an' she wasn' gonna have the cops comin' to her place to arrest him in fronta her *niños*."

"So, you think you could find him?"

"Porque?"

"You don't need to know why I want to talk to Freddie. You just need to look. You find him, I make it worth your while. *Comprende*?"

"Yeah. OK. I find Freddie, I call you."

"Right. Come on, Carolyn." And before I knew it, I was out of the pool hall, which was good news, and out on the street, which was not.

"Did you know that *hoodlum* is a San Francisco word?" I asked, feeling shaky and in need of ordinary conversation. "It meant young ruffian or criminal and evolved, perhaps, from youths who shouted "huddle 'em" when they were about to stone Chinese, which was evidently a favorite pastime."

"I doubt that Spider stones Chinese. No money in it, and it's frowned on these days."

"Shanghaid is another. Men were knocked unconscious with clubs or doped on the city's docks and carried aboard to serve as sailors on ships to Shanghai—"

"Yeah. It was a rough town in the old days. So I'll take my phone back," said Sam. "That must have been some call you made inside. You came over looking like you were gonna bite someone."

I shrugged, returned the cell phone, and donned a helmet. "I'm just a bit peeved. Jason left a message saying he wouldn't be taking me out to dinner. I don't know how he expects me to make my expenses tax deductible if I don't go to any restaurants I can write about."

"You want to try Japanese? I'm meeting Paul for sushi at Ebisu tonight."

"You're inviting me along?" What a bizarre idea. Was Paul his lover? Would he resent my inclusion? "Is it good sushi?"

"Best Dragon Rolls in town."

"I've never had a Dragon Roll."

"So hop on."

"Why not?" I agreed, climbing on behind him and feeling much more cheerful. Wouldn't Jason be surprised to find that I'd had sushi, which he loves, with two gay men? Maybe I wouldn't mention that they're gay. Then, as we roared off, I began to wonder what Paul looked like. Hopefully nothing like Mr. Morales. "What does Araña mean?" I shouted at Sam.

"Spider," Sam yelled back. Zipping in and out of rush-hour traffic, we came to a very lovely park with twisted trees. It was amazing to remember that San Francisco had been built on high sand hills. All these trees must have been planted, and if they were planted in sand, wouldn't they all fall down with the next earthquake? Not to mention the buildings. I remembered the plates and food dancing on the table at Citizen Cake and shivered. That had definitely been a tremor, even if Margaret Hanrahan had paid no attention. And surely a tremor foretold an earthquake.

27
Delicious Dragon

Carolyn

The weather was turning cool when we reached Ebisu on Sunset, and I was glad to get inside, where we squeezed into a booth—well, Sam sat beside me, so I was squeezed. His friend Paul Labadie arrived fifteen minutes later, after we'd been served a Dragon Roll and Asahi beer in giant bottles.

Now, a Dragon Roll is a work of art, a sight to see, and even better to taste. Besides the usual rice and wasabi, the body of the dragon contained crunchy shrimp (tempura?) and, I think, cream cheese. The skin was green with overlapping slices of avocado, and the crowning glory of the roll was a line of orange salmon roe peaks running along the spine. The chef had sliced the whole into pieces and reassembled them into a sinuous, delicious dragon.

Sam and I had finished one and ordered another by the time Paul arrived. Then dinner was one long series of surprises. Paul proved to be a tall, slender man with white-touched black hair and a slightly Asian look. His father had been a career military officer who met and married a

Korean lady while he was stationed there. And Paul, who never used rough language as Sam did, was, of all things, a venture capitalist. He played the stock market, and had since his college days at Berkeley, making money even in the bear market that preceded and followed the destruction of the World Trade towers. With this money and more that he raised, he funded dot.coms that often succeeded and biogenetic companies that discovered amazing drugs. He had even made an early investment in Yasmin Atta's Nightshades.

At one point, during the demolition of several salmon skin rolls, we discussed the latest book by Mario Vargas Llosa, whom I loved for his hilarious novel *Aunt Julia and the Script Writer,* Paul admired for his style, and Sam detested because he claimed that Vargas Llosa was a fascist. During this discussion I realized that the Sam talking trash at Tres Hermanos and the Sam talking literature at Ebisu seemed to be two entirely different men. I commented on the change.

Highly amused, Paul said, "Sam's a chameleon. He can fit in anywhere—a locker room full of football louts, a fund-raiser for the symphony, a gay bar in the Castro."

"Bad metaphor, buddy. Chameleons blend into the scenery," said Sam. "I stand out. Hard not to when you're my size."

Paul shrugged. "You can talk the talk, and your size keeps people from giving you grief or brushing you off before they find out that you're actually almost civilized and reasonably well educated, for a guy who went to a party school to play football."

"Who says Stanford's a party school?" Sam demanded.

"Were you a college football player?" I asked. Given his physique, he might well have been good. "Did you get to play much?"

Paul hooted with laughter. "Sam was an all-American linebacker in college and an all-pro linebacker for the 49ers."

My mouth dropped open. "Wasn't it rather difficult for you—with all those football players—because you're . . . ah—"

"Gay?" Sam grinned. "It wasn't a problem. I didn't want to have sex with them; I just wanted to crack heads and win games."

"Oh. What did you major in at Stanford?" If I had expected to hear physical education, I had another surprise coming.

"Geology," said Sam.

Well, that explained his store of information on earthquakes here and abroad.

"And literature. That was a minor. I had to put in a few summers to graduate."

"I majored in history," I said lamely.

"And Paul majored in business. Now is one of us supposed to ask you out on a date, or do you want to know our signs first?"

"Mind your manners, Sam," said Paul. "Did you think she'd take in the size and the Harley, see you in action at a pool hall, and conclude that you're a Renaissance man? And why are you dragging the poor woman around on a motorcycle?"

"Yes, why are you?" I chimed in. "Do you have a more comfortable vehicle?"

"Well, chickie, I like the bike. Just like I liked playing football and getting an education on the side. I like to have fun."

"And luring a sedate professor's wife onto a Harley strikes you as hilarious?"

"Right on, chickie. Let's have some green tea ice cream, unless you want another Dragon Roll."

"Maybe you could call me Caro if you don't like Carolyn, because I don't care much for *chickie*. I find *chickie* demeaning."

"Sexist?" Paul asked.

"No. Well, yes, but I hadn't thought of that. It's that chickens are so stupid. I'm not."

"Good point," said Paul, "and as for another Dragon Roll, if anyone gets another, I'm the one who should. You two started in before I got here."

"You insist on driving a car through rush-hour traffic, you gotta expect to be late and miss the Dragon Rolls."

"I wasn't late," Paul protested.

"And I couldn't eat another thing," I added. I don't like green tea, so I presumed that I wouldn't like green tea ice cream. Sam ignored me and ordered for all of us.

"Tell you what," he said. "Paul can give you a ride home in his car if you want, and you can spend the evening waiting for your mother-in-law to call from jail or your husband to get home from a scientific evening with the boys. Or you can get back on the bike with me and see what we can find out in the Haight about Martina L. King."

"Actually," I retorted, "I have an engagement at moon-rise, but I think I can work in a bit more investigation."

"What happens at moonrise?" Paul asked.

"The Interfaith Women at the center have offered to put me in touch with Denise or my late mother after they hold their goddess worship ceremony in the backyard," I replied.

Paul muttered, "Here I've got a great BMW, and I'm spurned for a jock on a Harley and a bunch of channel-ers."

"They only have one channeler, but I might find something out by talking to people during the social hour."

"You might find out that they're a bunch of flakes," Sam retorted. "Did you learn anything from Bebe?"

"She thinks Charles Desmond was in Denise's office before he started flirting with her in the kitchen and that he left by the backdoor, so he must have been gone by the time Denise was killed. Also I learned that there are un-locked doors and windows all over the center and that the older Russian, Alexi, spends all his time in the toilet. He's the man who walked in on Yolanda Minarez and precipitated the lawsuit." Sam was eyeing me quizzically. "Well, no matter. Bebe said the son, Vassily, spends his time flirting with the younger clients and no time on security. What did *you* find out?"

"Marcus Croker was on duty that night, but his partner said Croker takes an hour off every Thursday to have sex with his wife. I'll have to check that out."

"How?" I asked.

"By skulking in a doorway until he gets out of the squad car and then following him," Sam replied.

"Can I go, too?"

"What about your husband?"

"I don't think he'll want to join us."

"Finish your ice cream. We want to hit the shelters before they close the doors."

Surprisingly, the ice cream didn't taste like tea. It was green, but creamy in flavor and texture. I'd have to ask Sam for pointers on other interesting places to eat. The man had good taste, even if he was a gay ex-football player/private eye with interests in science and literature and the lover of a Korean American financial genius with beautiful manners. Paul held my chair for me and helped me on with my jacket before we pushed our way through the mob of people yearning for Dragon Rolls.

The first time I ever tasted a Dragon Roll was in a horrendously crowded restaurant in San Francisco. It was absolutely wonderful, not to mention beautiful to look at. I suppose one could fix it at home. What would you need? *Crispy shrimp* (tempura presumably, which you could buy at a Japanese restaurant and take home). *Sticky rice,* which you'd spread on a piece of wax paper with the shrimp positioned with their tails sticking out beyond the rice. Then you'd roll the wax paper so that the rice coats the two shrimp. After that, *thin slices of avocado* overlapping down the body of the dragon. Then *salmon roe* formed in little peaks along the spine, or (lacking salmon roe) little green horns of *wasabi* at one end from which you'd cut off a shrimp tail. If your dragon is horned rather than spiny, *thin carrot tusks* stuck into the head end of the dragon, and *voila*! A Dragon Roll! Of course, you have to cut it carefully into edible sections, and put it together on the serving plate.

How hard can it be? Well, pretty hard in my estimation. Better to find a restaurant that serves them. I actually found one at home in El Paso. Never cook if you can find a professional to do it. That's my advice.

Carolyn Blue,
"Have Fork Will Travel," *Cincinnati Herald*

28

The Tale of Martina L. King, Jr.

Carolyn

As we headed for Haight-Ashbury, a breeze blew drifts of fog through the streets. I paid attention because I'd heard so much about the Haight when I was young—the hippies, the Be-In at Golden Gate Park, the Summer of Love, the long hair and beads and drugs, Jefferson Airplane and the Grateful Dead. My father disapproved of flower children, college protesters, drug users, and me, if I didn't meet his expectations, although I was none of the aforementioned. The area didn't look dangerous. It contained a number of shops called Planet this or that, and the people on the street were mostly young, although there were some middle-aged, hairy individuals like the man with a ponytail halfway down his back. The most sinister sight I saw was a shaven-headed youth dressed entirely in black and walking a rottweiler, but for all I knew he might have been one of those neighborhood militia types.

At the shelter, which had windows blanked with brown paper and a worn sign, we interviewed a woman named Corky. She weighed three hundred pounds and wore shapeless black. In reply to Sam's inquiry after Bad Girl, a.k.a. Martina L. King, Jr., Corky said, "Stay here sometime. Not tonight. This is a ridin' night for her, best I remember. An' she don't use the junior."

Corky sat in a sagging chair of indeterminate color. On her lap rested a sign-in chart, in her hand a pen. She faced, at a distance, a small black-and-white television fronted by folding chairs in which were seated various shabby-looking people. We were invited to sit on a sofa that matched Corky's chair.

"Whatchu want with Bad Girl?" she asked Sam.

"We're investigating a murder at the Union Street Center. If she was there, we want to ask if she saw anyone."

"What kinda murder? *Split, you cain't nurse that baby in fronta my TV. Git on upstairs.*"

"Shit, Corky, this is my favorite program," the young woman whined.

"You make me git outa my chair, you outa here, girl." Corky had a voice that carried. "Person git beat up, shot, or what?"

"Knifed," Sam replied. "Last Thursday night."

"Whoa. Bad Girl got a thing about knives."

"So we heard."

"Yeah, her daddy killed her mama with a knife. Right in front of the poor child. She about nine or ten. Mama went into the ground, daddy into jail, and Bad Girl in foster care. Never said another word 'til she start hearing her mama an' daddy talking to her. Schizophrenic like her daddy. Not sure how she end up here. She stay in hospitals and group houses in the nort' till she eighteen an' get turned out by the system. Musta heard it din' git cold here on the Bay. That's important when you homeless."

Sam turned to me. "I thought you said she was a teenager."

"Over twenty-one," said Corky. "She skinny an' little cause she don' eat right. Don' see many fat folks in shelters an' on the streets."

"Do you think she might have killed someone?" Sam asked.

"Could be. Like I said, she gotta thing about knives. Never seen her havin' one she didn' draw on paper an' keep in her pack, but if she mad at someone an' off her pills an' see a knife, could be. If the voices tell her to knife someone. Voice tole her daddy to kill her mama. Tha's what she say."

"Was she here last Thursday night?"

Corky paged back though the grimy, X-marked lists of people who had enjoyed her hospitality. "Nope. Like I say, Bad Girl spend her time on the bus. Get a month pass. Then ride an' ride. Talk to her voices. Guess they likes the buses too."

Shades of the past in San Francisco, I thought, when tickets on the horse cars could be bought cheaper in quantity or for five cents a piece. "How can she afford a bus pass?" I asked, having read about the cost. "Does she have a job?"

"Hard to git a job when you half the time talkin' to folks no one kin see. Wish she'd take them pills, but she like to stay in touch, an' she don't hear no voices when she takin' pills. She don' have no trouble gittin' her a pass. Ain't a real one, but she knows a guy who makes 'em. Sure hope he don' have AIDS. She get that, she dead. She never be able to keep up with all them medications."

"Isn't there a hospital or group home where she could stay off the streets?" I asked, horrified at the plight of Martina L. King. If she'd killed Denise, maybe they'd put her in an institution that provided continuing treatment.

"That girl like the streets. She don' usually come here less she feel like talkin' to a real person, or it be rainin'. Bad Girl more interestin' than TV. You cryin', Miz Blue?" Corky asked me.

I was. I couldn't help thinking how terrible the child's life was and how much better it could be if she had a home, a family, and regular treatment. After all, that mathematician they made the movie about managed to get his life together and win the Nobel Prize. Poor Martina L. King would probably end up one of San Francisco's many suicides. The city was known as the suicide capital of the country.

"No use cryin' for Bad Girl. She doin' the bes' she can, like the res' of us. Gov'ment ain't gonna do nothin' for her. Got no family. So she make do. She like ridin' the bus, conversin' with the voices. Pro'bly the drivers and riders don' like her, but she ain't hurt no one I know of, so she kin keep on ridin'.'"

"Any way we could find out if she was on a bus that night?" Sam asked.

"Well, she like them buses go up to the park an' the golf course. Maybe she sleep up there in the trees. She bring back them golf balls an' give 'em to me. Say they pay for her bed when she stay here." Corky laughed robustly. "Like I got any use for golf balls. I jus' gotta hide 'em cause my clients, they throw 'em at each other, they get holda one. Had to call in the cops one night."

"I wonder if Ms. King attends any center activities other than the Monday afternoon art class," I mused. "Has she, by any chance, brought you artwork on days other than Monday, Ms. Corky?"

"Ms. Corky. Ain't that somethin'? By artwork you mean them pictures of knives, can be any day at all she comes in here, but they so folded an' smudged by the time she give 'em to me, couldn't say when she done 'em. Golf balls an' pictures of knives. Poor girl. Kinda nice she think to bring me a present even if it ain't something I got any use for."

"Perhaps she sees you as a mother figure," I suggested. Corky, for all her tough talk, struck me as a kind-hearted woman.

Corky scowled, shifted her considerable bulk, and plucked a whistle from the bosom of her dress. "Time to close the doors. If you all don' figure to stay the night, you best get on now." Corky then blew a blasting shriek on her whistle and used a remote to turn off the TV. Her guests, bundles in hand, obediently rose and shambled away to their beds, shepherded by a burly Latino who emerged to direct traffic. Sam and I bade Corky goodbye, thanking her for her time and information, and went into the street, whose population had increased while we were inside.

"She seems to run a structured operation. Are the beds clean?" I asked Sam.

"Never been in one," he replied. "You still want me to drop you off at the center to hang with the witches?"

"Are Goddess worshippers necessarily witches?"

"Probably. There's a lot of Wicca activity here in San Francisco."

"Really? Do you have warlocks in the Castro?"

"Jeez, Caro, how would I know? Do I strike you as a guy who would go in for that stuff?" We were both on the motorcycle by then and checking our helmet straps.

"How would I know, Sammie?" I retorted. "I just learned that you were a pro football player, a geologist, and a reader of Mario Vargas Llosa."

"Not since he got into politics." And off we roared toward my appointment with the Interfaith Ladies, whatever their faiths might be.

We had been traveling ten minutes or so, zipping around cars in such an aggressive and intimidating fashion that I was becoming more nervous than usual. Suddenly the motorcycle began to bump and jiggle in a terrifying way. "Sam," I shouted. "You have a flat."

He ignored me and sped up, steering through the crazy bumping. When we were once again moving with reasonable smoothness, he turned his head sideways and shouted, "That was a tremor, not a flat."

"God help us," I cried.

"You better go on home to Texas if a little tremor's going to scare you."

That sounded like a good idea to me. Maybe I could get a plane out before the airport became inaccessible. My taxi had crossed bridges over water to get me to the Stanford Court. I'd hate to be on one of those bridges if the Big One hit.

Sam pulled up to the center. "No need to panic," he advised. "I'd feel more comfortable with a measly little tremor than an evening with a bunch of witches."

"Marigold Garland is not a scary woman," I assured him, "just a little eccentric."

"Better you than me," he replied. "Pick you up tomorrow at nine." And off he went before I could make up my mind to ask for a ride to the airport.

Oh well, the ground seemed steady under my feet, so I decided to attend the meeting. Maybe the Goddess would warn us if an earthquake was in the offing. I thought about climbing the front steps, but I was so stiff from the motorcycle riding that I walked around the corner to look for the gate into the backyard. That was a mistake. It was very dark, and when I actually peeked in, the only light emanated from the rising moon and the candles held by chanting women in white robes.

Obviously, I was late. Should I turn around and go home? That flitting movement they were executing didn't look like anything my aches and pains would allow me to imitate. Well, too late. Marigold had spotted me and was dashing in my direction, chanting something about another sister come to join the circle. What did my mother-in-law think of these people? Had she ever been asked to join in? Marigold thrust a candle into my hand and led me toward the coven. Isn't that what groups of witches are called?

29
Earth to Moon

Jason

By 11:30 I had been in the apartment for an hour, torn between the fear that Carolyn might have been kidnapped by the pizza delivery man and the suspicion that she had gone out and stayed away to worry me because I hadn't taken her to dinner. Lately she seems to think that going out to eat is more important than an exciting research project.

At any rate, she bounced in, breathless, all smiles, saying, "You won't believe the day I've had, Jason."

Instead of listening, as would have been sensible, I said, "And you wouldn't believe the hour I've just spent worrying about you. Where the hell have you been? You were supposed to order out for pizza and——"

"Be waiting for you like a good little homebody? No wonder your mother is a feminist—a feminist, I might add, who is now in jail. I've been trying to get her out, and I have columns to write, so I went out to dinner. Do I complain when you don't come home until late because you're writing a paper on something highly toxic?"

"You went out to eat by yourself?" That wasn't like Carolyn.

"No, Jason, I had dinner with Sam and a friend of his named Paul Labadie. He's a handsome venture capitalist with lovely manners. It's really too bad you couldn't get free, because we had wonderful sushi. Have you ever had a Dragon Roll? They're—"

"You had dinner with two men, neither of whom you know at all? How did you get to this place?"

"On Sam's motorcycle. That was after we interviewed a man named Spider at a pool hall and before we visited a homeless shelter in Haight-Asbury to get information on a schizophrenic client at the center."

I must admit I had been a bit jealous at the idea of my wife dining with handsome venture capitalists, but motorcycles, pool halls, and homeless shelters? "Carolyn, do you have any idea of how dangerous places like that are?"

"I was with Sam. Did you know he was a professional football player?"

"Of course. He was a linebacker for the 49ers." Which should have been enough to make my wife run in the other direction. Her reaction to football is usually expressed in winces and hurried departures from rooms where it's on the TV screen. "And Mr. Flamboise could be twice as large and unable to protect you from someone with a weapon. Dad hired the man so you wouldn't—"

"Oh, I was perfectly safe. Except for the earth tremor. Those make me very nervous. I don't care if Sam *is* a geologist and thinks the ones this week aren't worth worrying about."

"Our private detective is a geologist?"

"Yes, his degree's from Stanford, where he played football. Oh, and Jason, I hope you won't be angry—"

"I already am."

"But not for a good reason. I have a right to go out to

dinner with friends if you're not available and to talk to
people about possible suspects in Denise Faulk's murder.
Goodness, I did a lot of my detecting on the telephone this
morning, and this afternoon I interviewed a Japanese
American window designer who took me to a store that
had a perfect rug."

"Perfect for what?"

"For us. That's why I'm apologizing, but you've been
so busy, I was afraid you wouldn't get a chance to look at
it with me, so I bought it."

"What did it cost?"

"Jason, you can be so stingy. It cost eight hundred dol-
lars. I'll pay for it myself, if you think that's too much.
She told me about a place here that has wonderful South
African dining room sets, too."

"I don't want a new dining room set."

"Fine. I won't look for one. Don't you want to hear
about the rest of my evening?"

"With Sam?" I asked sharply. "Or Paul?"

"Why, Jason, are you jealous?"

"Should I be?"

"Not really. They're a gay couple."

For God's sake! Did my wife actually think Sam Flamboise, the all-pro linebacker for five years running, was
gay? "Carolyn, Sam is not gay." I tried to sound patient
and nonpatronizing. "Whoever told you that—"

"He told me. Even Spider at the pool hall knew it. He
made some smart remark, and Sam scared him half to
death with a look and a couple of words. He's called Spider because he has them tattooed all over his arms. A perfectly disgusting man, but he knows Freddie Piñon, an
abusive husband who came to the center to find out where
his wife was, and Denise was the one who had got Graciella, Freddie's wife, into a shelter. So Freddie might
have killed Denise, don't you think? I saw a television
show about an abusive husband who attacked a woman
who had helped his wife."

"Carolyn, for God's sake, you can't associate with people like that. It's dangerous."

"So you're not mad about the carpet? Good. Bebe Takashima is really quite safe and has wonderful taste in rugs. But I haven't told you about the end of my evening. I've been at the center with the Interfaith Women. Sam dropped me off."

Relieved, I said, "Well, that sounds all right. Who brought you home?"

"Marigold Garland. She's a witch or a goddess worshipper or some such. We danced around under the rising moon in the backyard, holding candles and chanting things about herbs and spices. It's really rather relaxing, once you get over feeling silly. The idea was that the Goddess might tell us who killed Denise, but she didn't, so then we had tea and nasty whole-grain cookies, and a channeler tried to put me in touch with Denise, but she couldn't because I never met Denise. She was quite put out when she heard that because she'd used up all her powers on me and couldn't try it with someone who had known Denise.

"Then this lady who reads people's auras told me whose aura had looked murderous lately. I don't know how useful that will be, but I'll pass the names on to Sam. Frankly, most of the people she mentioned I could have guessed: the director Marina Charez-Timberlite; the schizophrenic art student, Martina L. King; Freddie Piñon; Mr. Timatovich, the security guard, but not very often; Marcus Croker, who's a policeman; and—oh—your mother."

"Now you've decided that my mother's guilty?"

"No, Jason. If I thought that—well, I don't know what I'd do, but it wouldn't be an investigation of the murder. That would be horrible—for me to prove that your mother did it."

"You must be very tired, Carolyn, after all these peculiar activities. Let's go to bed."

"I think I'll have a soak in a hot tub," Carolyn replied. "Riding a motorcycle is not easy on the muscles and bones."

"Good. If you stay away from Sam, you won't be riding on any motorcycles. My God, Carolyn, people in motorcycle accidents end up dead, or worse, brain dead."

"That's why we wear helmets," my wife replied and limped off to the bathroom.

I'm ashamed to say that I was relieved to know that she was in pain. Carolyn is not one of these people who subscribe to the no-pain-no-gain school of thought. She thinks I'm slightly mad because I like to run before work. In fact, she personally dislikes exercise of any sort. She probably thought riding a motorcycle wasn't in the exercise category and, having learned better, would now avoid them, and Sam Flamboise.

Could the man really be gay? Not that I'm a homophobe, but he came off at Eliza as the least-gay person I've ever met. On the other hand, if he and this Paul were gay, I had no reason to be jealous of my wife having dinner with them.

Shaking my head, I went into the bedroom and lay down. Witches, pool sharks, Dragon Rolls, schizophrenics, gay private investigators. I'd have to suggest to Dad that he have a talk with Flamboise about Carolyn's participation in the investigation. If I hadn't been so tired, I'd probably have lain awake all night worrying about my wife.

Carolyn

Ah, the hot water was so comforting. I could feel the aches melting away. I leaned my head back against the rim of the tub and floated. Until the water began to slosh. But I hadn't been moving. Which meant—*earthquake*! I leapt out and wrapped myself in a towel, ready to awaken Jason and flee down into the street. Except that nothing was now happening. I peered into the tub. The water was still. Disgruntled, I dried off, donned my nightgown, and went to bed. San Francisco is not an easy place to visit. Imagine living here!

30
Froggie and the Snitches

Sam

Paul liked Carolyn so much he called her at 7:30 the next morning to give her restaurant advice: Foreign Cinema for trendy, La Folie for French, and Delfina's for Italian. He even told her to use his name so she could get reservations on short notice. Paul entertains and gets entertained expensively. I heard this conversation as I was wandering into the kitchen for breakfast. When he saw me, Paul put his hand over the receiver and said, "It's Carolyn. You want to talk to her when I'm through?"

I'd already gathered that she is a woman who doesn't like getting up early. If she was pissed at Paul for calling, she'd take it out on me. "I'm outa here," I said. "Desk piled at the office." I scrambled away like a quarterback about to be sacked.

My desk actually was deep in paper; topmost was a report from the computer guy I'd set to research the Faulk will. His printout said: $7,000,000 estate, family business sold before death with provision of continuing executive position for son Ray. Wife Denise got two-thirds of the stocks and cash in a life trust with provision to leave it to the son, son's wife, and their heirs in any way she saw fit as long as they got it. Son got last third and the job. Feds got their share.

OK, money and murder. If Ray wanted it all right now, he'd have a reason to kill his stepmother. Faulk had just become a serious suspect, filed upstairs at Flamboise Central. I attacked the non-Blue stuff, only to be interrupted by Spider Morales. I never knew he got up so early.

"Hey, Sammie, I got news about Piñon. His cousin saw him Saturday night. For a fee, which you gotta pay me along with the two hundred you promised, he's saying Freddie wants to hide out at his place, but the cousin can't let him 'cause he's got a hot girlfriend don't like Freddie. She'd move out if Freddie moves in. Get the picture? Anyway, Freddie's pissed 'cause he's sleeping rough in some condemned building, but he gives the cousin some cash an' tells him to buy a gun. Freddie'll catch him in a couple a days, an' pick it up."

"Where'd Freddie get money?" I asked. "He's just out on parole."

"I don' know, man."

"Where's Freddie hiding out?"

"I ain't heard that yet."

"I'll up the ante if you do."

"OK. Gimme your cell number. I'll catch you later."

I gave him the number and thought about Piñon, who had cash to buy a gun. If there had been cash in Denise Faulk's office, that would explain Freddie's surprising affluence, and also his need to hide out from the police, even if the only place he could get was some boarded-up dump full of rats and rubble. Suspect number two. I filed him and went back to business.

By quarter to nine I'd cleared my desk and begun to call around for a name on someone who made counterfeit bus passes. Didn't sound like a very lucrative business to me, but I supposed there were enough illegal aliens and college kids in this town to keep him in bed and board, especially since the name I got, Froggie, had an address in the Tenderloin. Definitely low-rent. Froggie sounded like someone I might want to visit without Carolyn, whom I was supposed to pick up—right now.

My phone rang, news from my Russian snitch. Timatovich evidently liked his vodka and talked too much when he was drinking. He'd let it be known among his closest friends that he'd overheard a telephone conversation where he worked and had the goods on the accountant, who was cooking the books for fun and profit. So the bitch couldn't get him fired, according to Alexi, because he could get her fired. In fact, he was going to horn in on her scam and get rich, send his kid off to college in style with a car and money for a fraternity. Did they have fraternities at Cal Tech?

That was last week's news. On Sunday Timatovich was crying in his Smirnoff with his good friends because someone had killed the bitch, so she couldn't get him fired, but she wasn't going to make him rich either.

That pretty much wiped him out as a suspect. He'd had good reason to keep her alive. I called Carolyn to say I couldn't make it until ten. She wasn't pleased, but since I had a call on another line, I had an excuse to get off before she could enlarge on her displeasure. My next caller was in-house, my second computer hacker. Eric Timberlite was rumored to use mob guys to drive poor tenants out of rent-controlled buildings that he wanted to restore or tear down. The rapidity with which these buildings had cleared supported the rumors, in Simon's opinion. Also some of Timberlite's less-successful real estate ventures had burned down in the past. Suspicion of arson. Last, my hacker had heard from a software engineer who worked for the great man that Timberlite had been overheard ordering his wife to make the Women of Color stop protesting. If she didn't get it done, she'd have to resign, stay home, and give up her connection to the socially prominent Nora Hollis.

Didn't put him in a very favorable light, but the information didn't implicate Timberlite in Denise Faulk's murder. So, mark him off unless others didn't check out. I told my secretary I was leaving and headed for the Tenderloin. If Carolyn thought the Tres Hermanos neighborhood was scary, she'd have had a heart attack over this one.

Froggie lived and worked in a third-floor walk-up. The halls and stairs smelled like piss, but his place was clean and stuffed with electronics, tools of the modern counterfeiter. He had a bed, unmade, in a second room, which also doubled as a kitchen. Great quarters. "You oughta look into one of those loft-living spaces they built for the dot.commers and never managed to sell," I advised Froggie after introducing myself. "They're goin' cheap."

"Not cheap enough for me. Anyway, it's the work I like. I don't give a shit about the accommodations. So, what can I do for you? You need a passport or something?"

"Information. You know a woman named Bad Girl?"

"Why you wanna know?"

"She's gone missing. I'm trying to find her for a friend named Corky." A little timely lying is an important talent for someone in my business.

"Sure, Corky. Runs a shelter in the Haight. If Bad Girl sleeps inside, which she don't do much, she sleeps there or with me. How long's she been outa touch?"

"Corky hasn't seen her since last week." I didn't mention that Carolyn had seen her Monday.

"Huh." Froggie turned to a printer and inspected the slowly emerging product. "I seen her last Tuesday week. She come in for her bus pass and our monthly fuck."

"Yeah, I heard you get it on with her. That must be something. Doing a schizo."

"Well, it's weird 'cause she talks to herself. Even when we're in bed." He gestured toward the twin bed in the other room. "An' I'd like it better if she'd take a bath. I offered her my bathroom, but she don't like to take her clothes off. Hell, how many girls you know do it wearin' their sneakers?"

Using a magnifying glass, he examined the finished page. I politely refrained from getting close, being more interested in information than his business activities.

Froggie nodded his head approvingly. "You ever need a passport or a birth certificate, anything like that, I'm your man."

"Thanks. About the girl."

"Oh yeah. Well, looking like I do, it's not as if I can afford to be too choosy. Anyway, I kinda like her. She's different."

It was easy to see where Froggie got his nickname. He had the squashed-in face and croaky voice that went with amphibians that spend time sitting on lily pads. Maybe Martina L. King thought he'd turn into a prince one night. "So you got any idea how I could find her?"

"Ridin' the bus. That's what she does. That's why she puts out for me. She's got no money, an' she wants to ride the bus."

"Last time she was seen was late afternoon. Does she have any favorite evening buses?" I asked. If she'd been on one last Thursday at the right time, she hadn't killed Denise Faulk, or if she'd been on one later and had killed Denise, she might have been seen with blood on her by passengers or driver.

"She likes the number eighteen that goes up to the Legion of Honor. The driver don't hassle her, an' she says her folks like the view up there. That's who she talks to, but they ain't here. They're dead. Old man died in prison after he killed the mother. Gotta feel sorry for a girl don't hardly talk to no one but dead people. She's probably jus' ridin' around and sleepin' up on the golf course. That's what she does."

"Thanks." I bought a fake driver's license just to be

friendly. Then I went back to the street and my bike, which was being circled by two would-be bike thieves. I picked one up by the back of his belt and lifted him, screeching, away from my Harley. The other one ran. Well, I had a bus number. All I had to do was find whoever had been driving last Thursday night. Not that I considered Bad Girl much of a suspect. Too pathetic to be a successful murderer. I glanced at my watch. Almost ten. I'd have to shift out of Froggie language to appease Carolyn.

31
Abuser and Wife

Carolyn

Some mornings are impossible. After that tremor that didn't wake Jason, he woke me before sunrise to say goodbye, promising to be back by 6:30. Then Paul Labadie called at 7:30 and woke me up again to give me the names of three restaurants he thought I'd want to try for my column. While taking down Paul's recommendations, I noticed the answering machine blinking, something I'd forgotten to look for last night.

The message was from Vera. "Be sure that they're expecting Jesusita at the center. She'll be out of jail by noon and go straight over. And Carolyn, Margaret tells me that you showed up at the center on a motorcycle and joined the Interfaith Women for one of their peculiar meetings. I suppose you know by now that they think they're witches. Still, I'm relieved to hear that you've taken up new interests. Your father-in-law and I enjoyed riding his motorcycle when we were young and foolish."

That was news to me.

"At least you've given up investigating the murder for

pursuits less dangerous, although motorcycle riders should wear leather clothing, which protects their skin, if not their bones. Of course, nothing protects the head except a helmet. I hope you have one. I'll let you know when that female detective arrives to apologize and release me."

Ah, Vera, I thought, *how little you know.* I called the center to remind them about Jesusita. Working Women wasn't open, but the director's secretary, back from childbirth, took the message. She advised me not to come in myself because the director didn't like me and was in a foul mood. I had no more than thrown myself back in bed and closed my eyes when my alarm went off. I rose, grumbling, to dress for my nine o'clock appointment with Sam, who called at 9:00 to say he wouldn't be by until 10:00. So there I was with an hour to waste and nothing in the house for breakfast. Fine. Sam could buy me breakfast to make up for arriving late. I started calling restaurants and got, by using Paul's name and my profession, reservations at Foreign Cinema—what an odd name—for tonight, La Folie for tomorrow, and Delfina for Friday. Then I called the airline and confirmed our reservation to fly home Saturday evening after the anniversary celebration at the center. With luck Sam and I would have cleared Vera by then.

Sam showed up at 10:10 and took me down the hill to Bob's Donuts, and here I'd been fantasizing about Eggs Benedict. While we were waiting for said donuts, I told him about one Frank Marrayat, who couldn't afford eggs for breakfast in San Francisco during the Gold Rush, so ordered the less-expensive "Fricassee de Lapin," which turned out to be squirrel, not rabbit. "He liked squirrel, can you imagine?"

"Sure," Sam replied. "He's the guy who was so hungry he said he wouldn't have refused a 'fat Sacramento rat.'"

"You know everything, don't you?"

"Well, I know we have to go next door for coffee." He

picked up the Sam-size bag of donuts, and we left. Next door I discovered that Sam had ordered me an apple fritter; it was large enough to feed a family of four. While I nibbled, he told me of his morning calls and his visit to a counterfeiter named Froggie, who had given him the number of a bus route Bad Girl was known to travel. I complained about being excluded from the Froggie visit, which sounded quite interesting—I've never met a counterfeiter—but Sam said he was saving me for Ray Faulk's wife. He considered the stepson an excellent candidate to take Vera's place in jail and thought a respectable woman more likely to get information from Mrs. Faulk than a scary man like himself. How could I argue with that?

En route to Mrs. Faulk's house, Sam actually took a call on his cell phone. If people got killed talking on cell phones while driving cars, how much more dangerous to do so on a motorcycle. I tried to get him to hang up, but by the time I'd secured his attention, we'd stopped at a red light, and Sam told me to shut up—not very polite—because his snitch was reporting on Freddie Piñon.

"We may have lost Freddie," he admitted gloomily as we parked near the Faulk house. "He was seen standing drinks for some of his gangbanger buddies and bragging that he was going to buy a car and drive to LA." Sam sighed. "Unless we develop some good evidence against him, we won't be able to get him back."

"My poor mother-in-law. She could go to prison because we didn't catch Freddie Piñon before he left town."

"We don't know he's gone yet. It's not that easy to buy a car when the cops are looking for you. And if he killed Denise, he's going to think they are, and living in a vacant building isn't the place to hear about who's been arrested instead of you. My snitch says Freddie can't read, so he's mostly got no access to news.

"Now about your talk with Mrs. Faulk. Remember he's abused her so she's scared of him, and with Denise dead, she's got no one to protect her. You'll have to be careful, but what you want to find out is where he was Thursday night. I'll be in that coffee shop across the street, keeping an eye on who goes in and out of the house. Ask for him. If he's not there, say you want to talk to her. If he answers the door, say you got the wrong address. If she goes to get him, run. If he comes home, I'll follow him in to be sure you stay safe. OK?"

It was frightening to think that Mr. Faulk might attack me, but if he was the murderer. . . . Still, I felt reasonably safe with Sam as my protector, and I didn't have to tell Jason about this. Sam headed for the coffee shop and I, for the narrow row house.

As I climbed the steps, I cast a last glance at the coffee shop that held Sam and then one through the front bay window. San Francisco must have more bay windows per capita than any city in the United States. I could see into the living room where a woman in a gray dress sat on a sofa with her hands folded in her lap. She was perfectly still. I rang the bell twice before she answered. When I asked for the "man of the house," she replied that he was at work. When I followed my first request with one to speak to her, she nodded and motioned me in without even asking my business. A strange woman.

Glancing at a card I took from my purse, as if consulting the printing there, I said, "Are you Mrs. Teresa Faulk?" She nodded. It's hard to strike up a conversation with a person who has nothing to say. "I'm from the Union Street Center." At that she looked up, and her eyes glistened, perhaps with tears. "My name is Carolyn Blue." She nodded. "My mother-in-law has been arrested for the murder of yours." *What a subtle approach, Carolyn.* "I'm so sorry about Mrs. Faulk's demise."

"Denise was a wonderful woman," she said. "And I'm sure your mother-in-law is a fine woman. I am sorry for her predicament."

"Thank you. I wondered if you or your husband have

any idea who might have disliked Mrs. Faulk enough to kill her."

"My husband did not like her. He did not even allow me to go to her memorial service. However, he was at work the night she was killed, as he is every night after dinner."

"I believe she was attacked between 8:30 and 9:00."

"Then he was at the Faulk Building south of Market Street. It is still called the Faulk Building although my father-in-law sold the company before his death. Now my husband works harder than ever."

"I'm sorry to hear that," I said politely. "I understand that your mother-in-law was very helpful during a time when you had some . . . ah . . . trouble with your husband."

"Yes, my husband broke my jaw and arm because he was very angry that I went back to work. However, you should understand that we were happy for many years. I came to San Francisco from the Philippines to work as a nurse in a hospital. There I met my husband, who was having his tonsils out. Removal of tonsils can be very troublesome for an adult. I felt very sorry for my husband, and we fell in love."

She spoke in a monotone, staring at her hands, her face quite expressionless. Was this typical of an abused wife? "But he did not want you to work after you were married?"

"I only found that out when I secured a job as a nurse in a doctor's office after our second child began school. I did not have enough to do and thought he would be pleased to have the extra income since we had just bought this house. Such was the way in America, I thought. But my husband beat me for displeasing him. The second time this happened, I had to quit my job to keep secret my shame."

"I'm so sorry, Mrs. Faulk." Good grief, the woman sounded like a zombie.

"Yes, but the third time there was no keeping of secrets because I had to go to the hospital for treatment. Broken bones do not heal without medical attention, and my children were very frightened. When my mother-in-law came to see me, I confessed my problem, and she said to my husband that if he beat me again, she would go to his father, who would be very angry. My husband was angry with both of us, but he stopped beating me because, even though his father was sick, Raymond was afraid of him. I then took care of my father-in-law, for which he insisted on paying me, which again made my husband angry."

"Your husband sounds like a . . . a ferocious man."

"He was not always so, but he has changed. When his father died and left much money to my mother-in-law, my husband forbade me to see her anymore or to leave this house. He comes home for each meal to be sure that I am here. I think I will divorce him. As you are from the center, which looks after the welfare of women, perhaps you can advise me on how to go about this."

"Divorcing your husband?" I had no idea what to tell her. "You could ask Margaret Hanrahan. She's their lawyer and handles cases for clients."

"Yes. That would be the first thing. A lawyer. And then a job so that I can support my children."

"What the hell are you talking about, Teresa? And who the hell are *you*?"

The last was addressed to me. Ray Faulk had evidently come home for lunch. How clever of him. It was only 11:30. "I came to extend my sympathies to you and your wife over the death of Mrs. Faulk," I improvised. If I hadn't been sitting on their sofa, I'd have fallen down in fright. "Such a terrible thing."

"Get out!"

"This is Mrs. Blue, Raymond," said Teresa. "It is her—"

"As in Vera Blue? Why are you nosing around here?"

"Take it easy, Ray, old boy." Sam had come up behind

him and laid a giant hand on his arm. "The lady is paying
a courtesy call, and you're not being very courteous."

Ray Faulk whirled aggressively, took a good look at
Sam, and backed up. "I don't know you."

"No. Well, I'm a private detective. Sam Flamboise."

"The linebacker?"

"Was once. So now that we're buddies, how about you
tell me where you were when your stepmother was getting killed?"

"I don't have to tell you anything, and I resent the im-
plication. They have the murderer. Are you two trying to
put the blame on an innocent, grieving relative?"

Teresa Faulk looked so astonished at her husband's description of himself as a grieving relative that he moved
menacingly in her direction. Sam grabbed my arm and
pulled me toward the doorway. "You know better than to
let strangers in the house," Faulk said, grabbing his wife's
arm. She gasped in pain.

"Ease off, Faulk, we're leaving. But maybe you should
keep in mind that violence against any woman, particularly another member of your family, would make you
look like a good candidate for your stepmother's murder."

Faulk dropped Teresa's arm, and she cowered away
from him. Had it finally come home to her that her husband might actually have killed the woman who had res-
cued her? "We can't leave her alone with him, Sam," I
whispered as he held the door open for me.

"You wanna come along with us, ma'am?" Sam asked
Teresa Faulk.

"No," she said. "It would be better if my husband left."

"I'm not going anywhere, you dumb wog."

"Please do not call me a wog. If you do not leave, I
will call the police and report that you have injured me."
She held out her arm, on which angry red fingerprints
showed. "I know where to find the files of my previous
injuries, and there are hospital records. I do not think you
will wish to stay under these circumstances, Raymond.

Especially, if you killed Denise, for which I will never forgive you."

"But I didn't—"

"Thank you, Mrs. Blue and Mr. . . . ah . . . Sam for the insight you have given me on this matter." With that she went to the door to shake our hands. There being little else we could do in the circumstances, we left.

"Aren't you afraid he'll hurt her?" I asked.

"I doubt he's got the guts," said Sam. "What did you find out?"

"She said he was at work when Denise was killed, that he always goes back after dinner, and that she's not allowed to leave the house."

"That's a woman who needs to get a divorce, and we need to find out if he *was* at work that night."

I was pleased to see that Raymond Faulk had left the house too. He cast us a furious look, climbed into his car, and roared away.

32

Zaré: Lunch with a Fashion Plate

Carolyn

"**C**an we get to the financial district by one o'clock?" I asked Sam. "I'm meeting Yasmin Atta. She was at the center when Denise was killed."

"Right, and Zaré should provide a column," Sam suggested.

"Well, that's good news. Ah . . . did you want to come along?"

"I've got to check out if Raymond Faulk was really at his office that night."

"Good idea." Then I had an idea myself—leather pants. Vera hadn't mentioned pants particularly, just leather as the fabric of choice for motorcycling, and Bebe had said Recycled Chic had reasonably priced leather pants. "Why don't we meet at the center at 3:30? Do we have many stops to make this afternoon? Jason and I have reservations at Foreign Cinema for 7:30."

"There's one interview I want you to do—Marcus Croker's wife."

Ah, the mean policeman. As long as he wasn't there, I

didn't mind talking to his wife, and Officer Croker worked 4:00 P.M. to midnight according to Sam. Just then we passed the Transamerica Pyramid, shining glass from its base to its tip high over the financial district. The Montgomery Block Building had stood there until 1959, filled with low-rent studios for artists and writers. Did the office workers there now hear the ghostly whispers of the city's cultural past?

Yasmin Atta was fifteen minutes late, so I had time to peruse the menu and admire the décor at Zaré. Which was beautiful, especially the copper ceiling swathed with filmy white scarves. I sat on the wall side of a banquette done in a grosgrain fabric with colors ranging from dark red to peach. After ordering a glass of pino grigio, the Crab Cakes in Whole-Grain Mustard Sauce caught my eye. I do love crab cakes.

My lunch companion arrived, escorted to the table by the proprietor, Hoss Zaré, dark-haired and charming. And Yasmin Atta—what can I say? Slender, over six feet tall with a long, graceful neck, close-cropped black hair, satin dark skin, and the carriage of a princess. And her clothes! They flowed and shimmered. I've often felt too sedately dressed, but never before too short.

We introduced ourselves, she immediately chose the Wild Mushroom Soup from the list of specials mentioned by the Chinese waiter, and then she recommended it to me. Although I had ordered crab cakes, I took her suggestion as well. Unfortunately, Ms. Atta did not order anything else; she did tell the waiter to bring her soup immediately. Then she apologized for being late and, in advance, for leaving early because she had a meeting with someone who had developed a new line of lip creams for women of color.

"Oh my goodness, that's what Nightshades means," I said.

"What did you think it meant?" she asked.

Now I was embarrassed. "Well, my husband does research on toxins. I'm afraid when I heard the name of your company, my mind immediately jumped to—the poison," I finished in a small voice.

"There's a poison named nightshade? Lord help us. That could be a problem when we launch the IPO."

"What's an IPO?"

"Initial public offering. Of stock in the company. I want to raise money to expand."

"Congratulations," I said, glad she didn't want to expand a company that made poisons. Since she was leaving early, I got right to the point. "I'm investigating the murder of Denise Faulk, and I wondered what you could tell me about that night, or if you can give me the name of anyone who might have had reason to murder her."

The waiter put down her soup and my crab cakes. Did they specialize in the fastest service in San Francisco, or were they accommodating her schedule? The latter evidently, because I heard a woman say, "Aren't those *my* crab cakes? *I* ordered before *she* did." I quickly took a bite before the waiter could take mine away, and oh, my! They were wonderful! Crispy outside, deliciously flavored inside with crab and yummy taste enhancers, and served with an ambrosial mustard sauce, garnished with watercress.

I wondered if watercress might be the winter purslane called miner's lettuce in gold rush days. Ten thousand miners died of scurvy in three years, but many survived by eating purslane. Sailors dying in a city hospital were told by a visiting minister to walk out on the hills and collect the lettuce for salads with vinegar. Because of his advice, they lived.

Ms. Atta took a sip of her mushroom soup and sighed with pleasure. "I really shouldn't order this," she said. "But it's so mushroomy! And the cream! Well, I don't even want to know how many calories are in this bowl.

"So, last Thursday. Well, I was on another floor teach-

ing a class in makeup and clothing selection, so I didn't
see anyone go into Denise's office carrying a knife, and
I didn't go downstairs until after the fuss was over. Then I
took the middle stairs and the old ladies' ramp because I
had a meeting.

"Let's see. One woman left my room as soon as the
screaming started. Cammie somebody. She's a policewoman, so she'd be the person to ask. All I know about
her is that she's got good skin but dreadful taste in
clothes.

"As for motives, money would be my guess. Since
Denise took over, no one can get funding for anything. I
don't mind providing Nightshades for the black and
brown women. It's good publicity for my product, although I'd have preferred to send an employee to teach
the class. But Nora Hollis got hold of me, and nobody
says no to her. But the white women can't use Nightshades, so *I'm* buying the makeup for them. If I didn't,
there'd be accusations of reverse discrimination. I have
to hire token white girls at my business for just that reason.

"And it's not that I can't afford to buy the white-girl
cosmetics. It's the principle. But Denise said she didn't
have an extra penny to give my class. Now how could that
be? Nora's the best fundraiser in the city, and Myra, before she had to drop out with cancer—God, I need to call
her. I've got her the name of a woman who makes breasts.
Well, Myra got lots of grants. So where did all the money
go?"

"Is there anyone besides you who's upset about
Denise's handling of the finances?" I asked, attacking
another crab cake and swishing every bite through the
sauce.

Yasmin took another tiny sip of her soup and said,
"The lesbians. I'd check them out. They're furious because Denise said there wasn't enough money to pay an-

other staffer in the lesbian and transsexual group. They don't think poor Kara really represents their interests.

"Now there's a woman with clothes problems. I gave her a few tips yesterday on how to overcome the width of those shoulders, but when push comes to shove, Kara's going to end up looking like a pro basketball player in drag. Not that the lesbians care about her shoulders, but they purely hate the novels she writes, which aren't half-bad. I told her she ought to write one with a black heroine, and we could do some sort of joint promotion.

"Also the lesbians are miffed because they're upstairs with the witches, who they consider kooks, but no one on two will switch with them, and Denise said the center couldn't afford to hire furniture movers even if the Women of Color would agree. I think Bertha refused to swap because she's a devout Christian and considers gays and lesbians flouters of God's laws.

"Well, I've got to run." She glanced at her watch, waved to the waiter, and gave him her credit card.

"Please," I exclaimed, "let me pay."

"I wouldn't dream of it. I know you're trying to help Vera Blue, and she's the one person I *don't* think would have killed Denise, not that Denise wasn't a popular staffer until she had to give up Battered Women for finances. Is Vera a relation?"

"Mother-in-law," I admitted as Yasmin signed the credit card slip and rose.

"Lucky you," she said. "If I were married, she's just the person I'd want for a mother-in-law. Someone who likes to see women making it in business. You can't imagine how much more fun it is to run your own business than it was to be a model, where you're just meat on the hoof. Of course, I'd prefer my mother-in-law to be black." And she was out the door just as the waiter served my mushroom soup, which was really superb. Was that truffle oil floating on top? I ate every drop.

These two recipes from Zaré in San Francisco can be made at home, but do visit the restaurant if you're in the city. The food is wonderful, the décor gorgeous, and the service friendly.

Zaré's Wild Mushroom Soup

Serves 4 to 5 people

- Heat a large sauté pan and add *2 tbs. olive oil.*

- Sauté meripoir (*1/3 cup each finely diced celery, onion, and carrots*) until translucent.

- Add *1 to 1 1/2 lbs. cleaned wild mushrooms* (*oyster, shiitake, button, morel, porcini, etc.*) to the same pan and sauté until soft. The mushrooms can be rough cut or left whole.

- Add *1 or 2 sprigs of lemon-thyme, 1/2 tsp. mild curry, 2 cloves peeled garlic, salt, and pepper.* Sauté another minute and deglaze with *1/2 cup white wine.* Let liquid reduce by half.

- Add *1 1/2 cups chicken stock* (*or water*), and let simmer over low heat for about 1/2 hour.

- Add *1/2 cup heavy cream* and continue cooking another 10 minutes.

- Puree the soup, and adjust the salt.

- Refrigerate overnight.

- Bring soup back to a boil to heat through and then finish with drizzle of *truffle oil* on top.

Dungeness Crab Cakes

Serves 4 people

CRAB CAKES

- Mix gently in a large bowl *1 lb. fresh crab meat, 1 whole egg, 1/4 cup bread crumbs, 1/4 cup finely diced red and yellow bell peppers, 1/8 cup diced chives or green onions, 1/4 cup lemon-garlic aioli, salt and pepper* to taste. If mixture falls apart, add more aioli or bread crumbs as needed.

- One portion is roughly equivalent to an ice-cream scoop made into a patty. Coat each patty in breadcrumbs.

- Heat *2 tbs. vegetable oil* and sauté patties in hot pan for 15 to 20 seconds on each side.

- You can keep the patties in a 400 degree oven for a few more minutes to ensure cakes are heated through.

SAUCE

- Reduce *1/2 cup white wine* with *1 whole finely diced shallot* until only a few drops of wine remain in the pan.

- Slowly add *1/4 lb. butter* in small portions until mixture is smooth. Finish by adding *1 tsp. whole-grain mustard.*

- Once mixed, adjust for salt and pepper.

- Place sauce in center of each plate. Place two crab cakes and arrange *sprigs of watercress* in between as garnish.

These two recipes were provided by Chef/Proprietor Hoss Zaré of Zaré, a restaurant in the financial district of San Francisco.

Carolyn Blue,
"Have Fork, Will Travel,"
Oak Bluffs Gazeteer

33
Leather Chic

Carolyn

When the cab dropped me off at Recycled Chic, I went inside with some trepidation. I'd never shopped in a secondhand store before. Was the clothing sized, or did one have to guess? What about dressing rooms? Their showroom space was long, narrow, and crammed with racks, both on the walls and running into one another and the customers on the floor. I asked a salesgirl for the leather section, and she shrugged. "Feel free to look, but we don't carry anything kinky."

Kinky? Gingerly, I approached the left-side wall rack that began beyond the checkout counter. After spotting numerous sequined blouses and T-shirts with more down the line, I tried the other wall. In the center section I found three black leather jackets, none of them sized, so I tried on the largest and was able to zip it up. It barely reached below my waist, but it did fit, so I draped it over my arm and began to search the racks in the center section, while passing shoppers brushed me into tightly packed clothes. I don't know how many times I said *excuse me,* more often than other customers said it to me. After a half hour, I was very tired and hadn't come upon any leather pants.

About then I discovered a box of boots under the sequin section, and in it was a pair of beautiful, soft leather boots. If I couldn't find pants, the boots were long enough to give me some protection. First, I clung to the rack rail and held the sole of a boot against the sole of my shoe. It looked about right. Have you ever tried on a long boot while standing up? I managed, but I fell down once. The lady at the cash register heard the clunk and came over to help me up. "If you're injured, don't figure on suing us," she warned. "We got a sign up front. *Not responsible for injuries or thefts of personal property.*"

I groaned and leaned on her, still clutching the second boot.

"Why don't you use the dressing room?" she suggested. "It's got a chair."

"Where is it?"

"All the way in the back. You'll see the line."

"Do you have any leather pants?"

"Second rack from the back. Center. That's a great jacket. You better hang on to it. We don't have that many tens."

She returned to the register, and I went in search of the leather-pants selection. They had two in red with fringe; one in yellow, size two; and four in black, no sizes. Without much hope, I took the two biggest pairs to the fitting-room line—six young women loaded down with skimpy tops and skirts that might cover their underpants if they were short-waisted.

I waited at least a half hour to get to the head of the line, then another fifteen minutes, checking my watch frequently, because the girl ahead of me had half the store in her arms. When she exited, I went in and found two other women in there with me.

I turned my back politely. One of them said, "If you don't start undressing now, you won't finish in your fifteen-minute allotment." I started undressing. First, the pants. The smaller pair I couldn't get into. The larger I managed, but when I looked in the mirror, I considered them too tight.

"Perfect," said a redheaded girl in her underwear. Then she pulled a sheer slip—perhaps it was a dress—over her head.

"Yeah," agreed the second occupant of the room. "I wish I could get a pair of leather pants that fit me that well. In fact, those might. If you don't want them, let me try them on."

They fit me properly? I turned again in front of the mirror. *Well . . .* I pulled the leather jacket on over my blouse, shoved the blouse tails up underneath the jacket, and looked at myself. I'd never in my life worn anything like this, but it was . . . different. Sort of . . . interesting. And it would protect me from scrapes if we had an accident.

I glanced at the boots. To get into those, I'd have to sit down. Could I sit down in these pants? Gingerly I bent to pick up the boots. So far, so good. I could bend. Then I went to the only chair, which was piled with clothes.

"Hey," cried the redhead, and ran to rescue her selections.

I sat down. No embarrassing sounds of ripping, and the leather seemed to have some give to it. I struggled into one boot and then the other, stood up, and peered at myself. I must say that I looked like another woman and had to stifle the urge to laugh with pleasure. Did I have the nerve to actually wear these clothes in public? Would Sam make fun of me? Would Jason have a fit? Well, he didn't have to see them. And didn't I deserve to buy something outrageous once in a while?

With rebellious determination fueling my courage, I gathered up the slacks and matching jacket that I had worn in. Behind me I heard the redhead say, "Did you ever see a woman her age look that cool?" I wasn't *that* old, I told myself and went up front to pay. "I'm wearing the jacket, pants, and boots out," I told the woman at the register when, after another lengthy wait, it came my turn. "The blouse is mine, as are these." I displayed my linen-like jacket and slacks (real linen wrinkles horribly).

"Nice color," said the cashier. "How much do you want for those?" Nonplused that she was interested in buying my slacks suit, I decided to sell so I wouldn't have to carry it home. "Fifty dollars," I said.

"Twenty," she countered.

"Forty-five."

We settled on thirty-five, which came off my leather bill, and I walked out in time to hear Sam pull up in front of the center two blocks away. He was taking off his helmet when I caught up, and he said, doing a double take, "What happened to you?"

"My mother-in-law advised me to get leathers if I was going to be riding on a motorcycle," I said primly.

"Yeah? Well, Carolyn, that's the hottest pair of rider's leathers I've ever seen."

"Thank you," I replied, taking that as a compliment, but not necessarily sexist since Sam is gay. Then we put on our helmets and set out for the interview with Mrs. Croker. During a wait at a traffic light, I told Sam what Yasmin had said, that the murder was probably over money because no one could get Denise to come up with any since she took over. "Doesn't that add credibility to what Mr. Timatovich overheard and took to be evidence that she was stealing?" I asked at the next light.

"Yeah, but we'd have to find out who knew besides the Russian and why they'd kill her instead of turning her in."

"A person who helped in the theft," I suggested.

In front of Crokers' duplex, he said, "We'll get into Denise's apartment and see if we can find any evidence."

"Won't it be locked? Maybe even taped off by the police?"

"Tapes can be untaped and locks picked."

"You're going to break into her apartment? Sam, I can't—"

"So you go home, and I'll do it."

"Well, on second thought—" I began, no doubt having been lured into criminality by my leather clothing.

"Right," said Sam. "Now you follow the same routine with Mrs. Croker. Is he home? No? Good, it's her you want to talk to. Tell her you're a cop." He laughed. "Tell her you're a motorcycle patrolwoman, and you heard about her husband coming home Thursdays when he's on duty for a romantic fuck, and you'd like to know how she got him to do that, because you'd like to get some action from your husband. I'll be out here, keeping my eyes open for Croker."

I do not consider *fuck* a romantic word, or even an acceptable one. Would a motorcycle policewoman actually say *fuck*? Well, I wouldn't.

34
Carolyn Undercover

Carolyn

Mrs. Croker was neither well groomed nor a good housekeeper. I doubt that she'd have let me in if she hadn't liked my outfit. We sat in her living room with the television playing, amid a litter of magazines, dishes, and overflowing ashtrays, to which she added liberally in the time I was there.

"So you're with the motorcycle cops? That don't look like any cop clothes I ever saw." Without offering me one, she fixed herself a bourbon and water. Perhaps she'd been offended when I refused a cigarette.

"These are my civvies," I said, hoping that was the term for a police person's off-duty clothes.

"Mighta known. If they had uniforms like that, I mighta joined myself. I always liked motorcycles. What kinda bike you ride?" she asked.

"A Harley," I replied because I was unable to name any brand but Sam's.

"You don't look like you could keep one a them big

bikes from fallin' on you. An' aren't you a little old for the
bike patrol?"

"My sergeant doesn't think so," I said, smiling coyly.
"Say, the reason I stopped by, Nadine—you don't mind if
I call you Nadine?—there's a rumor going around that
your husband takes off every Thursday night just to come
home and have . . . ah . . . sex with you."

"You with IAD?" she asked suspiciously.

I'm sure I looked befuddled, but then I remembered a
police show: Internal Affairs—they investigated other officers. "Not me," I said. "I just wanna know how you
managed it. Like, I wish I could get my husband to come
home for a . . . a quickie now and then. We're never working the same shift, my husband and I." *Quickie* was a
good touch, but I should have used *me,* not *I.* "A girl likes
a little surprise in her love life. Know what I mean?" That
was better. Or maybe not. She was glaring at me again.

"I don't know where you heard Marcus takes off
Thursdays for me. So the question is: who *does* the bastard take off to see? Maybe I better catch up with that
damn Arbus and find out what's goin' on."

Oh dear, if she did that, Officer Croker would know
someone was asking questions about him. "Well, isn't that
just like a bunch of guys," I improvised. "I bet they told
me that so I'd make a fool of myself with my own husband. That really . . . ah . . . sucks. I'm gonna get my partner good for this one." Was I convincing her, or making
her more suspicious? "Look, I'm sorry to bother you, Nadine, and I wouldn't want to be the cause of acrimony between you and your husband—" Too much Carolyn-speak
again. How did Sam do it? Switch from street language to
normal language? "Just because my partner and his buddies are . . . practical joker . . . assholes." I can't believe I
said that, but she looked more convinced. "Guess I'd better be going. Sorry if I—"

"Oh, forget it," said the terribly blonde Nadine. She lit
another cigarette, and I headed for the door.

"He doesn't come home to *her* Thursday nights," I reported to Sam, and we headed toward the apartment of the late Denise Faulk. I'd never have believed how easy it is to pick a lock if I hadn't seen Sam do it. When I commented, he told me that a credit card was often good enough, but Denise had good locks. Then we went into a space that already seemed dusty and depressing. Sam put on gloves and gave me some.

His first disappointment, although he wasn't surprised, was the missing tape in her answering machine. Then I took the drawers in her bedroom, and Sam took her desk. I didn't know exactly what we were looking for, but Sam found it in a kitchen drawer under a counter that held a second telephone. "Bingo!" he said. Since I heard him from the bedroom and was tired of looking through her coat pockets and shoeboxes, I joined him at the kitchen table, where he sat holding a small notepad.

"What does it say?" I asked.

"Notes on various ways to siphon off money that isn't yours. Bills paid to nonexistent companies, departments at the center that get money regularly and aren't mentioned in their brochures. Consultant fees for nonexistent consultants."

"So she was stealing?"

"And it looks to me like she was getting advice from someone named Jacob."

"If we can find Jacob and he was a coconspirator, maybe we'll know who killed her."

"It's worth a shot," Sam agreed, "but it sure would be easier if we had a few less suspects. She's got telephone numbers written on a list here," he said, reaching back to the drawer and flipping another notebook to me. "You take this one, and I'll check the desk again."

Of course, I got the unimportant list. The only Jacob on it was annotated with the words *good lettuce*. She didn't even include his last name. Still, I wrote his number in my notebook. I was going to have a difficult time transcribing these scribbles when I got home because they were of different sorts. Usually I put my food notes in the computer and write columns the very night that I've eaten the food. In San Francisco, I'd never had time.

"You find anything?" asked Sam, coming back into the kitchen.

"I think she has a green grocer named Jacob," I replied dryly.

"I found a Jacob Rylander with an office downtown. Rylander, Stork, & Penfold. His card was in her desk and his number in her address book."

"What does he do?"

"Card doesn't say. Maybe he's so famous nobody has to ask."

"Or involved in secret criminal activities."

"Worth finding out." Sam called Rylander's office, but the answering machine suggested that he call during office hours, 9:30 to 5:00. He then looked Mr. Rylander up in the residential pages, called, and got Mrs. Rylander, who said her husband was out of town. Since Sam hadn't identified himself as anyone she'd ever heard of, she refused to say when Mr. Rylander would be returning.

"Now there's a bitchy woman," he muttered.

"Maybe he's skipped town with all the center's money, thinking if the theft is discovered, Denise will take the blame. It would be a perfect crime."

"There are no perfect crimes," Sam replied. "So let's get you home. You're going to Foreign Cinema, right?"

I glanced at my watch. Oh my. Not only was my husband waiting for me, but we'd be lucky to get to the restaurant in time to use our reservations.

35
No Place for Scientists

I ordered a beet, avocado, and endive salad at a San Francisco restaurant because I'd never eaten the combination, although Californians probably eat it all the time. I liked it, and experimented at home until I came up with this very pretty salad. Try it.

Star Salad

DRESSING:

- Heat a small, heavy, dry skillet over moderate heat until hot and toast *2 tsp. coriander seeds,* stirring until fragrant and a little darker, about 2 minutes.

- Grind seeds to coarse powder with mortar and pestle.

- In a bowl whisk together powder, *4 tbs. fresh orange juice, 4 tbs. sherry vinegar, tsp. salt,* and *4 tbs. light olive oil.*

• May be made a day ahead, covered, and chilled.

BEETS

• Trim stems of *4 small beets* to 1/2 in.

• Simmer beets in water to cover until just tender, about 30 minutes. Drain.

• When cool enough to handle, peel beets flat on five sides and slice crosswise into thin pentagons. While still warm, toss beets in *1 tbs. sherry vinegar* and chill, covered.

• Can be made two days ahead.

ASSEMBLE SALAD ON FOUR PLATES:

• Separate leaves of *4 endives* and arrange on the plates in star formations with the thick ends in the center. Point tips equidistant toward the edge of each plate.

• Arrange 4 beet pentagons in the center of each endive star.

• Peel and thinly slice *1 or 2 avocados,* and slide the slices into the curled endive leaves.

• Drizzle with dressing.

Carolyn Blue,
"Have Fork, Will Travel,"
Montgomery Post

Jason

It was after 7:00, and Carolyn hadn't arrived, although we were to join my dad and Morrie Straub for dinner and a very important meeting at 7:30. Straub would not be impressed if we were late. So where the devil was she? And what kind of a place was Foreign Cinema? I'd been hoping for a quiet restaurant with good food, a place that lent itself to serious conversation. If my dad and Straub could reach an agreement, my research group would be funded on a fascinating project. I could hire more post docs. Of course, I'd have to get the university to find space for them, but the project would be a lure to graduate students and a feather in the university's cap. *Oh my God!* "Carolyn, what is that you're wearing?"

"Leathers," she replied, breezing in fifteen minutes before reservation time. "Your mother said I'd better get some." She dropped her handbag on the dining room table and gave her hair, which was in disarray, a hard shake. "If you're worried about the cost, don't. I got these at a secondhand shop."

I hadn't even thought about the cost, only my wife's outlandish appearance and the dinner reservations. "You don't have time for a bath, and you certainly can't wear that outfit. Do you have any idea what time it is?" I couldn't remember a period when Carolyn, the light of my life, had been so continuously troublesome.

"There's no time for clothes changing either," she said, heading for the bedroom.

"Carolyn, that outfit is not appropriate for—"

"Oh, it'll be fine with a scarf and—what?—jewelry! Call a cab."

After I called, I returned to the dining room where I could see her dumping her travel jewelry bag out on the bed and flipping through her suitcase until she came up with a long scarf. Pale green with flower tracings in black. Where had she got *that*? It was at least six feet long.

She brushed her hair quickly, twisted it into a roll on the back of her head, pinning it with a green and gold comb, and wrapped the scarf around her neck with the long ends trailing front and back. Then she zipped the leather jacket halfway up after unbuttoning her blouse halfway down and clipped dangling gold rings to her ears. She looked—unlike my wife. Dumping the contents of the handbag she'd been carrying into a black purse with a long gold chain, she said, "Let's go."

We had ten minutes to get to Foreign Cinema, the address of which Carolyn gave the driver. She advised me to keep my eyes open in case we passed the Mission Dolores, which had been founded in 1782 by Father Juniper Sierra—we didn't see it—and the famous Hispanic wall murals. We didn't see any of those either, and the driver didn't see the restaurant, which was in hiding. Carolyn identified it by its metal door and portholes. There was no sign. By then we were five minutes late and feeling our way down a long hall lit only by votive candles on ledges.

"Are you sure this is the place?" I muttered.

Evidently it was. At the end of the hall was one large room inside with a window wall looking out on a table-filled patio, on the back wall of which a film was projected.

"Blue," said Carolyn. "Party of four. We'd like to sit on the patio."

"No, we wouldn't," I said. "There's a movie playing out there. We can't talk business in the middle of—"

"*Annie Hall*," Carolyn supplied. "I do love that movie." But after glancing at me, she said, reluctantly, "Oh, very well. We'll sit inside, Jason, but you're ruining the fun."

"Morrie Straub isn't the fun type."

"Then why did you invite him? Oh, there's your dad."

"Do you wish to wait at the bar, madam, while we prepare your table?" asked the man behind the reservation desk. He was eyeing my wife with so much interest that I felt like kicking him. Instead I chased Carolyn past the fireplace on the middle of the windowless wall to the bar, where my father and Morrie Straub were standing, sipping drinks, and looking around like two missionaries in the midst of a throng of cannibals. Carolyn kissed my dad on the cheek, shook Morrie's hand, hopped up on the only stool left, and ordered a Mojito from the bartender, after which she took down the recipe: muddle mint and lime, add sugar, soda water, and silver rum.

"Wonderful," Carolyn said to the bartender, a tall, blonde woman. "I think I had something like this in New York at Patria. I'll have to look at my notes. I'm a food columnist."

"Awesome," said the bartender. "Love your outfit. Where'd you ever get that jacket?"

Carolyn laughed. "You wouldn't believe it. A second-hand place on Union—Recycled—"

"Chic," said the bartender. "I've shopped there!"

"Maybe I should try it," said my father dryly. Then he turned to me. "This place is awfully noisy."

"I know," I replied glumly. "Sorry about that, Morrie."

"Well, it's different," said Straub.

Indeed it was. Cement walls, wooden floor, rust-red wood framing the windows, that raised fireplace, smoke-stained above, with enough logs to last a winter stored underneath, and dark, except where the bar and open kitchen were.

"It's very trendy," said my wife, who had turned around on her stool to take a picture of the restaurant.

"Oh, me next," squealed a pretty Japanese girl in a tight orchid dress that had a round hole in the middle exposing her navel and most of her midriff, and a very long slit on the side. She hugged my wife and said, "Very, very cool outfit, Carolyn. I'm so impressed. This is my date, Jaime. He's a flamenco dancer at clubs around town."

This Jaime kissed Carolyn on the cheek while my dad watched, astonished. Surely Carolyn hadn't invited these people along. She hadn't, but when the waiter, a tall, shaven-headed fellow in an apron, arrived to show us to our table, she did. Two more chairs were dragged over to our table by the window, and we sat down.

"Look at those chandeliers, Jason. The light bulbs on

long cords are like an upside down bouquet. They're just like the ones in the Guggenheim lunchroom."

"Which Guggenheim?" asked Bebe, the Japanese girl, who evidently dressed windows for a living. "I love them—well, Venice and New York—and I know I'll love Bilbao. Jaime, you should take me to Bilbao. It's in your homeland. Wouldn't that be awesome!"

"Basque country," said Jaime, who wasn't very talkative. "Terrorists."

Very little chemistry or business got talked that night. Morrie, for a wonder, was an admirer of the Spanish artist Murillo and the only person in the party to get Jaime into an extended conversation. Carolyn and my father talked about news of the investigation and the food. They'd both ordered duck, which was evidently good. She asked the waiter if their ducks came from the duck farm in Petaluma that had been founded in 1901 to supply ducks to Chinese restaurants and other buyers. He didn't know. Dad also admired Carolyn's choice of a beet and avocado salad, which sounded like a strange combination to me.

In the conversation department, I was the most overwhelmed because Bebe took a fancy to me and talked my ear off about the rug she and Carolyn had picked out, about how old-fashioned her mother was when it came to unmarried daughters living in their own apartments and dating non-Japanese men, about a delicious window she'd designed for a touristy pottery shop with coat-hanger figures dancing around, hanging off, and climbing into the pots. In between each new eruption of enthusiasm, she turned to my wife to tell her how cute I was, which I found extremely embarrassing. If my sardines hadn't been so good, I'd have given up on the evening entirely.

36
The Missing Knife

Carolyn

"Oh my God, Carolyn, I forgot to tell you," squealed Bebe over dessert. "My sashimi knife is gone! I was subbing for Kebra tonight in an ethnic cuisine class, and there it was!" She paused dramatically, waving a spoonful of *Pot au Crème Chocolat*. The *chocolat* landed on the table, but she didn't notice. "The slot for it was empty. The Japanese Consulate donated that set of knives. They're expensive! And if my father or the Consul find out, they'll be furious. They'll think I've been careless with an expensive gift, and I haven't. I always clean and put those knives away myself. I ask you? Who would want to steal a sashimi knife?"

"When did you last see it?" I asked. This missing Japanese cooking utensil might be of grave importance.

Bebe went into thought, putting her hands together and bowing her head as if in prayer. "It was there last Thursday when I put the sushi knives away."

"Was that before or after Denise?"

"Carolyn," Jason said into my ear. "I wish you'd drop that subject."

"Oh my sacred ancestors! Do you think the killer stole my knife? And . . . and . . ."

I nodded.

"What are they talking about?" asked Morrie, who was by then discussing the architecture of Gaudi with Jaime, both of them drinking cognac.

"A murder for which my ex-wife was arrested," said my father-in-law. "She's in jail."

"You're kidding me!" Morrie looked astonished.

"He's not," said Bebe. "It was awful. Blood all over both poor Denise and Professor Blue. She tried to save Denise's life and got blamed for the murder. Carolyn is trying to find out who the real murderer is."

Jason glared at both of us, but Calvin said, "Oh, stop worrying, Jason. She should be safe enough as long as she's with Sam. Let her have some fun. I made the mistake of trying to keep your mother in line and look how that turned out."

Let me have some fun? Now, that was almost as irritating as Jason trying to keep me from investigating at all. "That's important news, Bebe," I told her. "I'll pass this on to the detective as soon as we get home."

"That can't be soon enough for me," Jason muttered under his breath.

"I love this restaurant," I said defensively.

"I know," said my husband. "It's *trendy*."

"*Noisy* would be the adjective I'd pick," said Calvin. "I wonder if the cement walls, wooden floors, and the huge windows contribute to the din."

Mr. Straub glanced around at the other diners. "I think it's just that young people make more noise than people my age, and we are surrounded with young people."

Calvin laughed. "Maybe that's what Carolyn means by trendy—popular with raucous youths."

"I'm afraid this wasn't the serious business and scientific meeting we planned," said Jason apologetically.

Bebe giggled. "But you're having fun, right?"

I called Sam as soon as I got home. "Hi, this is Carolyn. There's an expensive sashimi knife missing from the center kitchen. Do you think it could be the murder weapon?"

"What does it look like?"

"I'll ask tomorrow. What's going on there? It sounds like a string quartet."

"It is. Paul's group comes here to play the last Wednesday of the month, and I have to provide the damn refreshments when they get through."

"Really. What are you serving?"

"Coquilles Saint-Jacques. Paul's idea, damn him. I'll give you the recipe."

"I do love that dish, but I must say I'd rather eat it than make it."

"You and me, too. That's why I'm giving you the only copy of the recipe. It's a real pain in the ass."

"Do you think you could moderate your language when you're talking to me, Sam?"

"Do you think you could provide more than half a clue, Carolyn? The knife being missing is interesting, but it would be a whole lot more helpful if we had it. Covered with blood and fingerprints."

If a private detective can make this recipe, so can you and I.

Coquilles Saint-Jacques

- Combine in a saucepan *1/2 lb. scallops, 1 small, finely chopped onion, 5 sprigs parsley, 1/4 bay leaf, 2/3 cup white wine, 1/2 tsp. salt,* and a *dash of pepper,* cover, and simmer 10 minutes.

- Cook *1/4 lb. mushrooms* in *1/4 cup water* and *1 tsp. butter* for 12 minutes.

- Drain broth from mushrooms and scallops and reserve. Finely chop mushrooms and scallops.

- Melt *2 tbs. butter* and blend in *2 tbs. flour.* Add broths and *1/4 cup milk.* Season with salt and pepper.

- Cook 5 minutes. Stir in most of *1/2 cup grated Swiss cheese.* Add finely chopped mushrooms and scallops.

- Pour into *6 scallop shells or a 3–cup shallow baking dish.* Sprinkle remaining cheese and *fine bread crumbs* on top.

- Heat in a 400 degree oven until bubbly (about 10 minutes).

- Serves 4 to 6.

Carolyn Blue,
"Have Fork, Will Travel,"
Boston Globe

37
Police Liaison

Carolyn

Jason jostled me awake to inform me that he wouldn't be dining with me that night. It seems that by selecting an interesting place to eat and inviting an interesting couple to join us, I had undermined the purpose of the evening, business and science. Therefore, he'd have to meet tonight without me.

Wasn't that mean? To reproach me when I was half-asleep and unable to defend myself. It served him right when I burst into tears. I was very hurt, although not repentant. I thought it had been a delightful evening, and I sniffled into my pillow that I was sure Mr. Straub would agree. Jason did apologize, but he didn't change his mind about excluding me from his plans or retract his objections to my association with Sam Flamboise. Now I'd have to cancel tonight's reservation, because I couldn't go by myself.

I had another good cry before getting up to dress, eat breakfast, and wait for Sam's call. And what did Sam have to say? That he had a crisis to deal with. Dumped twice. At least Sam had the good grace to suggest ways that I could carry on the investigation in his absence.

That cheered me up. However, I wouldn't be wearing my motorcycle outfit, which I had become quite fond of, having received so many compliments on it yesterday. Forty-plus and still *cool*. Even Mrs. Croker had liked it, not that I considered her a paragon of good taste. Perhaps it was just as well to wear regular clothes. I did have to meet the eminent Mrs. Hollis at the museum.

While I was debating wardrobe choices, Sam told me what he wanted me to do. "First, find out what that sashimi knife looks like. Maybe they've got a picture at the center or you can find it in a department store and take your own picture. I want you to show it to Harry Yu. He'll know, or the medical examiner can tell him, whether it could have been the murder weapon. That's the second thing. It's time we brought Harry up to date, so you'll be our police liaison. We've got good suspects now, and we can use his help."

"We've done better than he did," I objected. "He just arrested my mother-in-law without looking any further."

"Listen, Carolyn. I'm a *private* detective. I like to keep my relations with the cops amicable, and Harry's a good guy. Tell him about Faulk, who wasn't at his office the night his stepmother was killed, although a few people there thought he might have been at a poker game. You could call his wife and see if she knows who he plays poker with. And tell Yu about Freddie. Spider called late last night with an address on the little mutt. They can send some uniforms after Senor Piñon." He dictated the address. "But don't mention Croker. That might piss Harry off since they're both cops. Like I said, I'll see what Croker's doing from 8:00 to 9:00 tonight."

"I'll go with you," I offered. "Jason didn't like last night's restaurant. It was too noisy to talk chemistry, so I'm not invited to dinner tonight. You can pick me up at the center at 7:30 when my cake class ends."

"Look, Carolyn, what with that class and all the other stuff you've got to do today, why don't you let me follow up on Croker."

"Absolutely not. I'll expect you at 7:30." I hung up and looked for Raymond Faulk's number in the telephone book. When I dialed, the telephone rang until I couldn't stand to listen anymore. Why didn't she answer? Had he come back? What had he done to her? And the children. Well, they should be in school. She'd mentioned the name, so I looked up the number and dialed.

At first, because I hadn't claimed family status, they wouldn't tell me if the children were in school. "I'm their aunt," I objected, "and I can't get hold of my sister-in-law. I'm worried about her. And the children. I don't see why you can't just tell me whether they're there. Then at least I'll know they're safe. My half brother is a dangerous man. If you don't help me, I'll have to call the police, and think how embarrassing that will be if nothing's wrong. He'll be furious, and since he doesn't like her to leave the house, he'll be furious with her and—"

I either convinced the secretary that I was the children's hysterical aunt, or she got tired of listening because she agreed to check the attendance rolls. The Faulk children were not in class, and no one had called to explain their absence. "Oh dear, oh dear," I said. "I'll have to find their father." And I hung up. But someone else, preferably Inspector Yu, would have to find Raymond Faulk. I was afraid of him. I was, after all, the police liaison, not an armed officer.

Still fretting about Teresa Faulk, I went downstairs to consult Mr. Valetti on what bus to take to Union Street. I doubted that Calvin was planning to pay for my expenses as well as Sam's, although maybe he should have. No, that wasn't fair. Calvin had been quite gracious last night and interested in my discoveries.

Mr. Valetti was on his way to play bocce and gave me a ride to the center, fascinated by the information Sam and

I had collected. "My *professora,* she gonna be real proud of you, *Bellissima.* You're a good daughter to her. I'm-a be proud when you my daughter, too."

As if that's likely to happen, I thought as I climbed the steps to the front door. What a beautiful day it was. Every day had been. I couldn't believe that Anthony Trollope had grumbled about "rain falling in torrents" and sudden changes from "heat to cold" in one day. But then he had been a grumpy traveler.

Once inside, my first thought was to ask Penny Widdister in Battered Women for the records on Teresa Faulk. If I could get copies, Inspector Yu would be more likely to look for her and go after her husband. No one was at the sign-in desk, so I simply went upstairs and knocked. In a quavery voice, Penny asked who was there. Still frightened that batterers would come in and attack her. When I identified myself, she unlocked the door and let me in. I noticed for the first time that she was pregnant, probably about four months, and I felt sorry for my unkind thoughts. No wonder she was afraid. At first, she said she couldn't give me the record, but when I explained the whole situation, she began to cry.

"I hate those awful men," she sobbed. With shaking hands, she unlocked and shuffled through file cabinets. "I hope the police find him and beat him up." She plucked a manila file from the drawer and thrust it into my hand. "You take it right down there and make them help her."

I hadn't really anticipated that she'd give me the original, but I wasn't going to quarrel. "You're a good woman, Penny, and I'm sure Teresa Faulk will be forever grateful to you."

"Oh, don't mention me," she cried, alarmed. "I don't want him—Mr. Faulk—to know I . . . well, actually maybe I shouldn't . . ."

"I won't say a word. It's our secret. And thank you." I headed for the stairs before she could snatch the dangerous file back. It was safely in my shoulder bag before I reached the first floor.

"Oh, Mrs. Blue. There you are."

Marina Chavez-Timberlite. I hadn't thought much about that couple recently. Had Sam found out anything about her husband? What if *they* were running the scams mentioned in Denise's notes, and Denise had discovered it, and they had hired someone to kill her?

When I tuned in on Mrs. Timberlite, she was reminding me that I had volunteered to teach a class at 6:00 on the anniversary dessert. She hoped that I, being a culinary expert, had a wonderful recipe chosen. "Who's providing the ingredients?" I asked, nettled to be called a volunteer when I'd been blackmailed into the project. "No one's even called to ask what we'll need." Maybe she'd be too stingy to come up with the money and someone to shop. "I certainly don't have time for grocery shopping. I don't even have a car. I'm a visitor."

"Well . . . well . . ." She looked nonplused. "Perhaps you could dictate what you'll need to my secretary. Nutrition Central can arrange to have the materials delivered."

Phooey! I allowed myself to be shepherded into the secretary's closet, interrupted the nursing of the new baby, dictated the list, told Kelani to multiply it by ten, and went off to Nutrition Central to see if I could get a description or picture of the missing sashimi knife. Alicia Rovere didn't have a picture, but she did provide the manufacturer's name and the model number. "They sell them at Macy's. I don't know why Bebe made such a fuss. You'd think Japan was going to declare war because someone stole the Consulate's knife."

"If it was the knife that killed Denise, it's important."

"You think she was stabbed with one of our knives?" Alicia gasped.

"Maybe. At least it's something the police need to know.

"My goodness, Carolyn, have you been investigating all week? Vera owes you a big vote of thanks."

Alicia went off to oversee some other dreadful dish being cooked by the Food Stamp/Government Surplus cooks, while one young woman sidled over and advised me, if I was going to Macy's, to try the Tipper Gore cookies in the cafeteria. Then I returned to the secretary's office and asked her to call me a cab. I had to get to the Hall of Justice before Inspector Yu left to investigate another murder.

In the front hall a small group clustered around a young Hispanic woman. Dr. Tagalong called, "Hello there, Mrs. Blue. You'll want to meet Jesusita. Jesusita, this is Mrs. Carolyn Blue. She's the daughter-in-law of your mentor."

The girl actually threw her arms around me, saying, "*Gracias, gracias.*" When she recovered from her avalanche of thanks, she said, "Guess what I just got?"

"A job?"

"A tubal legation." She beamed at me.

"Ligation," said the doctor.

"I never have no more children. Even I get raped like my sister's boyfriend did to me, I have no more children. I get a job. I get my two kids back. Two's enough. I love Señora Vera. She is so good woman. You wanna see my scar? Jus' two little cuts. So easy I could almos' do it myself, no?"

"No," said Dr. Tagalong, "although the procedure has become less invasive."

Jesusita pulled up her blouse and tugged at the waistline of her jeans to reveal two BAND-AIDS. "Pretty cool, no?"

"Congratulations," I murmured. "Oh, that's my cab. So nice to meet you. Good luck."

38

Liaising with Harry and Cammie

Carolyn

I found the sashimi knife in the Macy's kitchenware department, displayed in a box with Japanese characters. It cost eighty-six dollars. Surely the Consul and Bebe's father wouldn't be that upset about eighty-six dollars. The knife was made of brushed molybdenum-vanadium steel and had handles with black holes in slanting lines, very contemporary. The attributes that impressed me most were the ten-inch length and the wide blade base. No wonder there had been so much blood. I took a picture with my digital camera, looked at it on the little screen, and received a suspicious stare from a saleswoman. "I'm investigating a murder," I explained.

"Well, it wasn't done with one of our knives," she retorted.

Then I located the cafeteria and bought two cookies: the Tipper Gore, as recommended (it had soft chocolate chips in it), and the M&M's. I remember hearing, as a preteen, that red M&M's were carcinogenic, but another rumor had it that they promoted breast development. I ate as many red M&M's as I could get my hands on in those days, but I'm still cancer-free and small-breasted.

I tried the cookies in the cab to the Hall of Justice. They were very rich, and I saved half of each for later. Both Inspectors Yu and Camron Cheever, to whom I was introduced for the first time, were in their shared Homicide cubicle. "You're the woman who set my daughter against me," said Harry Yu. "Until you told her, Ginger didn't know that Cammie and I had arrested the old lady. Now my own kid will hardly speak to me. She thinks the arrest was my way of keeping her from living in the dorms at Berkeley. So thanks a lot, lady. Oh, and my grandmother is now at that center teaching welfare mothers to make pot stickers."

"Is she?" If I'd had the time, I'd have taken her class. "I had pot stickers at the restaurant you recommended. They were wonderful."

"And I suppose you got my grandmother interested in organizing a Tai Chi class in the backyard over there."

"I had nothing to do with that. I'm here with information about your case. Sam Flamboise asked me to act as liaison between your investigation and ours."

"How do you know Sam?" Harry frowned. "Believe me, Mrs. Blue, he is not your sort of person. He's one tough cookie."

"Nonsense," said his partner. "Sammie's a sweet cookie. Not at all bitchy like some gays."

"I'd have to agree with you, Inspector Cheever," I said. "Except for bouts of unacceptable language, which he seems to be overcoming, at least in my presence—"

"You've been criticizing Sam's language?" Inspector Yu hooted with laughter. "How did he take that?"

"Very politely," I replied. "Do you want to hear what we've discovered?"

"I don't know. Do we, Cammie? Here we've got a good, solid case, and this lady wants to pin the Faulk murder on someone other than her mother-in-law."

"Family's family," said Inspector Cheever. "What have you got?"

She didn't look that fashion-impaired to me. She was wearing a perfectly respectable, tailored pants suit. It then occurred to me that Yasmin Atta had probably thought *me* fashion-impaired. But then she hadn't seen me in my leathers. "We have information on two suspects for you," I said and opened my notebook. "First is Frederico Piñon, an abuser of women. He's out on parole, which he has broken by failing to stay in his halfway house. He was seen at the center both the night before and the night of the murder, trying to frighten someone into telling him where his wife was. Since Denise Faulk originally arranged space in a shelter for the wife, we think it possible that he killed her when she refused to tell him.

"An informant named Araña Morales, who is covered with tattooed spiders, reported to Sam that Mr. Piñon is hoping to flee to Los Angeles but is presently residing in an abandoned building." I fished through my purse, forced to put my napkin-wrapped cookie halves on the desk in order to produce the card on which I had written the address.

"Are those Macy's cookies?" asked Inspector Cheever. "What kind are they?"

"Tipper Gore and M&M's, but I've already eaten half of each."

"I love the Tipper Gores. If you don't want the other half, I'll take it."

What could I say? I handed the chocolate chip half to Camron Cheever. Then Inspector Yu said he wouldn't mind trying the other one, so I gave it to him, reluctantly, hoping lunch at the museum would be tasty and substantial.

As Harry Yu munched my cookie, he stared at the address I'd given him. "I'll pass this on. You wouldn't know if he's armed, would you?"

"I think so. He asked a cousin to get him a gun and

some gang friends to find him a car. If you don't hurry, he could escape."

"We'll get on it, not that I'm saying he killed anyone, but he's breaking parole, going around scaring women. That's enough to pick him up."

"Our second suspect is Raymond Faulk, the stepson of the victim. He had two motives to murder Mrs. Faulk. She had control of two-thirds of his late father's estate during her lifetime, and she forced the younger Faulk to stop beating his wife, Teresa. Most frightening, Mrs. Teresa Faulk threw him out, and now she's disappeared with both children, and he didn't go to work today. A very dangerous situation, don't you think? He needs to be picked up immediately, even if he didn't kill his stepmother. We haven't been able to establish an alibi for him. He says he was at his office, but people there say he wasn't."

"Jeez, Harry, we're being shown up by a gay private eye and a professor's daughter-in-law," said Cammie Cheever. "I told you no way did a little old lady inflict those big stab wounds on Denise Faulk."

"Oh, that reminds me," I exclaimed, "I may know what knife killed her. I pulled out my digital camera and turned on the screen. "It's a Japanese-made sashimi knife. A center volunteer discovered its absence last night."

They both stared at the two-inch screen. "How big is it?" asked Harry Yu. "I sure can't tell from that postage-stamp image."

"Ten inches long, and two inches wide, maybe less, at the widest part. It costs eighty-six dollars at Macy's. And I might add that my mother-in-law has no interest in cooking or cooking utensils."

"If someone stole the knife from the center kitchen and took it away after the murder," said Cammie, "that sort of makes it a crime of opportunity, doesn't it?"

"Oh, hell," grumbled Harry Yu. "I knew you were going to be a pain in the neck the first time I saw you."

This to me. "We'll send a S.W.A.T. team after Piñon and put out a bulletin on Faulk. OK?"

I beamed at him. "Thank you so much. And could you keep me informed?"

"I'll call Sam. He's got a cell. I didn't see one in your purse when you were dumping it on my desk."

"There are places you can rent one by the day," said Cammie helpfully. "You could call Harry with the number."

Harry gave her a disgruntled look, but I was delighted. "I'll do that. Thank you again. And if you have no questions for me, could you tell me how to get to the Legion of Honor? It's a museum."

"Take a cab," Cammie advised.

"Well, I was hoping to take a bus so that I could inquire about a young schizophrenic who likes that bus and might be a suspect. She's obsessed with knives and was angry at Denise because Denise suggested that having someone like that at the center could run their liability insurance up."

"What's her name?" asked Inspector Yu.

"Bad Girl. Or possibly Martina L. King. She isn't black, but she has a—what do you call it?—cornrow hairstyle. It's so dusty I'm not sure of the color."

"This investigation must have been a real eye-opener for you," said Inspector Yu. "How'd you hook up with Sam?"

"My father-in-law hired him."

"The old woman's married?" He looked astonished.

"Divorced. Many years ago."

"Figures." Cammie Cheever grinned. "She doesn't much like men. You want me to call you a cab? You'll never get to the museum trying to take buses."

So I took a cab. The driver first drove to a cell phone establishment and waited while I rented one. This investigation was costing a fortune. Of course food, if it was interesting, was tax deductible, but none of the other investigation expenses were. During the drive to the park and museum, perched high over the city, I called Inspector Yu to give him my temporary number.

"I hate cell phones," said the driver as he accepted his fare and tip.

"And you're quite right to," I agreed. "My husband says they scramble your brains. I only rented this because I'm in the middle of a murder investigation and have to keep in touch with the police."

"Yeah, right," he said and drove away.

39
Lunch with a Philanthropist

Carolyn

The first thing I saw after leaving the cab was a bus heading toward the Legion of Honor. Second, I noticed the beauty of the building and its setting—trees, grass, flowers, and a clear view all the way across the bay to the Marin headlands. I took pictures before sprinting over to the bus, number eighteen, the one Bad Girl liked to ride. After the passengers climbed off, I climbed on and was told I couldn't do that. I had to get on at the proper stop. I ignored this reprimand. "Do you know a passenger named Bad Girl? She wears a black T-shirt, little braids, and—"

"Sure, the crazy one," said the driver. "Talks to herself. Scares the passengers."

"Were you, by any chance, driving this route last Thursday evening?"

"Nah, I'm senior. I don't do the night runs."

"Oh." How disappointing. "Could you give me the name of the driver who did drive this bus at night a week ago Thursday?"

"How would I know, lady? Now get off, would you? I gotta drive over to my pickup stop."

Oh well, it was worth a try. Because I had arrived a half hour early, I wandered through the permanent collection. They had some wonderful paintings: for instance, an El Greco of St. Anthony meditating on the crucifix, and a Lucretia stabbing herself, bare-breasted and ghostly of face, a painting to haunt one's dreams.

By then it was time to locate the café, where I told the cashier that I was to meet a Mrs. Nora Farraday Hollis for lunch. The cashier looked as if I'd said I expected to have lunch with the mayor. Another person was called to escort me to a table. On a day so beautiful I'd have preferred to sit in the brick courtyard with its live oaks, ivy, sculptures, and tables, but my escort said Mrs. Hollis never sat outside. I soon discovered why. She was a very tall, very thin, very distinguished-looking woman of eighty or so, wearing, without a sign of perspiration, a loose wool sweater with a high neck and a long wool skirt. If she was comfortable here in that outfit, she'd have thought herself in danger of frostbite outside.

We introduced ourselves and consulted our menus, from which I ordered their Heirloom Salad: red and yellow tomatoes, fresh mozzarella, excellent olive oil, and a marvelous balsamic reduction. Mrs. Hollis then insisted that I try one of the café's sandwiches, so I ordered roasted eggplant and zucchini on focaccio. After all, I had given my cookies to the Homicide Department and had no idea what, if anything, I'd get for dinner. Mrs. Hollis ordered smoked turkey with all sorts of wonderful accoutrements on a sourdough roll and had half of it wrapped up to take home. Then I felt like a glutton, but she didn't seem to notice. I ate, and she did the talking.

First, she told me that sourdough bread was made from

fermented starter dough, saved from day to day, and had probably been brought to San Francisco during the gold rush by Basques or Mexicans. Being the wife of a scientist, I had to wonder whether the yeast might not have mutated over the years, working its way toward toxicity. But my bread wasn't sourdough. She followed up the sourdough dissertation by telling me that the original Indians had made acorn bread, which was, according to some conquistador, "deliciously rich and oily." "Of course, they also ate insects, entrails, shellfish, and whatever else they could get, a diet that makes you appreciate our lovely café."

Then she told me with relish that the museum had been built on the bones of paupers from the gold rush era and that, in fact, the backfill for the café no doubt held thousands of skeletons, while their gravestones, which had been kicked over to build the golf course, were often found by nude sunbathers on the beach below. What was backfill, I wondered, and was my chair sitting on top of it? This was worse than dining with Jason when he got started on some dreadful subject like mad cow disease.

Third, she explained how she came to be associated with the center. She had given them the building, which had been the family home from the 1870s, her family being of gold rush origins and later prominent in banking. "When my ancestors moved on to a better neighborhood, the house was converted into apartments and rented out. In fact, the city was full of them in the old days, many identical to each other, the tract houses of the 1870s. The owners ordered all the fancy woodwork from catalogues or factories South of Market, and now people think they're so unique and delightful."

Mrs. Hollis chuckled at the foibles of the young and said that when the house finally came to her on the death of her mother, she gave it to the center because she was interested in the work they did and disapproved of the neighborhood in which they did it. Of course the tax deduction was welcome, as well.

Then she told me that she herself had started the arts program and talked Fiona Morell into directing it. "Poor Fiona is a very cultured woman, but she can't get used to the art projects that appeal to our clients: gospel choirs, Diego Rivera look-alike murals, poetry slams. Did you know that Diego Rivera was invited to a reception at the Chinese Revolutionary Artist's Club? Evidently, the event wasn't a great success. He arrived with a large group of friends and fans, overlapped the little chairs, didn't speak their language, and the food ran out much too soon. This was in the early thirties. Yun Gee, one of their founders, was quite good. We have Rivera murals here in San Francisco."

Mrs. Hollis was my kind of woman. I love historical trivia.

"But I was telling you about the arts program. I managed to get a grand piano for the gospel choir, and Fiona was sure it would fall through the floor. For that matter, Denise was appalled when she saw how the floor sagged under it. She worried about the insurance liability problems. And then Fiona was so hoping last month to bring in a string quartet of Asian youngsters, but the clients voted for a poetry slam. Fiona does have trouble mediating among so many different ethnic interests, and Marina can be a bit stiff-necked when trouble arises. I'm afraid the arts program has proved to be a problem, but I feel that art is important, even if it isn't traditional."

"Speaking of Denise," I murmured, having swallowed a bite of garlicky eggplant. This had an aioli on it. "As you know, I'm trying to find out who really killed her, my assumption being that—"

"Your mother-in-law didn't do it. Of course, she didn't. Have you come to any conclusions?"

"Well, we've . . . my father-in-law hired a private detective, Sam Flamboise, with whom I'm working."

"Oh yes, the football player. But my dear, are you aware that he's homosexual?"

"So he said." Didn't she approve of gays? Well, no need to get into that. "We've come up with several suspects, whose names we've passed on to the police, and there are also some questions. I hope you can shed light on one of them."

"Oh, my goodness, you don't think *I* killed Denise? No, of course you don't. Denise was my favorite person there. She saved so many women at risk from brutal husbands and boyfriends. You'd be amazed at how many women live with men to whom they are not married.

"It was a shame, taking Denise away from the battered women. She was wonderful there, but then Myra was diagnosed with—well, it was very sad, her affliction—and we had to have someone who understood accounting. Denise was very unhappy in that position, always having to deny people money that they needed to run their programs. And she made certain discoveries. Well, the less said about that the better."

"Discoveries?" Finally something that might be helpful.

"Yes. I'm afraid they were of a . . . possibly . . . criminal nature."

"Really? Did they have anything to do with theft of money, checks written for services never rendered or to center activities that didn't exist?"

"Why, how did you know? You and the football player must be excellent detectives. Poor Denise was poring over those books trying to find out where the funds had gone. I do raise a lot of money for the center, as do friends of mine, and we've been quite successful at getting grants. Denise shouldn't have had to stop funding activities, but the money just disappeared, and she couldn't tell how or where it went, although she'd developed some ideas. But then she was killed before she could identify the thief. I suppose I must go into it myself, but I've been so distressed by her death—"

"Do you think it's possible that Denise herself was stealing the money?" I asked.

"Absolutely not," said Mrs. Hollis, looking offended.

"But finances didn't get tight until she took over, according to the staff."

"Oh well, they're all devoted to their own areas of service. Women will bicker, you know. But it was not Denise's fault. I tend to think that when Myra became ill, someone took the opportunity to steal while she was too distracted and frightened to notice. Yes, I'm sure that's what happened.

"And now that you've finished your lunch, my dear, let me give you a personal tour of the Henry Moore exhibit. It's quite fine, and I do pride myself on an extensive knowledge of the artist and his work."

She was a veritable encyclopedia of Henry Moore information. I've always liked Moore's sculpture, but before I left the museum I'd been exposed to early work influenced by primitive Egyptian and South American Indian art he'd seen in the British Museum and to drawings of people huddled in London underground stations during the Blitz, drawings that brought him his first fame and popularity. I also learned that he'd been the last child in the large family of a British coal miner. There were drawings of men in the mines, too.

It was one of the best tours I've ever taken. Mrs. Hollis and I parted on very good terms, pleased with each other and Henry Moore. What a nice break from detective work. On impulse, I asked if Cliff House and the seals were nearby. At that moment I almost wished that I could spend the rest of my time in San Francisco playing tourist, but I couldn't, of course. There was my mother-in-law to rescue.

"Sea lions, dear," said Mrs. Hollis. "Not seals."

Do sea lions balance balls on their noses? I wondered nostalgically. *And why call the place Seal Rocks if there aren't any seals?*

40
Following the Money Trail

Carolyn

Since I had time before the cake course, I decided to visit Myra Fox. Even if the thefts had occurred when Myra was too ill or worried to catch on, still she might have noticed something, had some suspicion, be able to suggest who might have raided the coffers. Of course, I'd have to be very tactful. I didn't want the poor woman to feel that she had been negligent. According to someone, she had her hands full—what with horrible treatments, depression, and losing her hair.

I used my rental phone to call the center for her address, which I gave the taxi driver. Within twenty minutes we pulled up to a drab, pseudo-modern apartment building that made the city's bay-window-bedecked Victorians seem all the more desirable. Myra Fox lived on the fourth floor and answered the door herself. She looked terrible: emaciated, gray-faced, turban-headed, and exhausted. Still, she seemed happy to see me and offered to make tea. Of course I refused.

We sat in the living room, a pleasantly decorated space

in plum and blue-gray with fringed lamps and flowered chairs. "I never got to meet your mother-in-law," Myra said. "It was a great coup for the center to bring her in this summer. I actually made the initial financial arrangements. That was before I was diagnosed. I suppose someone has told you about—"

"Yes," I agreed hastily. "I'm so sorry for what you must be going through, but at least you have an interesting job to return to when your treatment is over."

She smiled wanly. "I do look forward to returning. So many good friends. And they've been wonderful to me, especially Charles. Have you met him?"

"No, but I'm sure he's been a great comfort. I heard how thoughtful he was about getting files for you to work on to take your mind off . . . well . . . work you love must be a welcome distraction." She looked a little confused, and I had to wonder if she'd been able to do any of the work her lover brought home to divert her.

"Actually, I'm hoping you can help me, and the center," I continued. "I'm looking into Denise's murder, and it's come to my attention that money seems to be missing from the accounts."

She turned pale.

"Not that anyone blames you," I hastened to add. "But I wondered if you'd noticed any discrepancies before you had to take medical leave."

"What kind of discrepancies?" she asked.

I thumbed through to the notes I'd made in Denise's apartment. "Payments to vendors who didn't actually provide any goods or services. Consultant payments that were . . . I don't know . . . fraudulent? I'm afraid I don't know much about accounting, so I may be describing these things badly. Did you suspect anything like that?"

"No! The books were in perfect order when I left."

"I'm sure they were," I said soothingly. I shouldn't have come. I was upsetting the poor woman. "Well, there are two ways to look at this. Papers I saw in Denise's apartment seemed to indicate she was setting up these schemes herself."

"Oh, surely not. I mean I know that Denise was a professional accountant for many years, so I suppose she'd know how to do something like that, but she always seemed to be a nice woman."

"Who's a nice woman?" A blonde man had let himself into the apartment, and Myra introduced him as Charles Desmond.

"Mrs. Blue has been telling me about papers found in Denise's apartment and—and possible theft of center money. It sounds impossible, doesn't it?"

"I should say so," said Desmond. "If they'd let you come back to work instead of showering you with false sympathy and making you stay home getting depressed, you'd soon get to the bottom of any funny business. I could have helped."

"Charles is a great believer in the benefits of working through good health and bad," said Myra, sighing. "He's very protective of my emotional well-being."

"Of course I am. Beating cancer is a matter of mind over matter. And good treatment, of course. I know all about how depressed one can be away from one's work. The tech disaster put me, and many others, among the unemployed."

"Yes, I've heard how hard it's been in San Francisco," I murmured. "As I was saying, the problem seems to be whether Denise was the thief or investigating a theft. I was hoping Myra might be able to help me."

"Of course she can. Just let her at those books, and she'll clear matters up in no time, won't you, love?" He had turned fondly to Myra, who looked more tired than eager.

"That's a wonderful offer, but I'm afraid the police still have the office sealed off, and the books with it."

"So the police are investigating this presumed theft?" he asked.

"Not really, although I'm in touch with the police, and I suppose Mrs. Hollis will bring it to their attention sooner or later. She thinks Denise was investigating the books."

"Nora's a wonderful fund-raiser and a generous patron," Myra admitted, "but she never pays any attention to what happens to the money after that, except to dash in and set up some new program from time to time."

"I wish we could be more help to you, Mrs. Blue," said Charles Desmond, "but if the books are unavailable, I don't see how. Still, it was very kind of you to visit Myra and solicit her help. She needs all the company and encouragement she can get. By the way, do you live close by, or can I offer you a ride home?"

"I'm staying at my mother-in-law's sublet, but actually I've got to go back to the center. I can call a cab."

"Nonsense, I'll drive you," he insisted. "Myra, is there anything I need to pick up at the market? Why don't you have a nap until I get back."

"I think I will," she said in a tired voice.

Desmond drove me back to the center, asking about the notes I'd seen at Denise's house and looking very concerned with my answers. "Good lord, you don't suppose Denise was actually stealing, do you? I wonder if someone was in it with her, and killed her to keep the profits for him or herself."

"I wondered about that myself, and I do have the name of a man named Jacob who seemed to be involved in whatever she was doing."

"Really? Well, they say there's no honor among thieves."

"I understand you were in the building that night, Mr. Desmond. Did you see anyone who shouldn't have been there?"

"Not that I remember. I talked to Denise about taking home work for Myra, but she refused, which I thought pretty hard-hearted at the time. Looking back, maybe she knew the files couldn't bear scrutiny by an accountant fa-

miliar with center business. The only other person I remember talking to was a young Japanese cooking teacher.
I suppose I must have seen people but didn't particularly
remark them because they were regulars."

We'd reached Union Street, so I thanked him for his
input and wished Myra a speedy recovery, then climbed
the stairs, thinking that he must be very devoted to her. He
was younger and quite good-looking, yet he'd stayed with
her through very hard times.

41
Chaos at the Center

Carolyn

After talking to Myra and Charles, it seemed that Denise might have been a thief, but Nora Hollis had said Denise was investigating possible thefts. Well, I'd discuss the information with Sam. If he'd gotten hold of the elusive Jacob, that might help.

At the sign-in desk I discovered a teenage boy, presumably the son, instead of Mr. Timatovich. His presence reminded me that the father had issues with Denise, fear of being revealed as an overtime thief, plans to blackmail her or force her to include him in the spoils. Maybe they'd quarreled that night, and he'd killed her. As Sam said, too many suspects.

I was almost relieved to reach the kitchen and face a group of women who evidently thought cooking something that didn't involve government surplus food would be a real treat. Some were dubious at the idea of cake made of finely ground walnuts instead of flour, but we progressed through the batter mixing and baking. Only when I went in quest of some pot holders and a knife with which to cut horizontally through the finished cakes did the unthinkable occur. I found, in a non-Japanese knife drawer in among the pot holders, the missing sashimi knife. It was coated with dried blood. I backed away from the sight in such haste that I tripped and fell. A blessing, evidence-wise. By the time the students had helped me up, I realized that no one must touch the murder weapon. Fingerprints had to be preserved. Accordingly, I slammed the drawer shut before the students saw its grisly contents, leaned against it, and instructed them to search the kitchen for suitable cake knives.

While they searched, I pulled out my cell phone, called Inspector Yu, and told him I'd found the murder weapon. He questioned me, then told me not to touch it or let anyone else near it. He would send crime-scene techs over to take it into custody.

My students found all kinds of things, including a number of useful knives and some duct tape. I taped the drawer closed and proceeded with my cake instructions. We sliced each cake in half horizontally, having refrigerated them straight from the oven in order to shorten cooling-off time. Then we slathered a thick layer of black raspberry jam on the bottom halves and settled the upper halves on top. Having reassembled them, we put them in freezers, and I demonstrated the preparation of the chocolate cream frosting, which they would have to make Saturday morning by themselves, while the cakes defrosted, and apply both between the two layers and then on the tops and sides of the four-layer extravaganzas. With the lesson completed, everyone milled around congratulating each other on how many compliments would come their way at the anniversary celebration. Some hugged me. Some asked if their names were going to be in my column.

When the crime-scene techs arrived, we had just started cleanup. Needless to say, the police presence and the untaping of the drawer distracted my students, but they couldn't see what was being taken out so carefully. And then it was over. We had returned to the cleanup of the processors, bowls, pans, and utensils when the shrieking started.

Dragging their hands from dishwater, abandoning sticky kitchenware, my students stampeded toward the sound. With trepidation, I followed. In the front section of the house we discovered a stocky, graying woman proclaiming to an ever-increasing audience that it was just as she thought: her worthless husband was not where he should be, and she knew just what he was doing instead of his job, which he had palmed off on his son, the treacherous boy who would make a fool of his mother by concealing his father's affair. She had a very distinct Russian accent.

At the sign-in desk the teenaged math genius kept saying, "Mama. Mama." He had no luck breaking into his mother's noisy lamentation.

"Gone last week. You think I don't see you sitting here in his place, Vassily, traitor son? Now gone this week. Your father is an animal. One woman not enough for him." She moaned and wrung her hands.

"It's the prostate, Mama," cried Vassily. "He's always in the bathroom when he's not working."

"In the bathroom. He is in the toilet now?" She rushed over to the door under the stairs and banged her fist on it.

"Just a minute please," called a female voice.

"Is the mistress," cried Mrs. Timatovich and hurled herself against the door, which sagged on its hinges and revealed Maria Fortuni of the Crone Cohort sitting on the toilet. Mrs. Timatovich then decided that her husband and the alleged mistress were copulating in some nearby office, so she pushed through the crowd to begin a search.

Maria pulled her knee-length underpants up under her dress, and said, "I should have believed Yolanda. People *are* breaking in on old ladies. We're not safe here. I'm going home." She picked up her purse and, cane thumping angrily on the floor, scuttled toward the old ladies' exterior ramp. Meanwhile, Mrs. Timatovich had broken through the police tape and into the untenanted business office.

"No, no, Mama," her son cried, running after her. "That's where the lady died."

The mother screamed and backed out into Vassily's arms. "I see bloody ghost. She still there in office." Mrs. Timatovich began to weep. Members of the crowd peered into Denise's office to see if they too could spot the gory sight.

I quickly pushed them away, explaining that the office was a sealed crime scene. As I closed the door and stuck the tape back up, I didn't see any bloody apparitions. Vassily put his mother into his chair behind the desk and tried to explain that his father was working another job, while he, Vassily, filled in here.

"Why he's not telling me about other job? He's spending the money on his mistress."

"No, Mama. It's so I can go to Cal Tech."

"Many good colleges here. Why not study here?"

Since their conversation did not seem to be winding down, I interrupted. "He wasn't here last Thursday?" I asked.

Vasilly looked shame-faced. "I called him before the police came, and he left his other job to come back so no one would notice that I'd taken his place."

"So where exactly was he when Denise Faulk was killed?" I demanded.

"He substitutes as a guard on Thursdays at the Faulk building. It's—"

"I know where it is." If this was true, Timatovich hadn't murdered Faulk, but he might know if her stepson had an alibi. "Did you kill her?" I asked the son bluntly.

The boy was so astonished that he couldn't speak. However, his mother could. "My son? You think my son is killing some woman? Having sex with some woman? Shame. Shame. He is good boy. Is virgin."

"Mama!" The son turned bright red.

Before I could pursue the matter, Sam burst through the front door. "Where the hell have you been?" he demanded. "I'm double-parked out front, and we've only got a few minutes left to set up surveillance."

"You won't believe what's been going on here this evening," I said as he hustled me down the steps.

"Tell me later," he responded brusquely. "If I miss Croker, I'm going to call your father-in-law and tell him, either you quit or I do."

"Goodness, you're cranky."

This is a very tasty cake, not too hard to make, and worth the effort.

Chocolate-Black Raspberry-Walnut Cake

MAKE A DAY BEFORE SERVING

Serves 10 to 12

- Preheat oven to 350 degrees. Butter and flour two 9-in. cake pans.

- Grind *9 to 10 oz. shelled English walnuts* to a fine powder (2 cups) in a food processor or blender.

- Separate *6 eggs*. In a large bowl beat egg whites until stiff. In a separate bowl beat yolks until lemon-colored and fluffy. Gradually beat *1 cup sugar* into egg yolks and fold into beaten whites. Fold in powdered walnuts.

- Pour batter into the prepared cake pans and bake 25 to 30 minutes or until the cake pulls away from the sides and is lightly browned.

- Invert pans on racks immediately and let cool slightly. Then remove cakes from pans and let stand 2 to 4 hours.

- While cakes cool, prepare chocolate cream frosting.

- Melt *3 oz. semisweet chocolate* in a medium saucepan over medium heat. Whisk in *5 tbs. sugar* and then stir in *1 1/2 cups heavy cream*. Stir constantly until mixture almost comes to a boil. Remove immediately from heat. Chill up to 2 hours, no more.

- Slit cooled cakes horizontally and spread cut sides with *black raspberry jam*. Put each cake back together.

- When ready to frost, beat the chocolate cream with an electric beater until it is the consistency of whipped cream. Spread between cake layers and then on top and sides of cake. If you wish, sprinkle top with *shaved chocolate.*

- Refrigerate overnight.

Carolyn Blue,
"Have Fork, Will Travel,"
Boca Raton News

42

The Elimination of Croker and Bad Girl

Sam

"**Y**ou brought a car!" she exclaimed, as if I'd brought roses.

"Yeah, it's hard for two people to sit on a motorcycle doing surveillance without being noticed by the surveillee." She gave me a don't-be-mean look, but hell, she knew we had to be in the area before Arbus stopped to let Croker out. I had to risk a speeding ticket to get us there. "If he gets picked up by another car, we drive after him."

"Is this your car?" she asked.

Just like a female, more interested in the car than the work at hand. If I hadn't been gay before, working with Mrs. Carolyn Blue would have done the trick. "It's Paul's car, and if we put so much as a scratch on it, he'll kill us both."

"Then you shouldn't have driven so fast."

"If you hadn't insisted on tagging along and then turned up late, I wouldn't have needed to, and if I'd gotten a ticket, believe me, you'd have paid the fine. Now forget about the car. If Croker starts out on foot, we walk."

"Of course."

She'd gone into that prissy, indignant mode. Pretty soon she'd be bitching about my language. "There he is."

The squad car pulled up across the street; Croker got out and started walking. "Get out quietly. We'll stay on this side. You hold my hand."

"I will not. I'm not afraid of a policeman."

She met me on the sidewalk, and I grabbed her hand, muttering under my breath, "We're trying to look like a couple. If he glances over at us, you look up at me and giggle or some damn thing."

"Oh, I see," she murmured grimly.

We didn't have to do any couple imitations because Croker never looked around. He walked half a block, turned right, walked a block over, and went into a place called The Barnum—hotbed hotel. I pulled the scarf from Carolyn's hair so it dropped around her face in an uncharacteristically messed-up way. She didn't look like a whore, but she'd have to do. "Quick, unbutton a few buttons."

"What?" She turned and gaped at me.

"Your blouse. You need to look like you're coming here to meet some guy. Get inside and see if you can find out what room he's going to. I'll be behind you but coming in the alley door so he doesn't recognize me." I watched her sashay in, actually swinging her hips and flipping her hair. A little overdone, but it probably wasn't part of her repertoire. I pelted around the corner to the alley and met her at the elevator.

"Two-oh-seven," she said. "The desk clerk knows him and the number. He didn't even pay."

"Right. He's a cop." I'd poked the up button on the elevator, while the desk clerk yelled, "Hey, you. You're not—" but he didn't catch us. I dragged Carolyn in and hit the close button.

So who was Croker meeting? Was he on the take and picking up a payoff? I patted the gun I'd stuck in my belt.

He wasn't going to be happy to see me, even if being caught did eliminate him as a suspect in Denise Faulk's death. We got off and headed down the hall to two-oh-seven. I could hear a female voice behind the door. Shit! It wasn't graft, and Carolyn was going to be embarrassed. If we were lucky, the woman wouldn't have taken off too many clothes before we got in. I knocked and said, muffling my voice, "Hey, Croker, it's Arbus."

Croker opened the door and tried to close it when he saw me, but I gave it a good shove and pushed him back into the room. The woman was already on the bed, buck naked, and Croker had his shirt off and his pants unzipped. Evidently they weren't into precoital conversation. Having followed me in, Carolyn gasped at the view.

"What the hell, Sam?" Croker snarled. His face was red, and he looked ready for a fight, which I could provide, although the ladies probably wouldn't appreciate the show. Or maybe the one on the bed would.

She said, "If you think you're bringin' your friends for freebies, Marcus, forget it."

He said, "Shut up, Lucille."

I said, "Sorry to interrupt this interlude, Croker, Lucille. I just want to know if you do this every week. Like last Thursday. Was Croker here with you last Thursday, Lucille?"

"What do you care, Flamboise? You wanna watch?" Croker sneered.

I glanced at Carolyn, who was frozen in astonishment as she figured out what was going on. "Maybe your wife hired me to follow you," I suggested.

"The fuck she did!"

"Listen, Croker," said Lucille, "this is too weird. Is he some I.A. guy who's gonna drag the both of us into court because I'm trading sex for protection? If I end up in jail, I'm gonna tell them the kinda stuff you do. I don't *like* bein' roughed up. Maybe I can file charges. Can I do that, mister?" she asked me.

"Shut up," said Croker.

"This wasn't my idea," Lucille whined. "He said I put out or he jailed me. Every time he saw me on the street, he'd pull me in and charge me."

"You meet him every Thursday this time of night?" I asked. Croker moved threateningly toward Lucille, so I pushed him against the wall. "That the deal, Lucille?"

"Yeah, ask the guy at the desk. I even gotta pay for the room. Last Thursday. This Thursday. Every Thursday since he decided I was the whore of the month. He gets here at 8:00, 8:15. An hour in the sack with this gorilla. I could do three guys in an hour an' make some money, but I gotta meet Mr. Let's-Try-All-the-Weird-Stuff here."

"Always an hour?" I asked. She nodded and stared defiantly at Croker.

"OK. That's what I wanted to know. You feel like reporting him, you got my permission, Lucille." I grabbed Carolyn's arm, and we were out of there.

"That's horrible," she whispered as we slipped into the elevator, which I'd jammed open. "And he's a policeman. Isn't that illegal?"

"You bet," I agreed, "but he didn't kill Denise. You want to catch bus eighteen with me and see what we can find out about Bad Girl?"

I figured she'd decide to go home, but she agreed. We walked back to the car with me keeping a wary eye out for Croker. Not likely he'd have any friendly feelings for me in the future. Carolyn was bemoaning the sad and seedy fate of prostitutes as we sailed along in the BMW. There wasn't much traffic on the streets, so we made it to a number-eighteen stop in about fifteen minutes, then parked and waited for the bus to show up.

When we got on, the driver, a friendly black guy, said, "First time I seen someone git outa a BMW and git on my bus. You slummin' or what, man?"

I paid the fare and described Bad Girl to him.

"Whatchu want with her?" he asked as the bus

chugged up a steep hill. "She mindin' her own business back there. Sleepin' most likely. Guess she back on her pills the las' few days. Don' bother the passengers so much. Nods off. Mos' nights we git to the park, I wake her up, she git off an' head out into the trees. She do like the trees. Say her mama sometime a tree."

"Would you remember, sir, if she was on your bus last Thursday?" Carolyn asked politely.

"My, oh, my. Ain't you a nice-spoken lady? Whatchu runnin' around with an ugly bald guy for? In this here town it's a real pleasure to pick up someone that talk an' look normal like you, ma'am."

"Thank you," said Carolyn.

"Lotsa strange folks live in San Francisco, an' I do think they all ride my bus."

"I suppose it's hard to remember one passenger who might have been on your bus a week ago," she said sympathetically.

"Oh, I'm not likely to forgit las' Thursday. Had to stop an' call an ambulance. Poor little Martina, she goin' plum crazy. Like to scare the white hair off this ole lady live near the end of my route 'fore I start up to the park. Girl screaming at the old lady 'bout knives an' such. Sayin' 'Don' let him git you, Mama.' I try to calm her down. Then I put in the call. She back on Monday, say, 'Mr. Bus Driver, why you send me to the bad doctors?' Guess they keep her in the hospital the whole weekend. She do hate that. She cain't hear her mama when the doctors givin' her them pills an' shots."

Carolyn sat chatting with the bus driver about what the kindest thing might be to do for someone in Bad Girl's situation. She didn't even notice when I went to the back of the bus to wake up Martina L. King, who seemed both sad and sane when I talked to her. She had indeed been in a psych ward for four days. When she got off at the circle fronting the museum, I had to restrain Carolyn from trying to take her home. The driver let us stay on and ride his bus back to Paul's car.

"Well," said Carolyn, "this has been a dreadful evening, but we have eliminated three suspects."

"Who's your candidate for innocent number three?" I asked.

"Timatovich. He wasn't at the center last Thursday. He was working another job at the Faulk Building. Of course, we'll need to check it out, but I think his son was telling the truth. So Timatovich may be able to tell us whether Faulk was at his office that night."

"Well, I can make it four. Harry Yu called me just before I picked you up. A S.W.A.T. team ferreted Freddie Piñon out of his rat hole and took him to jail. He's facing charges for shooting a clerk in a convenience store robbery Sunday night, and it turns out he was robbing another one on Thursday around the time Denise was killed. That clerk chased him out with a gun and identified him in a lineup tonight."

There were no spaces on Sacramento within two blocks of Carolyn's place, so I double-parked and walked up the stairs with her. She had her key in the lock when the first shot rang out. Because we were completely exposed on that stoop, all I could do was pull her onto the cement and roll us both down the stairs and into the shelter of a car parked on the street.

"What have you done to me?" she groaned. "Every bone in my body is broken."

I heard the third shot hit glass and hoped it wasn't a window in Paul's car.

43
Safe at Sam's

Carolyn

Can you believe it? Someone actually shot at us, Sam and me, right out on the street. There I was, huddled on the sidewalk by a car, shielded from further bullets by Sam's considerable bulk, and staring at the gun in his hand. Where had that come from?

Whoever fired the three shots evidently gave up and went away. After a moment of silence, we heard a door slam, and a car roared up to the brow of the hill and over. Sam was up as soon as he heard the slam, but he didn't shoot at the retreating car. "You got a notebook?" he asked as he helped me up. "Write down '98 Toyota Camry, four-door, dark blue or black, California plate 375."

"That's a very short plate number," I mumbled. I was shaking and badly bruised, although evidently I hadn't broken any bones.

"Lucky I got any numbers," he said, sounding rather short-tempered, and he took my notebook right out of my hands, flipped through, muttering curses, and wrote down the information he'd given me. "You OK?"

"No," I said, aggrieved. "I hurt all over."

"But you weren't shot?"

"I don't think so." I looked myself over under the street lamp but couldn't see any blood. "Unless a bullet hit the back of me. But I certainly am bruised."

"Well, I did my best to shield you on the roll down, Carolyn. At least you're alive."

"Me? Why would anyone be shooting at me? They must have been shooting at you. Or maybe it was one of those random drive-bys."

He was punching numbers into his cell phone. "The first bullet hit right by your head. If they'd been shooting at me, I'm a much bigger target, but they didn't come close." Then into the phone, "Yeah, my name is Sam Flamboise. Three shots were just fired on Sacramento. The shooter got away in a '98 Camry. I got partial plates. If you can contact Homicide Inspector Harry Yu, this is probably related to the Denise Faulk case. Drive-by shooters don't get out of the car, shoot, and get back in," he said to me. "Yeah, we'll wait here." He gave an address.

By then Mr. Valetti had joined us and wanted to take me indoors. Sam said we had to wait for the police. Mr. Valetti lamented the deterioration of the neighborhood now that criminals were attacking innocent tenants at his front door. A couple from the floor above Vera's sublet arrived and became alarmed when the situation was explained. People across the street were hanging or peeping out their windows as two patrol cars arrived and the officers began to interview us. I didn't have much to tell them except for the nature of my bruises. Other officers arrived and looked for bullets, one of which they dug out of Mr. Valetti's front door. A second was found in the backseat upholstery of Paul's BMW. In fifteen minutes or so, Harry Yu arrived. I pointed out to him that my mother-in-law, presently locked up at the Hall of Justice, was obviously not the person who had shot at us. Harry Yu said that maybe Sam had enemies, unconnected to the Faulk murder. Sam insisted that I had been the target. I started to cry. Mr. Valetti yelled at Sam, who yelled back.

"Could it have been Officer Croker?" I sniffled.

"Why would he shoot at you?" Sam demanded. "I'm the only one he recognized, and he's a good shot. He'd have hit me if it was him."

"What's this about Croker?" Inspector Yu asked.

"He's forcing a prostitute to have sex with him in return for not being arrested," I explained. "And he evidently has . . . unusual tastes."

Cammie Cheever arrived in time to hear that and said, "Why doesn't that surprise me? Everyone knows Croker is a thug."

"What does Croker have to do with this case?" Yu asked. "I told you he was on patrol the night of the Faulk killing."

"Nothing," Sam replied, "but we just crossed him off the list tonight. He was screwing a whore named Lucille when Denise Faulk got killed. It's his regular Thursday thing."

"The hell it is. The man's on patrol Thursday nights," Yu snapped.

"Like that means anything," said Cammie. "Let's go get him."

"I think I'll go in now," I murmured. "I don't like being out here on a street where people shoot guns in my direction."

"She can't stay here tonight," Sam said to Inspector Yu. "Guess I'll take her back to my house until you catch up with Ray Faulk, who's the only suspect left. At least I've got good security."

"What about Jason?" I demanded. "Someone could kill him when he gets home."

"Right," said Sam, who was dialing his cell phone again. "Tell Harry where your husband's eating or having his meeting. Harry, tell Dr. Blue to stay at the Stanford Court with his dad. His dad's still there, right?" I nodded. "Paul, I'm bringing Carolyn home with me. Someone just tried to kill her. She can stay in the guest room. . . . Oh yeah, I forgot about your mother. Would she mind sharing? . . . Good." He hung up. "Paul said for us to hurry up. His mom got in late, but she's about to serve turnip and black cod stew, and she doesn't mind sharing the room with you. You'll like her."

Turnip and black cod? It sounded awful. Inspector Yu saw us into Paul's BMW with its broken backseat window before I could tell anyone about another idea I'd had about who the shooter might be.

I was quite excited about going to the Castro. When the gays moved in during the seventies, they jump-started the preservation of the old Victorians and the advent of yuppiedom. I'd love to have seen the Street Fair or the Gay Pride Parade, or Halloween, which was supposed to be wild, colorful, and funny, with outrageously dressed drag queens and such. All Sam could show me was the Castro movie theater, a wonderful Art Deco relic of the twenties where, he said, the audiences knew and shouted out the lines of old movies.

Paul and Sam had an absolutely gorgeous gray Victorian with teal and black trim and amazing scrollwork. When I commented on the house, Sam said it was an Eastlake, which I took to be its style. What I noticed, even in the dark, were the flowering bushes that led up the steps to an arcaded doorway, the stained glass, and, once inside, the beautiful parquet floors and oriental rugs, and Mrs. Labadie, a stocky, graying Korean lady in an apron. She enveloped me in a motherly embrace that smelled of exotic spices, commiserated on my terrifying experience, and led me to a white paneled dining room and a table set for dinner—turnips and black cod.

The dish was so spicy I could hardly tell I was eating turnips, which I don't like. I chewed, smiled, complimented, drank white wine, and told Sam about my conversation with Nora Farraday Hollis, who didn't believe that Denise was robbing the center, but rather pursuing whoever had, and the later conversation with the cancer-ravaged Myra Fox and her lover, Charles Desmond, who supposed Denise could have done it; she'd have known how if she wanted to, but who'd have thought it of her? and so forth.

"Sam, it could have been Myra and Charles. He's out of work, younger than she, and good-looking. If he wanted her to, she might well have done it, thinking she could cover it up. But then she got sick and couldn't.

"He might even have helped her. He's some sort of computer person, and he said that between them, he and Myra could get to the bottom of it if they had access to the books. Myra looked pretty pale when I started talking about those notes we found in Denise's apartment, but then Myra looks pale anyway.

"And Charles was there the night of the murder. He said Denise wouldn't let him bring home files to take Myra's mind off her troubles. Maybe he was trying to get the accounts they'd used to steal money. Bebe thought he left through the kitchen door before Denise was killed, and maybe he did, after he stole the knife."

"What knife?" Sam asked, interrupting me for the first time.

"Oh, didn't I mention that? I found the missing sashimi knife early this evening and had the police take it away. It was covered with blood, and I was very careful not to touch it, so they may get some fingerprints. He could have come back around to the Crone Cohort ramp, killed Denise, scooted out to the kitchen, where classes were over, dumped the knife in the pot holder drawer, and left."

Paul and his mother were staring at me, open-mouthed. "Jesus, couldn't you have told me about this earlier?" Sam demanded.

"When? You wouldn't listen. You wanted to catch Croker, and then we got shot at and—"

"OK. You're right." He pulled out his cell phone, dialed, and said, "Harry, Carolyn's got another suspect for you." Then he passed the phone to me.

Thank God, I thought. *An excuse to stop eating turnips.* Except for them, it was quite a nice dish. I described the whole conversation at Myra's to Inspector Yu and added all the information I thought applicable. While I was talking, Sam had seconds, and Paul went into another room to answer another phone.

"Your husband, Carolyn," he called. "You can take it in the parlor."

Parlor? How quaint. But then this is an Eastlake Victorian, so perhaps parlor is the best term. "Jason?"

"My God, Carolyn, some policeman just called and told me to stay here at the hotel with my father because someone was trying to shoot you. I asked you, I begged you not to get involved in—"

"Calm down, Jason, I'm fine. Really. No gunshot wounds. And we're down to two suspects. Your mother should be free today or tomorrow."

"And you're staying with that damn detective?"

"Yes, dear. He says they have a top-of-the-line security system, and I'll be sharing a room with Paul's mother. She's very nice. Korean. She and Paul's father met when he was stationed—"

"Carolyn," my husband groaned.

"There's absolutely nothing to worry about, Jason.

She's even offered to lend me a nightgown. She keeps clothes here for her visits. I hope it's full length. She's a lot shorter than I am."

"Caro, will you stop talking about nightgowns and—"

"Right. Of course. The thing is, you mustn't go back to your mother's sublet until the murderer is caught. Just attend your meeting. Aren't the best papers always on the last day? Except for the plenary addresses, of course. I'll call you as soon as we get him. I've rented a cell phone so I can keep in touch with Inspector Yu as the investigation comes down to the wire. Since I found the murder weapon, maybe there'll be fingerprints to distinguish between the last two suspects, one of whom must have been trying to shoot at us tonight."

"*You* found the murder weapon?"

"Yes, while I was teaching the cake class for the anniversary celebration on Saturday. We'll have to attend that, but there's time before our plane leaves. And the cake is your favorite—chocolate-raspberry-walnut. Everyone's hoping your mother will be able to attend. It would be a shame if you didn't get to see her before we leave. Will your dad still be here?"

"Carolyn, I'm going to bed. For God's sake try to stay out of harm's way. Give me your cell phone number, and leave messages for me at the meeting desk."

"Of course I will, Jason."

When I returned to the dining room, dessert had been served, and Paul was telling his mother that he and Sam might take in a foster child. She became very excited and said she'd always hoped to be a grandmother.

Sam remarked wryly that if Child Welfare gave them a foster child, it would probably be some messed up gay kid. Mrs. Labadie said they'd make wonderful parents for just such a child.

I was fascinated. What an interesting household it would be: two gay men, a Korean grandmother, and a child in need of a nurturing atmosphere. One could only hope that the child would be civilized enough to respect the beautiful furnishings. I couldn't imagine Paul appreciating loud rock music emanating from upstairs or Coca-Cola stains on his oriental rugs. And Sam would have to clean up his language if he was to be a good role model. I reminded myself to mention that to him the next day.

44
Cell Phone Tag

Sam

Carolyn looked amusingly relieved when Paul and his mother produced an ordinary breakfast. She had mentioned in a whisper her fear of being served "little tentacled creatures" as we walked toward the breakfast nook. Evidently the "tentacled creature" had been a breakfast experience of her husband's in Japan.

Her cell phone rang just as pancakes and scrambled eggs appeared on the table, and she said, "Oh, hi, Jason. You'd have loved what we had for dinner last night. Spicy turnip and black cod Korean stew." She beamed at Mrs. Labadie, although I knew Carolyn hadn't liked it. Women are sly. "Well, why don't you call me in between meetings if you're so worried. . . . No, I can't promise to stay home. The apartment isn't safe. . . . I suppose I could stay here for the day, but what if I have to go out to help the police. It's my duty to do it, Jason. She's your mother, after all. . . . Good. You have my number and I don't have to return the phone until tomorrow. . . . It's not that expensive, Jason, and it's an investigation expense. Get your father to pay for it."

This is the conversation I picked up with half an ear, while Paul's mother was suggesting that Carolyn and her husband might like to come over for dinner tonight. Carolyn heard it too and said, when she'd hung up, "That's so kind of you, Mrs. Labadie, but Jason and I have reservations at Delfina." Paul's mother then decided that she'd leave for home at noon.

Pleased that Carolyn had been able to get the reservations, Paul invited the two of us along so she'd be sure to order the right things. He called on the spot and changed her reservation to four, never realizing that Jason wouldn't be crazy about having us along on their last dinner in San Francisco. Carolyn was enthusiastic.

"You know," she said, "there's a woman at the center I wish I could get a date for. Kara Meyerhoff. Poor thing. She's head of the lesbians and transsexuals."

"Well, we might be able to scare up a lesbian," said Paul. "You want to see if we can get a table for six?"

"But she's not a lesbian; they aren't even friendly to her. They don't feel that she represents their interests because she used to be a man. Now she's a woman, and she'd just love to have a date, but she's tall and very sensitive about her wide shoulders. On the other hand, she's very feminine and has a pretty face, and she writes romance novels, which was her profession even before she became a woman."

"That's—" Paul choked. "Well, Sam and I will have to give it some thought, but offhand—"

"We don't know anybody," I finished for him.

"Or maybe we do."

"Whatever you're thinking, Paul," I interrupted, "forget it." That twinkle in his eye was mischievous.

"So where do we start today, Sam?" Carolyn asked. "One thing we need to check out is whether Mr. Timatovich saw Ray Faulk at the Faulk Building that night.

And Jacob from Denise's address book. Maybe he's home by now, if he hasn't skipped town with the ill-gotten gains."

"And my office, where there's work waiting for me. You can come along for safety's sake and make calls from there."

"If people are shooting at you, maybe you better take the car again," Paul suggested.

"Oh dear," said Carolyn. "Did you tell him?"

"Tell me what?" asked Paul.

That's when Paul found out about the bullet that went through his window last night and had to be dug out of his upholstery by police techs. He was not happy, although I offered to foot the bill for the repairs, at Calvin's expense, of course. We did take his car. The idea of being on the bike with Carolyn behind me and someone taking pot-shots at us wasn't appealing.

"May I speak to Mr. Rylander?" Carolyn listened and signaled to me that he was in his office. "It's about the death of Denise Faulk." After that she had a very short wait before Jacob Rylander picked up. I signed letters, went through the telephone messages, and eavesdropped. Rylander evidently denied any knowledge of Faulk's death.

"You were her lawyer, then? . . . Oh, her estate lawyer. Tell me, Mr. Rylander, how did her stepson react to the division of property when his father died? . . . That bad? Do you consider him a dangerous man? . . . Yes, I did hear about his wife. In fact, she and the children have disappeared. The police are looking into it, but what I wanted to talk to you about was some notes we found in . . . ah . . . that Denise made."

Good, she'd had enough sense to keep our illegal search of Denise's apartment to herself.

"About ways to steal money. That's what they seemed to be. Do you think Denise could have. . . . No, money from the center. . . . Oh, I see." Carolyn listened and made notes for some time. Then she said "thank you" to Mr. Rylander and hung up. "Denise found discrepancies in the accounts and talked them over with him. He handles estates and trust funds, that sort of thing. Evidently he explained what was probably going on: fake accounts and made-up consultants. He said we should have the police Fraud Squad go over the books."

"Call Harry Yu, and tell him."

Before she could, she got a call on her cell. "Of course I'm all right, Jason. I'm sitting safely in Sam's office while he signs papers and I call people trying to get information. By the way, we're going to Delfina tonight. Seven o'clock. It's supposed to be wonderful. Sam and Paul are coming along to be sure we order all the right things. . . . OK, I'll expect to hear from you in another hour."

"Call Harry," I said.

"As soon as I call Mr. Timatovich. I want to know about Ray Faulk and where he was that night." She dialed, and I signed more papers. "Could you call Mr. Timatovich to the phone, please? . . . This is police business. I'm afraid he'll have to leave his post to take the call." She put her hand over the receiver and said to me, "As if he's ever at his post. Yes, Mr. Timatovich. This is Carolyn Blue. I understand you have a part-time job as a security guard on Thursday nights at the Faulk Building. . . . Oh yes, you do, so please don't bother to deny it. This is, after all, a police investigation, and you've already lied about being at the center when Denise Faulk. . . . Not when she was killed, you weren't. Your son called you over. Now what I need to know is if Mr. Raymond Faulk was in the Faulk Building before you left for the center. . . . Well, did he sign in that night? . . . How often did you have to leave your post to go to the men's room during that period? . . . Don't you use that language with me, Mr. Timatovich. If you don't want to talk to me, I'll just give your name to Homicide Inspector Yu. . . . I am not pretending to be a policewoman. You met me. I'm Vera Blue's daughter-in-law. I told you my name when you picked up the phone, so don't threaten me. . . . She did not, and we might know who did if you were a better security guard." She slammed down the receiver and said, "What a dreadful man. I hope they do fire him."

I'd clapped a hand over my mouth so she couldn't see me laughing during her conversation with Timatovich. "I have to tell you, Carolyn, people don't appreciate being harassed about their language."

"That reminds me, Sam, if you're going to take in a foster child, you'll have to stop swearing."

"Jesus Christ, just call Harry, will you?"

She did and gave him so much information that by the time she finished, Harry had promised to have the Fraud guys audit the center books and increase the efforts to find Ray Faulk. He said he'd go over himself to talk to Myra Fox and Charles Desmond if such a visit was merited when the reports on the books were in. Her next call was from the anxious husband again.

"Really?" she said. "That does sound like an interesting toxin. Where does it come from? . . . Plants? Did I tell you that I met a woman whose company is named Nightshades? I thought it was the poison, but they make cosmetics for women of color. . . . Really? Toxic face powder? What century was that?"

I shook my head. Conversations at their house must be downright surreal.

45
Crab Cocktail and the Faulk Story

Carolyn

I must have been getting on Sam's nerves because he pushed back the last pile of papers and said, "OK, I'll take you out for lunch. Then we'll come back here, and you can write a column."

"Where are we going?" What a terrible woman I am. Just a minute before I had been fretting about the safety of Teresa Faulk, and it took only the promise of lunch and a column to focus my mind on food.

"Swan Oyster Depot," he replied. "It's an institution; founded the early part of the century by four Danish brothers. Great ambiance, great oysters—"

"Actually, I don't care for oysters. Do they have anything else?"

"How about a crab cocktail that will send your taste buds into swoons of ecstasy?"

"That's very poetic, Sam."

We stood outside the Oyster Depot looking into the front window, which was packed with fish and shellfish. "It looks like a grocery store," I said.

"Fish market and oyster bar," Sam responded.

"Freshest fish in town," said a man who had stopped beside me. "You can tell by looking at the trout's eyes. They're not cloudy." I wasn't sure which, among the many fish, the trout were, so I took his word for it, and Sam and I entered. Ambiance indeed. It was like a football game with fish. Behind the long marble bar was a team of burly men shouting happily to one another, mixing sauces, and serving fish. On the customer side were tall stools filled with enthusiastic seafood lovers. We found two rickety seats for ourselves at the far end of the narrow enclosure. A glass case of fish loomed in front us with only a narrow eating area. Framed pictures of fish covered the walls.

"Sammie," shouted one of the dark-haired owners. "The Nova Scotia Malpeks are great today."

"OK. Six of those and eighteen of whatever else. I leave it to you, man." They slapped hands. "The lady will have a crab cocktail with your special sauce. We'll both have the Heinekens on tap."

Our particular brother—Sam introduced us, but I've forgotten the name—mixed the cocktail sauce with great speed and flair, naming ingredients as he put them in, and then tossing the sauce into about a pound of crab chunks. Then he fixed Sam's oysters, explaining to me that he and his brothers cut the oyster from the small half of the shell and transferred it to the large half, which had all the juice.

"Best way to do it," Sam said and began to fork up oysters and toss down the liquid from the shells. He was Jason's kind of man; I could tell from the way he ate oysters, which my husband loves.

And Sam was right about the crab cocktail. My taste buds swooned. I was so enchanted that I didn't want to abandon the cocktail to answer my cell phone.

"Better get it," Sam advised. "Might be Harry."

It wasn't Inspector Yu; it was Jason. "You won't believe what I'm having for lunch." I described my cocktail and Sam's plate of oysters. Then I read the list of the day's oyster selections from the wall. Jason was so envious. "Why don't we come here for lunch tomorrow before the anniversary celebration?" I suggested. He agreed.

"Are you being careful?" he asked, sounding worried now that he'd stopped thinking about oysters.

I glanced up and down the row of customers at the counter, then behind at those waiting to take our seats when we finished. "Not a murderer in sight," I whispered into the phone, "and Sam's got a gun, so you needn't worry."

"Oh, great," said Jason. He doesn't like guns and won't have one in the house, which is perfectly all right with me.

Having reassured my husband and given him oysters to look forward to, I gave Sam the benefit of my pretrip research. "Did you know that there weren't any oysters here in 1850, and people really wanted them, so someone went searching up and down the coast, found some, brought them back, planted them in a bed, and fed them bran for a year?"

"Yeah, I read that book. They were small, tasteless, and worth their weight in silver. Thank God Swan's gets them from all over the place." He forked up another.

I beamed at him. A fellow reader of local histories. "Well, did you know that the first settlers to the Bay area were Ohlone Indians who left over four hundred shell mounds?"

Sam grinned and said he was working on his own right here at the Oyster Depot.

"Not one six hundred feet long, I hope. We'll never get to the center to give the Fraud Squad Denise's notes."

"You didn't give them to Harry yesterday?"

"We were looking at different suspects then. Freddie and Ray Faulk. Don't you imagine the financial investigators are there by now? Denise's notes might be very helpful, not to mention the ones from my talk with Mr. Rylander."

"All right," said Sam, without enthusiasm. He drained his beer, paid the bill, and off we went to the center, where two plainclothes policemen were ensconced in the business office. At first, they tried to get rid of us, but I persevered and secured their interest. They looked at the notes. One said to the other, "Look up this name on the computer, Ross."

"Oh boy," said Ross. "This looks promising." He had been skipping from one file to another on the screen. "Records of payouts for food, but no records from Nutrition Central of receiving the deliveries. Colin, go into the file cabinets and see if you can find paper receipts under Nutrition Central for a load of fish on 2/20 this year."

Colin looked. "Nothing here," he said.

"OK," said Ross, "we'll concentrate on these notes. Thanks." Then they forgot about us, so we left.

"See," I said to Sam.

"So it was a good idea," he admitted. "Just be glad they didn't ask how we got those notes."

"I never thought of that, but I've got another idea." He groaned. "Now, don't be that way. I can't stop worrying about Teresa Faulk. What if she's in that house, injured or dead? I think we should go over and . . . well . . . break in, if we have to."

Sam slapped his forehead with sardonic drama. "I've turned a respectable professor's wife into a criminal. Anyway, the front door's not in an empty apartment hall. It's right out on the street. We could get arrested."

"Well, we could at least peek in a window. That's not illegal."

"The hell it isn't."

"Then we'll drive by and ring the bell. You can see into the living room from the front door."

"You're incorrigible." But we went, and when we got there, I could see Teresa sitting on the sofa, just as she had been before, except that two children sat on either side of her, and she was reading them a story. She had a black eye. Sam said, as I rang the bell, "Looks like Ray's been back. She didn't have that shiner before."

"She didn't," I agreed. Teresa peered through her peep-hole and then let us in. "What happened?" I asked her. "By the way, this is Sam Flamboise. I didn't get to intro-duce him before. He's the investigator on Denise's mur-der. And he carries a gun." They shook hands. I could tell Teresa was trying figure out where his gun was. I didn't know myself.

"Raymond came back from work the night after you were here and beat me up," she said angrily. "Then he told me to get him some dinner. The children and I ran out the backdoor, caught a cab two blocks over, and went straight to the shelter Denise told me about last year."

She motioned us to seats in the living room and sent the children off to play in their rooms. "We stayed a day and two nights, but this morning I decided that I wasn't going to be driven out of my own house, so I went to the police, filed charges against Raymond, and got a restrain-ing order. They brought me home in a police car, but he wasn't here, thank goodness. I had the locks changed."

"Good for you," I said.

"They're driving by every hour, and they gave me a telephone that connects me right to the police station in case he shows up. I can't believe how helpful they've been."

We didn't mention that they were looking for Ray for more reasons than wife abuse. Sam said, "Mrs. Faulk, does your husband play poker on Thursday nights?"

"Poker?" She looked startled, then outraged. "Gam-bling? He's been gambling? Well, that's the last straw. He knows my father ruined our family by losing everything at the casinos in Macao. He knows I hate gambling."

"We don't know that he's been gambling, Mrs. Faulk," said Sam gently, "but someone at his office suggested that might be the case, because he wasn't there the night Denise was killed."

"He wasn't? And you think he killed her." Tears rose in her eyes.

"We don't know that," I chimed in.

She picked up the telephone by the sofa, dialed a number, asked for her husband, then asked for someone named Hank. "Who does Ray play poker with, Hank?" she asked, evidently got an answer, said "Thank you," hung up, and dialed again, asking for someone named Gaskin. "Mr. Gaskin, this is Teresa Faulk. Was my husband playing poker with you a week ago yesterday? . . . You're sure? You may have to tell the police that, so you can't lie about it. . . . Thank you. Goodbye." She turned to us. "He was playing poker from 7:30, which was just after he left the house, to 11:00. Can you believe that? I'm going to divorce him right away."

"I would," said Carolyn, "and since he evidently didn't kill Denise, he's going to inherit the money his father left her. He wouldn't have got it if he'd killed her. I saw that on TV. Isn't that right, Sam?"

"Yep. TV is a great source of information on criminal law."

I ignored the sarcasm. "I think you should call a lawyer right away. In fact, I can give you the number of your father-in-law's estate lawyer."

"There might be a conflict of interest there if Ray is the heir," said Sam.

"Mr. Rylander?" asked Teresa. "He's a very nice man. He had a talk with Ray once about hitting me. Ray was furious, but it helped. I'll call him right away."

We said goodbye to Mrs. Faulk and went back to the BMW. "Well, that's about all we can do," said Sam. "I'll take you back to the house. You'll be safe enough with Paul."

My cell phone rang, Jason I surmised. I was wrong. Inspector Yu was calling to tell me that information I'd given the Fraud detectives provided enough evidence to get a warrant for Myra's arrest and one to search her apartment. Inspector Yu and his partner were leaving momentarily. "What about Charles Desmond?" I asked. "He must have killed Denise. Myra couldn't wield a knife. A conversation wears her out."

"We'll see what we find at the apartment," said the inspector.

"Sam, we need to get over to Myra Fox's. The police are on the way to arrest her and search the apartment."

"Believe me, Carolyn, we won't be welcome. We've done as much as we can."

"Nonsense. What about Charles Desmond? He's the murderer, and they don't have a warrant for his arrest."

Sam stared at me for a moment, then said, "Oh, what the hell," and put the car in gear.

46

The Apprehension of a Cancer Victim

Carolyn

When we arrived at the Fox apartment, Myra was weeping hysterically and Cammie Cheever hovering over her muttering, "Calm down, lady, calm down. We need to ask you some questions." Policemen were tearing the place apart and putting things into bags under the direction of Harry Yu, and Charles Desmond was nowhere in sight. Harry told us to go away and wait for a call. On the other hand, Myra Fox was glad to see me. In fact, she threw herself into my arms.

"What am I going to do?" she cried against my shoulder. Cammie gave her partner a significant look, and he backed away.

What could I say to her? On the one hand, I felt sorry for her. Breast cancer and its treatment were troubles I wouldn't wish on anyone. On the other hand, she had probably stolen money and was going to jail for it, not to mention being responsible directly or indirectly for Denise's death and my mother-in-law's incarceration. "Where's Charles?" I asked. "In times of stress the presence of a loved one is the greatest solace." Police conversation ceased, waiting for her answer.

"I don't know," she whimpered. "He left this morning. He's looking for work, you know." She sounded defensive. "He'll certainly be home by dinnertime. He's going to bring home steamed crab."

She looked so lost and afraid, and I was not convinced that Charles would be coming back. "This must be terribly stressful for you." I got her seated on the sofa and patted her shoulder. "Do you have any tranquilizers?"

"In the bathroom." She dropped her head into her hands and recommenced weeping.

"I'll get you one," I offered and rose to do it, motioning with my head for Harry Yu to follow me. Sam did too, and we went to the bedroom, where officers had the couple's underwear out on the bed and were moving on to the closets.

"He's in the wind," said Sam.

"Can't be sure of that," Yu replied without seeming convinced.

"If you mean he's left town or plans to, he'd need money, and he doesn't have a job. So we should find out if he has access to Myra's funds," I suggested.

"You talk to her," said Harry. "By the way, we picked up Ray Faulk and jailed him for spousal abuse. He'll get bail, but his alibi for the Faulk murder checks out."

"His wife has changed the locks," I said and went into the bathroom to look for a tranquilizer. Valium. That had to be it. Hoping she hadn't already taken one, I shook out a pill, filled the bathroom tumbler, went back to Myra, and doped her up. Then I said, "Myra, I hate to suggest this, but are you sure that, under the circumstances, Charles is coming back?"

"What circumstances?" she asked, still sobbing lightly.

"After I visited you, someone took a shot at me in front of Vera's apartment. Well, three shots. That was . . . around 8:30. Was Charles home then?" I could tell by the look of dread in her eyes that he hadn't been. "Does he have a gun?"

"Only the one he bought me," she replied.

"When was that?"

"Yesterday. He gave it to me when he got home last night. For protection."

She was staring at me like a deer caught in the headlights. Deer do that in Texas. They freeze. If you hit a deer, the damage to your car is substantial. "Where did you put the gun, Myra? Or did he put it away for you?"

"I put it in the bedside table."

So it had her fingerprints on it. "Which side?"

"Left. Charles sleeps on the right."

"Harry," I called to the homicide inspector, "have them look in the left bedside table for a gun."

"What kind is it?" I asked Myra.

"I don't know. It has a trigger and a hole in front for the bullet to come out." She giggled. "And a handle. I think it was silver."

"Myra, does Charles have his own bank account?"

"We share one." She smiled dreamily. "We share everything."

It wouldn't do much good to ask to see her checkbook. It wasn't likely that he'd entered any checks he might have cashed. "I want you to call your bank and ask them the amount of the last ten checks written on your account."

"Aren't they closed?" While I worried about that, she reconsidered. "I never go there anyway. I pay all my bills by computer."

"I do too," I said. "Isn't that a wonderful service? I look at my account everyday, just to see how much money's in it."

"You do?"

"Myra, I'd like you to do that. Look at your account to see how much money's in it." I took her arm and raised her gently from the sofa. Obediently she shuffled into the second bedroom to an elaborate computer setup, toward which two officers had been making their way. Myra sat down in front of the machine.

"You can't do that, ma'am," said one of the men.

"She wants to look at recent withdrawals from her bank account," I said, sending him a warning glance. "That's all right, isn't it, Inspector Yu?" He'd followed us in. "It's really important to keep up to the minute on one's account," I said, "especially a *joint* account."

"It sure is," Cammie agreed. She'd come in, too, and Myra was looking from one to the other in confusion. "You poor lady, you're so tired, aren't you?" She came up right behind Myra. "Do you need any help?"

"No." Myra stared at the keys. "It's in my favorites list." She pulled up her Internet service, which took forever to come onscreen. The wait didn't seem to bother her, but everyone else in the room was tense. Then she scrolled down her favorites list and clicked on her bank. Wells Fargo. After another interminable wait, the account came up. She stared blankly at the name and password prompts.

"You remember the password, don't you?" asked Cammie encouragingly. "Think a minute."

The minute seemed like five, but Myra did get into her account and clicked on "checking." Then she stared blankly at the numbers. "Where's my money?" she asked, puzzled.

He had left her fifty dollars.

"How much did you have in there?" Cammie asked.

"Forty thousand dollars, with access to sixty in the savings account." Myra seemed to have come out of her fog. "It's not insured if you get over one hundred thousand." She was clicking again, and Harry Yu moved forward, but Cammie waved him away. "It's gone," said Myra. "It's all gone."

"I think he cleaned you out, honey," said Cammie.

"You got any idea where he might have gone with your money?"

"There's more. Much more." Myra began to click rapidly, to fret over the slow advent of screens. By the time she'd accessed three other banks, she was in tears. "How could he?"

We took her back to the living room. Harry called in an all-points bulletin for Charles Desmond, thirty-two, blonde, brown eyes, six-two, 190, driving a dark-blue '98 four-door Camry. Myra gave him the license plate number. It was her car. Charles had had to sell his Miata. Every airport in the area was alerted to stop him if he tried to fly out.

"I guess he's never been arrested?" asked Harry.

"Not that I know of," she replied, trembling pitifully. The tears had stopped.

"That explains why we didn't get a match on the prints from the knife."

"What knife?" she asked.

"The one he killed Denise Faulk with," said Sam. "You didn't figure that out? That he was the one who killed Denise?"

She gulped. "If he did that, he did it for me. So no one would find out about the money I stole."

"But he took the money, didn't he?" Sam persisted.

It broke my heart to see him keep after her, but we did need to know.

"I guess he did," she admitted, sounding infinitely weary. "He even told me how to steal it. He was going to invest when the market got better, and then we'd put it back."

"Has he invested?" Sam asked. "The market's coming back."

"I don't know. I've been too sick to worry about it," she said.

"Well, you'll have to testify against him," said Harry. "If we catch him."

"I couldn't do that." Tears rolled down her face again. "I love him."

"Honey," said Cammie, "don't be a sucker. Cut a deal with the DA. You're going down for the theft, but it looks like he left you to take the rap for the murder, too."

"I didn't do anything to Denise," Myra cried.

"Maybe, but your prints are on that gun he gave you, and dollars to donuts, that's the gun he tried to kill Carolyn with last night."

"Oh dear, oh dear. How could he? I did everything he wanted me to. I can't help it that I got cancer and had to stay home for a while."

"Myra, you couldn't have kept up the stealing much longer," I pointed out. "The center doesn't have enough for the programs anymore, and if he hasn't made any investments, that means he never planned to pay the money back. He may well have planned to take it and leave you behind."

I think she believed me. Goodness knows why. If she'd thought about it, she'd have known that my visit yesterday had spelled the end for them. Desmond had certainly figured it out and tried to stave off being caught by trying to kill me. Myra was handcuffed and taken away. They copied everything on her computer and carried off the disks and the computers, along with anything they thought Desmond might have left a fingerprint on.

Jason called me twice while we were there, checking on my safety. The second time Sam got on the line and told him to meet us at Delfina. Jason did not like that at all, but he agreed. That's how I happened to visit a wonderful restaurant wearing the same clothes I'd worn the day before. At least my husband would be happy to see that I wasn't wearing leather.

47
Delfina

Jason

I was the first to arrive, anxious to see for myself that Carolyn was safe. I sat at a brushed aluminum table for four. People were eating at a sort of bar above me, looking down, possibly resenting the fact that I had a table all to myself.

I glanced across the room so that I wouldn't have to look at the watching diners. Mirrors, yellow walls, modern paintings. I ordered a glass of merlot, smoky and oak flavored, and studied the menu. Paul Labadie showed up next, a nice enough fellow, but I didn't have much in common with a gay venture capitalist. I wondered if he got as much pleasure moving money around as I did investigating toxins. He carried the conversation by telling me about my wife's attempts to pretend she liked turnips.

"If you see any new lines on Carolyn's face," he said, "just chalk it up to the muscle tension she exerted to keep from wincing each time she put a turnip in her mouth, not that she didn't fool my mother. If I weren't gay, Mother would be hinting that Carolyn is wonderful matrimonial material. She was quite taken with your wife."

Carolyn arrived just then, accompanied by Flamboise, to whom I'd taken a hearty dislike without much evidence to support that opinion. Not very scientific. Carolyn was bubbling with news about their investigation.

"I just know your mother will be freed any minute," she said, leaning over to give me a kiss. That was certainly welcome. It seemed like months since she'd kissed me. "We do know who did it," she continued. Flamboise pulled her chair out before I could get up to do it. Damn crowded restaurants.

"We *think* we know," Flamboise temporized, sitting down himself. Given his size and the relative delicacy of the light wood chairs, I was anticipating that his would collapse under him. It didn't. He accepted a menu and reminded Carolyn that the fingerprint matches hadn't yet come in.

While we looked at the selections, Labadie offered advice, lamented certain items that were not available that evening, and generally played host to a meal I'd probably have to pay for. At least Carolyn could take hers off the taxes, unless it was dreadful. I almost hoped it would be.

Carolyn ignored advice, listened to the waitress, and ordered something called Pappa al Pomodoro. It seemed to translate "Pope with tomatoes," but it turned out to be a yellow soup with bread in it, and she loved it. She and Labadie tasted her soup in turns, discussing what ingredients the chef had used besides tomatoes and bread. Olive oil, vinegar, onion? I had prosciutto with figs, which was, I'll have to admit, quite delicious. It put me in a better mood, that and a mild, fruity savignon blanc I chose myself. Carolyn, alight with good humor, said it was perfect with her soup and kissed me again. As he was finishing up some calamari on a white bean salad, Flamboise's cell phone rang. I really dislike cell phones in restaurants.

"It's Harry," he said. "Desmond's prints are on the knife, and the markings on the bullets in Valetti's door and Paul's upholstery match those the crime lab fired from Desmond's gun."

Carolyn beamed. "*We* solved the crime! Give me the phone." Flamboise handed it to her. "Inspector Yu, I hope you plan to release my mother-in-law tonight. We'll come down to get her as soon as . . . you have to catch him first? I don't see why. *Her* fingerprints weren't on the knife. . . . Oh, all right, but could you hurry? She's been in that jail for over a week now. . . . Well, if she's causing so much trouble, you have all the more reason to let her go." She hung up and said to me, "Can you believe that? They won't free your mother."

"Don't get on Yu's case," Flamboise advised. "He can't speed the system up, but he can sure slow it down if he wants to."

"But we closed his case, and we saw to it that he and Cammie get all the credit. It seems to me that he could do me this one little favor." She turned to me. "Jason, maybe we should call a lawyer. Has your father gone home?"

"At noon."

"Oh." She looked disappointed, and I felt rather guilty. My wife had put herself in harm's way and run around all week trying to help *my* mother, who had never been particularly nice to her in the twenty-plus years of our marriage. And I couldn't think of anything to accomplish the release. I knew very well that my mother would be in jail until they got good and ready to let her go.

A busboy cleared our first courses, and the waitress served the entrees. Flamboise chose plank steak, Labadie had ordered halibut on a fig leaf, I got roasted Tuscan spareribs, and Carolyn immediately dug into her grilled salmon.

"Oh, this is wonderful," she cried. "The salsa verde is so yummy. Here, try some everybody." Labadie did and pronounced it superb; I had to admit that it was excellent; and Flamboise said, "Forget it," when Carolyn tried to give him some. Then she tried the things around the fish and said, "What is this? It's delicious. I didn't even write down what it said on the menu." Labadie got her a copy of the menu. Evidently she was eating charred gypsy peppers. My wife was a very happy woman—taking pictures of the restaurant, making food notes, wondering if she could deduct her expenses when she hadn't written a column all week. "Will it count if I write them when I get back to New York?" she wondered.

The company proved to be quite pleasant. Labadie and my wife discussed the Henry Moore exhibit at a museum she'd visited. Flamboise and I struck up a conversation about football. He had a number of very funny stories to tell about his years in pro football, most of which reflected badly on him, and I have to say I found the man quite likable, even intelligent.

During dessert, a piece of Bittersweet Scharffen Berger chocolate cake jumped right off Carolyn's plate as she was lifting a forkful to her mouth.

"Oh my God, it's an earthquake." Carolyn dropped her fork and hurled herself toward me.

I must admit that I was taken aback. It was the third tremor this week. I held her tightly and noted the mixed desserts on the table and the large frosted bulbs swinging on black cords above us. What I didn't notice was the queasy sensation an earthquake usually engenders. I'd been through one in LA.

"I don't think there's any cause for alarm," said Flamboise calmly. "You'll notice the natives aren't fleeing into the streets."

"Oh, you're just like that minister in 1865 who told his congregation not to worry; it was all over," snapped Carolyn. "He got out faster than they did by going through the vestry."

"Do you see me heading for the vestry?" Flamboise asked cheerfully. "It's just a bit of movement along the fault."

"Heywood or San Andreas?" Labadie asked.

Flamboise looked thoughtful, then said, "Beats me. You want me to call a friend at Stanford?"

"I'm such a wimp," my wife said in a trembling voice as she edged off my lap. I let her go with some reluctance. Although I'm not a man for public displays of sexuality, I'd missed my wife this week.

"Nonsense, Carolyn," said Labadie. "Enrico Caruso lost his voice during the 1906 earthquake and never came back here."

"It *was* an earthquake?" She turned to Sam. "But you said—"

"And John Barrymore went on a monumental drunk," said Sam. "You want a drink? How about some grappa?"

"Wonderful idea," said Carolyn sarcastically, but now she was smiling. "Then when the big fire starts, I'll combust spontaneously."

I assured her, not for the first time, that grappa is not akin to diesel fuel.

"Since they haven't got Desmond in custody," said Flamboise casually, "I think you two better spend the night at our house. Paul's mom's gone so the other twin bed is empty, and Desmond might have a gun, other than the one he tried to palm off on his girlfriend."

"Oh, no," said Carolyn, "I am not going to wear the same clothes for another day. This is worse than the time they lost our luggage in Paris. We'll have to go back to Vera's."

She was so upset that the other two men looked taken aback. I knew how much my wife objected to being unable to change her clothes at least once a day, but I did think the nervous outburst had more to do with the tremor we'd experienced than the clothing problem. When the busboy finally arrived to clean up our table and the waitress to offer fresh desserts, my wife said, "Absolutely not. This is the second time I've had a dessert jump off my plate. I'm not going to risk a third."

"Fine," said Flamboise. "I'll take you two and Paul back to our place. Then you can give me the keys to the Sacramento Street apartment, and I'll bring back whatever you want."

"Then *you'll* get shot," Carolyn objected.

"Is there a backdoor?" he asked.

"Well, yes. It's off the little side street and through the gate."

"You got a key to it?"

She admitted that she did. And so it was arranged. Carolyn and I stayed the night in a rather fussy Victorian place that didn't seem like Flamboise's style at all, although I'll admit the leather chairs and cognac in the den were to my liking and obviously to his. I wasn't pleased to discover that the outfit he brought for her to wear the next day was that outrageous leather thing, but since the man was willing to creep around at night so we wouldn't get shot by the murderer, I couldn't very well complain, and Carolyn obviously loved it. Could that be some menopausal anomaly? Like men with their midlife crises, buying sports cars and chasing young women?

Once in the bedroom assigned to us, Carolyn donned a peculiar nightgown, evidently the property of Labadie's Korean mother, and asked if she could sleep with me. I looked at the twin beds, calculated how much space there would be for each of us in one of them, and agreed with alacrity. Obviously, my wife had forgiven me for whatever sins I'd committed this week.

While ordering dinner in a San Francisco restaurant, I chose Pappa al Pomodoro. "Pope with tomatoes?" my husband asked, perplexed. Pappa means mush, actually, and the soup was thick and delicious. I decided immediately to try it at home. Bad decision. Using standard recipes, I came up with something that tasted good, but was lumpy and unpleasant in texture, unlike the restaurant's version. Also, it persisted in sticking to the bottom of the pan during the hours of simmering. After several tries, I devised my own version, nv*Pappa al Pomodoro for those of us with little time and less patience.

*new variant

Easy Pappa al Pomodoro

- In a heavy-bottomed soup pan, sauté *1 peeled, thinly sliced onion, 8 cloves thickly sliced garlic, and a scant 1/4 tsp. red pepper flakes in 1/4 cup olive oil* until onion is golden and garlic slightly browned.

- Add *two 14.5 oz. cans of yellow roma tomatoes.*

- Season with *salt* and add *1/2 bunch fresh basil* torn into tiny pieces.

- Crush tomatoes, stir, and cook, stirring frequently, until the tomatoes fall apart.

- Stir in thoroughly *1 cup fine unseasoned breadcrumbs.*

- Add *4 cups water* and stir thoroughly.

- Add *rest of basil,* torn into tiny pieces, and simmer, stirring occasionally for about 1/2 hour until soup is thick but not lumpy. Add salt to taste.

- Refrigerate and heat later until warm but not hot.

- Serve with a splash of olive oil and *1 to 2 tbs. grated Parmigiano cheese* on top of each serving.

- 4 to 6 servings.

Carolyn Blue,
"Have Fork, Will Travel,"
Yuma Sun-Times

48

Chocolate Quake

Carolyn

What a beautiful morning it was when we awakened in Sam's house. Jason and I showered—together—feeling very good-humored and pleased with each other, and dressed, I in my leathers, which I still loved, and Jason in a pair of slacks and a sport shirt Sam had chosen. Then we went down and had breakfast overlooking the soaring, terraced rock garden: scrambled eggs with hot sauce, flour tortillas, and Mexican sausage, made by Sam in our honor. Coupled with a piece of good news, it was an auspicious beginning. Sam had heard from Harry Yu. Charles Desmond had been picked up at an airport trying to use tickets that would have taken him ultimately to Rio de Janeiro. Instead he was being processed into the county jail. Maybe he'd meet Vera on the way out. "What about Jason's mother?" I asked Sam.

"I assume they'll release her in due time," he replied.

"In *due time*?" I took out my cell phone and dialed, murmuring to Jason, "We have to remember to return this before we leave. Could I speak to Inspector Harry Yu, please?"

I waited. Then I said, when he came on the line, "This is Carolyn Blue. When does my mother-in-law get out of jail?" Jason was giving me that look of husbandly amusement, for which I could have kicked him. "We'll come right down to pick her up if you'll tell me when."

Inspector Yu couldn't say. There were formalities to go through. One of which was the interrogation of Charles Desmond. But she should be free today or tomorrow.

"We won't be here tomorrow!" I exclaimed. "I'm going to complain to the . . . the District Attorney."

He told me to "feel free," but the DA was unlikely to be in his office on Saturday. He liked to play golf when he got the chance. Then Inspector Yu wished me a good day and hung up.

Of all the nerve! I got out my notebook and found Margaret Hanrahan's home number, called her, and explained the problem. She, thank goodness, sympathized and said the least she could do for Vera, who had gone through a week in jail because of the Union Street Women's Center, was to move the process along, grease the wheels of justice, as it were, as soon as she finished her breakfast. I suggested that it would be nice if my mother-in-law were released in time to attend the anniversary celebration. Margaret agreed that Vera's presence would add immeasurably to the occasion.

Paul asked if all the staffers at the center would be present for the event. I was sure they would. Sam asked if he and Paul were invited. I said if they weren't, they could consider themselves invited by me. Paul suggested that they might have a nice surprise for me and then offered us a ride to Vera's apartment, since the apprehension of Charles Desmond made it safe to go there. Desmond hadn't had another gun, as it happened, but that was beside the point now. Jason and I did have a lovely night in the brass bed upstairs.

We also had a lovely morning. We packed and successfully took buses to the phone rental store and to the Legion of Honor so that Jason could see the Henry Moore show. I passed on all the artistic and biographical information that Nora Hollis had given me. Then we took a cab to the Swan Oyster Depot, where Jason feasted on a wide variety of oysters, and I had a lovely salmon plate and chatted with one of the brothers. From there, it being quarter to two, we took a cab to the center and arrived as the Women of Color, carrying placards, caught Marina and Eric Timberlite stepping out of a limousine. Bertha Harley and her indignant protesters besieged the Timberlites with sad stories about single mothers and elderly ladies who were going to be homeless because of the greedy machinations of Timberlite Ventures, Inc.

The director and her husband were completely surrounded and unable to get away until Mr. Timatovich rushed down the steps to rescue his employer. I heard her say to him, "Oh, thank you, my dear man. Don't let anyone tell you you're to be fired. I shall see that you remain our security guard as long as I'm the director here." Mr. Timatovich tried to help her up the stairs, but her angry husband was pulling her toward the limousine, and he prevailed over her objections by slipping Mr. Timatovich a twenty-dollar bill.

The upshot was that Marina didn't get to make her director's speech launching the celebration, but Nora Farraday Hollis was happy to take over and welcomed everyone to "this auspicious occasion." One of her remarks involved the debt the center owed to Sam Flamboise and me for our efforts in finding the murderer of "dear, dreadfully missed Denise Faulk." We received a round of applause, and Mr. Valetti stood up to sing, joined by a black contralto and the gospel choir, who sang in English and added some unusual flourishes to the gypsy scene in *Il Trovatore*. Then the pot stickers were served.

Grandmother Yu, who was there with Ginger, really knows how to make a pot sticker. I had two, not to mention burritos made by Jesusita Gomez, who attended with her children and wanted to know where her savior, Vera, was. I said that I hoped to hear soon that she had been released from jail. "Horse's ass cops," Jesusita muttered and went off to talk to Dr. Tagalong.

While we were sampling sushi, fried chicken and collard greens, Philippine delicacies I couldn't identify but liked a lot, and Ethiopian *injerra* with red hot dips, while I was introducing Jason to people I had met, including a rather glum but clean Martina L. King, Paul and Sam wandered over with a tall, handsome man. "This is Porter," said Paul. "He's a friend of ours."

Jason and I greeted Porter and recommended the Dragon Rolls, which weren't as good as those at Ebisu, but Jason didn't know the difference, and I was just happy to see them again. Even if they didn't have the salmon roe spine spikes, they did have wonderful carrot stick antennae sticking out the front. It was truly a shame to eat such works of art.

"Porter would like to meet your friend Kara Meyerhof, Carolyn," said Sam.

"Oh, my goodness. Aren't you a dear?" I gave him a hug and rushed off the find Kara. The fellow was tall enough, although I was afraid his shoulders weren't as wide as hers, but he seemed quite amiable, so maybe he wouldn't mind. I located her chatting with Dr. Tagalong and Grandmother Yu about the new Tai Chi class. "Kara, friends of mine have brought along a nice man for you to meet. His name is Porter, and he's very tall." Kara actually blushed with excitement and hurried after me.

I didn't know why Sam and Paul seemed so amused because Kara and Porter got along famously. I heard him suggest that they go out for dinner after the celebration. I'm ashamed to say I was eavesdropping—until a small band of people led by a priest burst through the gate and began to harangue the happy crowd.

"For shame," said the priest. "Urging a good Catholic girl to have herself sterilized." He had spotted Dr. Tagalong and was heading her way. For a wonder, the doctor, who had seemed so proud of Jesusita's tubal ligation, if that's what the fuss was about, turned pale. "You have led this young woman into grievous sin and endangered your own soul!" he shouted, his voice gaining volume. Poor Jesusita, who had been happily munching a tamale, burst into tears. Then her two children began to cry as well.

I considered his actions not just tactless, but unnecessarily cruel, and I was tempted to tell him the story of Dr. Scott, who was deported from San Francisco to New Orleans by his Union-sympathizing parishioners during the Civil War because he persisted in preaching favorably about the Southern cause. Dr. Scott had been taken directly from the church service to a waiting steamer on the docks for bringing the wrong message to a hostile audience, just as this priest—

"And who are you, Father, to tell any woman what she can do with her own body?" It was my mother-in-law. She'd just walked out of the kitchen with Margaret Hanrahan. "Until you've brought a child into the world, a child you don't want—"

"I love my children," said Jesusita defensively. She gathered them up in her arms. "I just don't want any more."

"Of course you don't," said Vera. "You can't support any more." She turned to the priest. "Have you chased down the fathers and insisted that they support these two children? Did you come to Jesusita's rescue when she was thrown in jail because of the crimes of one of those fathers? Did you insist that he marry her and support the children by honest labor? Of course your didn't."

The priest looked disconcerted. He tried to gather himself together, but my mother-in-law was not finished with him. "You, Father, are a trespasser here, where we *care* about the fate of women and the well-being of their children. This is private property, sir. If you don't leave immediately, we will have you arrested for trespassing."

Many in the crowd cheered. I couldn't help but feel a burst of pride in my mother-in-law, just out of jail and already on the front lines. The priest glared at her, but he did leave, his six followers trailing behind. Beside me, Kara was saying, "I have to tell you something, Porter. It's only fair that you know my name used to be Karl."

Well, there goes the dinner date, I thought, but I was wrong because Porter laughed and said, "You're kidding. Well, I have a confession, too. My name used to be Portia." *Oh my goodness,* I thought. *They're made for each other. I guess.* I wasn't sure how it would work, not being that familiar with transsexuality, and I wasn't about to pursue the matter, but I did wish them well. Sam, wouldn't you know, was grinning at me. I suppose he knew that Porter had once been female. Vera was giving Jason a hug, and then, for a wonder, me.

"I have to say, Carolyn, Margaret has been keeping me abreast of your activities on my behalf, and I'm impressed. You're a much gutsier woman than I would have thought. Maybe you should think about giving up food articles and becoming a private investigator."

"*Mother,*" protested Jason, horrified.

"Oh, don't be a goody-goody, Jason," she said and walked away, laughing, only to be accosted by the delighted and amorous Bruno Valetti. The two of us stared at each other, amazed. Such good humor was unlike Vera, and I, for one, doubted that it would continue unless she managed to get away from her admirer.

And then the cake girls came out of the kitchen in a row, proudly bearing their cakes to a table that had been set aside for them. Each of the ten cakes held a burning candle, representing one year in the center's history, and the young women had added decoration I wasn't expecting. On the end cakes were balloons outlined on the frosting with M&M's. On the eight middle cakes they had written, with good intentions but poor spelling, *Happy 10 Aniv ersery Unon St Womin Centar.*

We all clapped enthusiastically, and Nora announced that each head of department present would blow out a candle. Then the ground pitched under our feet, and the cakes slid apart, all four layers going every which way, balloon cakes falling off the ends of the table in pieces. I grabbed hold of Jason and held on for dear life, women and children started screaming, and Sam looked up at the house. It wasn't, thank God, falling down, but then the old Victorians survived earthquakes well because they were made of redwood. They just burned down afterward, for the same reason.

"It's over, folks," he shouted above the din. "Couldn't have been more than a three and a half. Just a little stress on the fault. No big deal. Help yourselves to some cake." Somehow or other, his words seemed to calm everyone. Except me. People began scraping cake bits off the table onto paper plates that had held the main courses. The cake plates had fallen off with the balloon cakes.

"Jason," I said, "this is really too much. I want to go straight to the airport before the Big One hits."

"OK," he agreed, "but which are you more upset about? The tremor or the destruction of your cakes?"

Now there was a question. "I'm not sure," I replied. "But I do think the tremor could have held off an hour or so. Those young women were very proud of their cakes. They worked hard."

"Well, their work is being appreciated." We looked at

the cake tables, which were almost bare, while a lot of children were smiling and smeared with chocolate.

"Just a typical day in San Francisco," Sam remarked, grinning, as he came up to give me a hug. Then Jason and I said goodbye to everyone, including his mother, and escaped out the gate.

"I never did get to see the sea lions at Seal Rocks," I lamented as we headed for Union Street. "I wonder how they feel about earthquakes. It's probably traumatic for a sea lion. One minute he's sunning himself on a nice rock. The next his rock is jumping up and down, maybe even breaking apart."

"He probably just slides off into the water and frolics around until it's all over," said Jason, hailing a cab.

"We should be so lucky," I mumbled. "I've now lost three very nice desserts to earth tremors. I'm not sure I want to come back here."

"Sure you do," said Jason, helping me into the cab. "You liked the food, and the chances are minimal of my mother being in jail the next time we visit, or even of another series of tremors occurring."

"You wanna go anywhere in particular, man?" asked the cabdriver.

"Sacramento Street, first," said Jason. He provided the address because we needed to pick up our luggage at Vera's sublet.

"Just what are the chances, would you think?" I asked. "Of more tremors if we come back?"

"I know a man in the Math Department who could figure it out, if you're really interested," Jason replied.

"That might be reassuring." *We in the academic world do have certain perks,* I thought. *Travel to interesting places. Access to all sorts of information—including my chances of losing another three desserts if I return to San Francisco, which, earthquakes aside, is a wonderful city. We could even visit Sam again if it didn't turn out to be too dangerous. And visit the sea lions.*

My husband has taken up cooking—well, one recipe—but he invented it himself, perhaps to show his appreciation for a favor I did his mother, perhaps because he got interested in yellow tomatoes after he saw me struggling to recreate a soup I ate in San Francisco, or perhaps he suddenly saw cooking as an activity related to scientific experimentation and couldn't resist a little hands-on lab work in the kitchen.

Quick and Scientific Pasta Sauce

- Mash *3 large or 4 small cloves of garlic* with *salt.*

- Add the garlic to *one 14.5 oz. can golden roma tomatoes* and pour into a food processor.

- Cut into chunks *1/2 peeled cucumber, 1/2 large onion,* and *1 yellow bell pepper* and add to the tomatoes.

- Add the *leaves from 1 bunch parsley, 4 or 5 dashes of balsamic vinegar,* and *4 or 5 dashes of olive oil* (or vinegar and oil to taste), turn on food processor, and process into sauce.

- Mix sauce with hot pasta.

Carolyn Blue,
"Have Fork, Will Travel,"
Abilene Herald

Recipe Index

Hungry for another
Hemlock Falls Mystery?

CLAUDIA BISHOP

Available wherever books are sold or
to order call 1-800-788-6262